EVERY LITTLE SECRET

EVERY LITTLE SECRET

A Novel

Mercedes King

Cover designed by HW Designs

Mercedes King
Visit my website at www.MercedesKing.com

Printed in the United States of America

First Printing: Jan 2020
Triumph Productions

ISBN-13 978-1-7343927-0-8

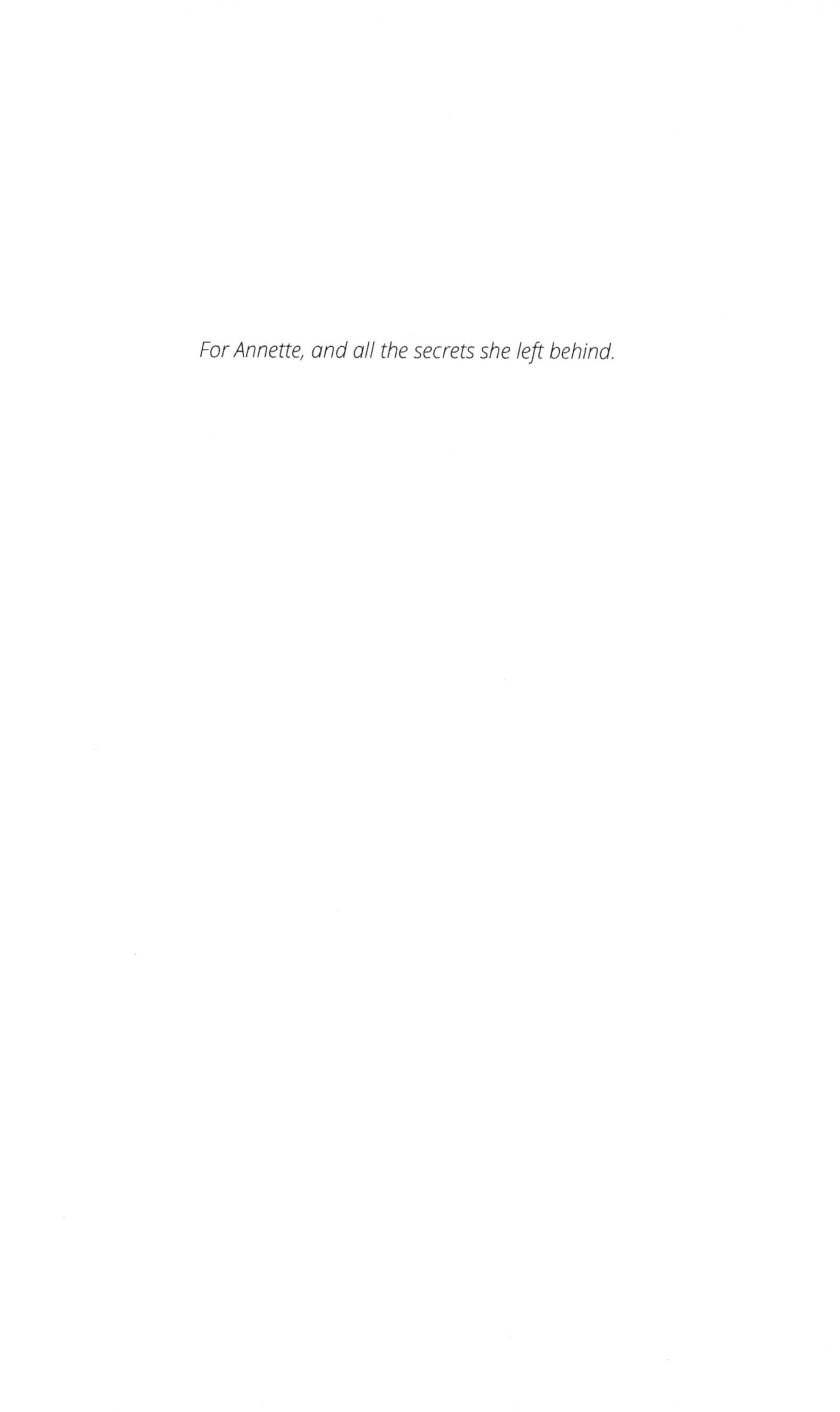

For Annette, and all the secrets she left behind.

CHAPTER ONE

May, 1992

Being born and raised in Eastern Kentucky, my mom was inbred and baptized with a plethora of hillbilly sayings and wisdom, if there was such a thing. One of her favorites being, “That’s life in the ghetto,” which I didn’t understand. If life here in Jefferson Meadows, an aging subdivision on the southern skirt of Columbus, was ghetto, why had we never left? My dad had left. Abandoned us, actually. Twelve years ago, but we never talked about him and why he’d walked out. Mom’s preference.

Mom and I had carved out a routine since it was only the two of us now. Well, us and Maverick, my four year-old pit bull. Yes, I was still harboring a crush on Tom Cruise since seeing Top Gun, but since I had little chance of marrying him, I’d found my own Maverick at the animal shelter. My brother had moved out a while ago, making life easier for me. Between work and school, though, Mom and I didn’t see each other much. Mornings, like today, being the exception.

“Roger asked me to marry him.” Mom hardly glanced at me when she said it. Sitting at her desk in what was once our living room and was now her real estate office, she continued rifling through papers and jotting notes.

“Again?” I asked, matching her nonchalant, flat tone. She liked doing that, dropping big news and acting like it was little more than a comment on the weather. Getting a reaction was a thing for her. By now, I knew this game well and didn't play along. I looked at Maverick and shook my head subtly. He gave me that innocent, wide-eyed stare and lazy tail wag.

My mom and Roger had known each other for years. Both worked at Columbus Realty. Their passion for real estate gradually overflowed into their business-friendship. But that made their love story sound dreamy. Annette Reed embodied many character traits; Danielle Steele-romantic wasn't one of them.

Most people couldn't believe my mom was in her mid-fifties. Petite all around, she had a spunk many her age lacked. She kept her hair dyed 'in-denial-blonde' and thanks to her regiment of Salems and homegrown vegetables, had maintained a slim figure. Part of her youthfulness, I think, was also due to the fact that she didn't come into her own until after my dad left. Saddled with a mortgage and, at the time, a job waiting tables, she'd survived. Yes, Gloria Gaynor sang my mom's theme song.

Few people connected us as Mother-Daughter. We shared the same hazel eyes, but I had a good four inches on Mom and long brown hair. Oh, I guess we also had the same shoe size, which came in handy when Maverick snacked on Mom's favorite pumps.

"So what did you tell him this time?" I readied my backpack for school, having only finals left in my junior year at Capital University. I'd graduate early, thanks to taking summer classes the previous two years, and I'd already been accepted into Capital's law school. Being a nerd paid off.

Mom shrugged. "I told him we'd have to wait and see. Too much going on now to even think about that noise."

Leave it to my mom to consider marrying someone and building a life together as *noise*.

Mom gathered what she needed and headed out. She probably mentioned where she was off to, a showing, meeting clients, or the like, and I gave a systematic reply about having a good day, but I wasn't listening. Notes from Abnormal Psych consumed my brain.

Dismissing her mention of Roger's proposal came easy. Every few years she won the heart of the guy she was seeing, but she'd end the relationship when it got too serious. She was holding out, she often said, for a man with no children and lots of money. Knowing her, she probably wanted him terminally ill, too. After what she went through with my dad, I doubted she'd remarry.

I grabbed a Coke from the fridge. My sustenance. It was only day two. That meant two more days before I allowed myself to eat. You control what you can in life.

As I headed out the door, after a quick kiss on Maverick's head, a car pulled into the driveway. I laughed to myself, thinking my mom had forgotten she was meeting someone here. Maybe Roger's proposal was stuck in her head after all, throwing her off a bit.

"Morning," said the young man who emerged from the car, now parked behind mine and potentially making me late.

"Hi. Can I help you?"

"Hopefully. I'm looking for Annette Reed." He smiled somewhere between friendly and cautious. If I had to guess, he was around my age, twenty-something. Nicely dressed in slacks and a button up shirt, he was crowned with an orange-blonde buzz cut, had plump lips for a guy, and wasn't wearing a wedding ring.

"You just missed her. Were you supposed to meet her here?"

"Ah, no. Actually, I'm with Columbus PD."

"Oh." I tossed my backpack onto the passenger's seat in my car. The thud matched the same feeling that hit my chest. "Is something wrong?"

"I'm working a case, and I wanted to talk to Annette. She might be able to help me out."

"Oh?" Yes, I was groping for words here. "She's my mom, but like I said, she already left."

"So you're Kyle? Kyle Reed—daughter to Gerald and Annette?" He pointed at me, as if making an a-ha connection.

Curiosity and a sliver of anxiety mingled inside me. I tucked my hair behind my ear, which I never do. A stranger—a police officer—pulls into my driveway, looking for my mom, and he knows my name. Maybe he picked up on my off-balance feel. He smiled and held out his hand.

"I'm Lance Turner. I'm part of a new division at CPD. We take a fresh look at unsolved cases, and right now we're looking into the death of Marty Cox."

"Who?" It stammered out as I withdrew my hand from his. Probably a bit too quickly. My knees suddenly felt wobbly. I leaned against my car in a flimsy attempt to appear cool and unphased.

"Marty Cox. She used to work over at the Junkyard Lounge, but it's been quite a while ago. Do you happen to know her, know the name?"

I hadn't heard that name out loud in almost a dozen years. And I didn't want to hear it now, not when things were going smoothly. My mom would be somewhere between Incredible Hulk angry and migraine sick to hear that name mentioned.

Marty Cox had started it all. She'd ramped up the discord between my parents, and when I was eight years old, she'd taught me more about life than I was ready for. She'd been the reason my dad left.

"Sounds familiar." That was all I wanted to commit to at the moment. I bit the inside of my bottom lip to counter the dread knotting in my stomach. Long-buried memories assaulted me. The scent of Jovan Musk perfume and purple eyeshadow snapped to the forefront of my mind.

Lance nodded in a way that said he'd go along, accept that less than helpful response.

Lying wasn't my strongest character trait. And to a cop? I might crumble, spill all the ugly, painful details if he pressed too hard.

"I just wanted to talk to Annette. See if there was anything she might remember that could help me out."

"I seriously doubt it." I sounded defensive, like I had something to hide. The whole thing with Marty had scarred each of us. We lived with it, but we never talked about what happened back then.

Lance looked at the ground, nodded more, and shrugged. "You never know. Sometimes when you start talking, think back on what's happened, you might realize something that got overlooked."

I stood frozen, couldn't think of a thing to say.

"Maybe I can catch up with her another time." He took a card from his pants pocket and handed it to me. "She can give me a call, if she wants. Or you can, if you happen to know anything more." His smile reappeared as he slid his hands back into his pockets and returned to his car.

I glanced at the card for no other reason than for something to do. As I watched him drive off, and reciprocated his wave, I wondered what had just happened. I felt buried by an emotional avalanche. Being young at the time, I remembered the angst between my parents more than actual events. Trepidation marched an icy trail through me. No mention of Marty led anywhere good.

Lance Turner had no idea the turmoil that might unleash. And why mention Marty's *death*? Why didn't he just come out and say it—the truth—Marty had been murdered.

By the time I left campus, the Abnormal Psych final was a blur in my mind. I hoped I got my name right at least. If I ended up getting a call from Dr. Gray about my performance and a recommendation to retest, I'd understand why. But how could I explain to Dr. Gray, or anyone else for that matter, that after twelve years, some guy showed up wanting to question my mom about an unsolved murder?

But I had to admit, when it came to Marty's demise, I'd been curious. She'd had a brief but intense affair with my dad. Then he'd left us. A short time later, Marty ended up dead. If this were the basis of an episode of *Unsolved Mysteries*, I'd be snuggled in my seat, glued to the TV, and placing my bets on the scorned wife because those were horrors that happened to other people. But in this case, that scorned wife was my mom.

Chills surged down my back and I chased the thoughts from my mind.

I cranked up the radio as Marky Mark rapped about *Good Vibrations*, trying to drown out any more foolish musings. When I pulled into the parking lot of Gantz, Salyers, and Worley, Law Offices, I knew I had to get myself together.

The building had been converted from a residence into offices about ten years before I came along. Sitting between the seedy south side and the edge of downtown, it was close to home and kept me out of the rush hour traffic mess that plagued the city. Bob Gantz and his buddy Ed Salyers owned the place. They'd bragged about how cheap they'd gotten the house for, but they lacked interior design skills, having covered the place with forest-green carpet and used furniture.

Who was I to complain, though? Bob and Ed hired me as a receptionist my senior year of high school. A year later, they took on Suzette as another partner, and being impressed with me and my passion for the law, she hired me as her assistant. Rather than doing time at McDonald's, I was already working with lawyers and getting a taste of how the legal system worked. Not as glamourous as *Miami Vice* and *L.A. Law* made it seem.

I walked in, feeling more like myself, and greeted Crystal, who had my old job. A tad younger than me, she definitely fueled the rumors that Bob and Ed preferred eye candy at the front door. Pretty, blonde, and friendly, her hair defied gravity and her skirts gave new meaning to mini.

"Hey, Crystal. Any action today?"

"On a Friday? It's dead as can be."

Hearing *dead* made my chest jump start. Not enough of a reaction that Crystal noticed, but I needed to let go of the jitters. Anyway, she was right. Most judges weren't in chambers on Fridays, which meant that Bob and Ed were usually out, too, making the day long and the office quiet. Dead.

"Suzette busy?" I asked.

"She's been on the phone all morning."

Unlike Bob and Ed, Suzette was a workhorse. She spent ten to twelve hours a day in the office, at the courthouse, or a flurry of places in between. I didn't know if it was because she was more passionate about what she did, or if it was because she was a new partner, and a woman, and felt like she had more to prove.

Although my desire to be a lawyer was solidified when I read *Helter Skelter* and *In Cold Blood*, Suzette inspired me even more. Thanks to a case we worked on last year where Suzette proved an accused man innocent on appeal, I hoped one day to work for an organization like the National Center for Victims of Crime.

I headed up to the second floor to Suzette's office, and like Crystal had mentioned, she was on the phone. Not that I'd travelled the globe, but I'd never met anyone like Suzette. She wore gold-trimmed glasses that were straight across the top and tinted purple. Heavy set, she adored donuts as much as her BMW, and always wore her waist-long hair in a braided ponytail. Deep in her 30s, I figured, she had a boisterous laugh you could hear from miles away, and if anyone could be defined as a split-personality, Suzette Worley fit the bill.

She waved me into her office and kept her conversation going. I'd grabbed my legal pad and pen from my desk before going in and doodled the date while I waited for her to finish. As usual, she punctuated the discussion with her laugh and with her serious tone. She finished, hung up, clapped her hands together, and sighed.

"So what's new with you, babe?" Suzette leaned back and laced her fingers behind her head, her chair screeching as she stretched.

"Survived my Abnormal Psych final. Two more to go next week."

"Good for you. Another year down. Should we celebrate?"

"Probably too soon for that." I didn't want to think about how my grade would turn out.

Suzette studied me a moment through those violet-tinted lenses. "You look peaked and gross. Finals wearing you out?"

"Is there any other way to look during finals?"

She let loose with the laughter. "I've been there, babe." She went on to update me on where we were with the Blair custody case, the Drumms' bankruptcy filing, and the Crawford case. For Suzette, there was no such thing as a lazy Friday.

I popped up from my seat to head back to my workspace but paused.

"Suzette, can I ask you something?"

"Anything, babe. You know that."

"Is there a statute of limitations on murder?"

With her elbows on her desk now, she slid her glasses down her nose and looked at me. "You're telling me you don't already know this, Ms. Third Year Criminology student?"

She was right. I already knew the answer and wouldn't be worth my scholarship if I didn't.

"There isn't one," I said.

"Not when it comes to murder, babe. Can't put a limitation on when we catch those bad guys, now can we?"

"No, I guess not." I muttered a thanks and went for my office before she had a chance to get wise with too many questions. I couldn't share about my earlier encounter with that guy Lance. It was still too new, too fresh, and I needed a chance to mull through it. Even so, it felt weird not telling Suzette.

Back at my desk, I let that no statute of limitation sink in. It made sense, didn't it, that the police wanted to solve every case. That a new unit had been set up for that purpose. So no matter how long it had been, no matter how long it took, CPD wanted answers—even justice—for Marty Cox. Maybe it was selfish or cruel, but I wished it didn't involve them showing up at my front door.

Although I'd only worked half a day, I was anxious for five o'clock's arrival. Suzette was on the phone again when I told her I was leaving, and Crystal had already skipped out. Other people's legal issues provided a temporary distraction, but custody battles and bankruptcy filings compared little to wondering if my mom would face a murder charge.

Despite the fact I was drained, I couldn't go home yet. I drove over to Brunswick Manor, a local venue people reserved for weddings and dinner parties. Shelia, my brother's fiancée, had invited me to join her and Trey for their cake-tasting appointment. It was great of her to find thoughtful ways of including me. She did the same for my mom, taking her along for wedding dress shopping and asking her opinion on everything from shoes to how she should wear her hair. Since we didn't have a big family with cousins, aunts, or our own father, Shelia seemed conscious of making the wedding about all of us and not just her and Trey.

"About time, little sister," Trey greeted me. Eight years older than me, barrel-chested like our dad, and topped with a yuppie cut, Trey had a knack for always making me feel self-conscious, even when there wasn't anything to feel self-conscious about. I wasn't late and they didn't have to wait on me to get started, but his snide comment gave me the same inward-cringe as the wet-willies he used to torture me with. Was it a special power that older siblings wielded over younger ones? A force that kept the sibling pecking order in tact?

"So glad you made it." Shelia hugged me and seemed oblivious to Trey's remark. "Long day?"

"Yeah, but that's not unusual." I think Trey hated it whenever I got attention. Oldest versus the Baby syndrome. Too much psychology pulsing in my brain today.

I never put much thought into the ideal woman for Trey, but if I had, Shelia would probably come close. With Sigourney Weaver-like cheekbones, chocolate-brown hair and eyes, she turned heads. Her fingernails were always sculpted and painted to perfection. What made her endearing, though, was the fact that she was a nurse who worked in the burn unit of Children's Hospital. Her love for kids meant I'd get to be an aunt one day, something I wanted more than having my own kids.

Maude, Brunswick's consultant, joined us and brought with her a tray of cake slices. Politely, she chided the couple for being slow in decision making with their wedding only two months away. Rather than offer up excuses or reasons, Trey and Shelia shifted in their seats and didn't look at Maude or each other.

I forked off a bite and held it to my lips. The fresh smell of cake batter and buttercream frosting almost made me faint. I'd had three Cokes today and nothing else. Cake was bad news. I'd agreed to come for moral support and not to actually eat the cake, but now that I was in this, I wasn't sure how to fake my way around it. Fortunately, Trey and Shelia were busy watching each other's reactions. So was Maude.

I casually crumbled my bite with my fork and while no one was looking, I raked the crumbs from the plate onto the napkin in my lap.

Then with a subtle swipe of my hand, the crumbs scattered onto the floor. I managed the same process with all the samples, because I knew if I tasted even one bite that my selfish cravings would take over and I'd eat all three slices. I couldn't let that happen.

I wasn't proud. Making messes wasn't my thing, and no way I wanted to peek at the floor. I had nothing against cake, but I couldn't sit there and shovel it in my mouth like it was harmless. Careful not to make a sound, I shuffled my feet back and forth across the carpet under the table to scatter the crumbs. I hated—hated—that I couldn't have some and wished I hadn't agreed to come.

"Which do you like, Kyle?" Shelia asked when she turned to me.

"Too tough to decide." I put my fork in my mouth as if I were taking in every morsel.

"I think we should go with the chocolate and raspberry filling," Trey said.

"Don't be an idiot!" Shelia snapped. "You can't serve chocolate cake at a wedding."

Maude and I traded glances but Trey didn't skip a beat.

"It's our wedding. We can do what we want."

"Yes, but not chocolate." Shelia smiled for Maude. "I want some things to stay traditional, so I think we should go with the white cake and buttercream frosting."

Trey shrugged. "If it makes you happy. They're all pretty good." He focused on finishing the chocolate cake.

"The white cake it is," Shelia said to Maude, who appeared to force a smile as she took notes. "Excuse me a moment, please." Shelia headed for the ladies' room.

"Can I get you some to-go boxes?" Maude asked Trey, who readily agreed.

Now that we were alone, I took Shelia's seat. I felt like I'd been trapped in a pressure cooker all day with the oddball visit from Lance Turner that morning and no one to talk to.

"Trey, I gotta ask you something."

"Shoot." His attention on the cake didn't wane.

"It's about Mom. Well, actually, it's about Marty."

Now he looked at me.

"This guy came to the house today, said he worked for Columbus Police and they're looking into Marty's case, like it's going to be reopened for investigation. He wanted to talk to Mom and see if she might know something or remember something from back then, but I really think he's trying to say that Mom might be a suspect." My words came out messy, like the cake crumbs from my lap. "Do you think Mom could've had anything to do with it, that she could've killed Marty?"

"Way to start a conversation."

"I know I'm screwing this up, but it's important. What if this guy comes back, starts asking Mom questions? Shouldn't we tell her and do something?"

Trey went back to the cake samples and forked in more bites. I could never read his face. Was he mulling the complexities of telling Mom or experiencing his own flashbacks of life back then?

"Sounds like you oughta be the one to bring it up," he said. "That'll really put her in a good mood, too."

He was right. I'd been the one to talk to Lance, even had his card. But resurrecting the past, talking Marty and my dad with my mom, well, nothing could be worse. Then throw in the bonus that she might be under investigation. Yeah, I wanted that job.

"I'm surprised though," Trey said, his plate nearly cabinet-worthy clean.

"About what?"

"Surprised it's taken this long for someone to come around asking about Marty."

CHAPTER TWO

I couldn't really talk to Trey, not there, not with Shelia coming back from the restroom and with Maude returning from the kitchen with to-go boxes stacked up to her chin. It wasn't the right time, but I felt a bit of relief, having told someone. Not that Trey made a point of making me feel better, or gave me the reaction I wanted, but that was typical of Trey.

After we finished up, and thankfully no one noticed the shower of crumbs I'd left on the floor, I was off to see my boyfriend Derek. I headed home for a pit stop. A walk and some treats for Maverick, and a quick change of clothes for me. Friday nights usually consisted of dinner (the one time a week I allowed myself a full meal) at Brown Derby, the latest movie, and time back at his place.

We'd been together a year, having met at Capital accidentally. I was walking across campus and heard yelling. Derek was about to be hit upside the head by a 2x4 because he was staring at me. His co-workers were hollering for him to look out. He ducked in time and moments later we were both laughing. As he approached me, his white t-shirt stretched to its limits, jeans torn at the knee, and just enough dirt on him to look rugged, I knew I was in trouble. I was bound to say the wrong thing or appear instantly love-struck. There was no way I could tone down my smile. We chatted about nothing and when he was called back to work, I handed him my number on a ripped piece of my Environmental Science homework. Few guys had asked me out, ever, so I didn't think we'd last past a date or two.

Even though we'd made it beyond a few dates, we weren't having sex yet, each of us for different reasons.

Derek was fairly religious and wanted to wait until he was married, or at least he thought he did. For me, being all-out-fat-naked with someone terrified me. So did making a mistake. Once I gave myself over to someone, there'd be no going back. Plus, my mom would never forgive me if I got pregnant.

Sex was a commitment of historical proportions to me. Losing my virginity meant giving away a lifetime piece of ownership over me. Although I'd been close with two other boyfriends, I wasn't ready. The other boyfriends being a perfect example of why. I wasn't with either one now. So I wrestled with how girls my age and younger gave themselves away so carelessly. Guys moved on when their interest fizzled and they'd had their fill. I hated the idea of being used and cast aside. This didn't make me any kind of example to others, though. Not really. I couldn't explain why, but I didn't want a string of ex-lovers littering my past and forever haunting my Little Black Book of Emotions.

The good news was that most people thought we were having sex, Trey and my mom included. Not that we ever talked about it, but my brother would look at me and wink when I first started going to Derek's, and my mom became near-spastic because she couldn't tell me not to go. Strange as it sounded, their impressions made me feel normal.

When Derek answered the door to his apartment, I stole a quick breath. His dark hair was matted to his head, his chest muscles heaved under his gray muscle-cut tank. Seeing him like that always made my heart beat like I'd completed a floor routine of gymnastics.

"Good timing." He smeared his face with a towel, then kissed me. "I'm just finishing up."

Derek's devotion to working out rivaled my obsession with not eating. Since he also worked at his dad's construction business, his physique reflected it. I never imagined I'd be spending my Fridays with a guy who looked this good, and who wasn't anxious to take advantage of me. He had his flaws though, like being too dependent on his family and careless with his money at times. Thanks to me, he'd opened a savings account and now put money aside.

"Won't take me long to get ready, if you want to go out." He rubbed the towel over his hair.

Inside the apartment, I plopped onto Derek's hand-me-down couch from his brother and admired him for a minute. Along with the couch, there was an equally-aged recliner and a TV in an entertainment center cabinet made of oak. His weight bench and dumbbells also took a portion of the room. Nothing matched. Being the youngest of four boys, Derek received all of the family's furniture cast-offs.

"Actually, we could just get a movie from Blockbuster and order pizza." Eating tonight would break my four-day rule, but I had a workable system for eating pizza. Two squares. I knew how to nibble, take my time, and with the amount of pizza that Derek ate, it was impossible for him to keep track of me. Not that he noticed my freaky habits.

"That works, too."

I wanted to unload the day's garbage, hear what he thought about the mess. He knew my dad had left when I was eight, but I hadn't gotten into details about Marty. It made me feel ashamed, like it meant there was something wrong with me if I told Derek everything. There was also the issue of trusting a person so completely, of making myself vulnerable by sharing that sketchy history. I wasn't there yet in this relationship. Keeping Derek at arm's length, both physically and emotionally, meant I was safe.

"You never think for yourself, do you?" Where that remark came from, I couldn't say. Looking at Derek, I knew his expression matched mine, and I knew it was too late to figure out what I was thinking.

Maybe the fact I couldn't talk about Lance had made me cranky. Being careless with words was, at times, my strength.

Derek had that easy going personality that was hard to ruffle. He had a playfulness about him that I'd gotten used to. It often helped loosen me up, like last summer when he'd nudged and begged me to ride my first roller coaster at King's Island, and he was never shy about taking his nieces and nephews to Chuck E. Cheese. But the grumpy side of me said that was trouble, that he'd never take anything serious. He'd never take me or our relationship serious.

"Hmm. Okay." Derek's words came cautiously, as if feeling his way through the landmine of my current mood. "Does that mean you want to go out now?"

I made a sound. Something between a disgusted sigh and a grumble.

"That's what I mean. You never have any ideas of what we could do. It's always me."

"I'm confused here," he said. "Did I do something wrong?"

This was my fault but I didn't know how to be anything but cruel and ugly at the moment. I couldn't explain what was bothering me.

"No, Derek, you're perfect." I said it with a flat, condescending tone. Another strength.

Derek didn't take the bait and explode into an arguing fool. He had a solidarity about him I admired. Deep down, I must be jealous of Derek and the fact he came from a good home. I didn't know what it was like, having parents that were decent to each other, loved each other, made family their priority.

"Why don't I take a shower first?" He tried disarming me with his smile since we'd played this game before: me being snarky and unpredictable, him innocent and confused. "Then we can start over."

I sat there with my arms folded, not looking at him, almost pouting. Derek headed for the bathroom. I clicked on the TV with the remote and turned up the volume to drown out the sound of the shower. A few minutes in, I couldn't take sitting there with myself and knew this wouldn't be a good night for me and Derek. It was best if I left, didn't bicker with him. He deserved better, and my head ached knowing that one day he'd figure that out.

I left Derek's without saying a word to him or leaving a note. A bit heartless, but I saved him from me. It was too early in the evening for me to go home, because then my mom would know something was up between Derek and me. On a Friday, I never made it home before midnight. That meant I had hours to kill. The bad thing was, I didn't want to do anything. Shopping, the movies. None of it held any appeal. Most of my friends had plans with their boyfriends, and I was supposed to be with Derek.

I wished I could talk to Trey, but he was with Shelia.

I ended up at the Southland Mall and forced myself to see a movie. *Deep Cover*, but I wasn't into it. To console myself, I sank into that mental funk I liked torturing myself with. I knew my irritations and wacky moods pushed Derek away. I told myself I was foolish for thinking our relationship could last. Guys like Derek didn't fall in happily-ever-after-love with brainy, scrawny girls like me. Heck, I had boobs the size of lemons, what was there to keep him interested?

After the show, my stomach groaned like a muffled animal. Decrying its missing Friday night meal, no doubt.

"Suffer." I actually said it out loud as I slumped into my car and drove home.

The kitchen light was on, an indication Mom was there. I wondered if I had the wherewithal to face her. Our house had an unusual layout, both inside and out. My parents built the garage after they moved in, back when I was two. Detached and roomy, the garage housed my Sunbird and my mom's Grand Prix comfortably, along with the Christmas decorations and a zillion tools that my dad left behind and my mom never touched. Since the garage sat in the backyard, we used the back sliding doors off the patio to come and go. Only strangers and salespeople touched the front door. Just more of the weird and quirky way our household worked.

When I stepped inside, I smelled the toast and hot chocolate, two of my mom's favorites for a late night snack. Maverick, ever the ladies' man, left Mom's side and wiggled his butt my way and rubbed against me. I greeted him with full-body scratches over his reddish-brown coat while his tail viciously slapped the table leg. His smooches dampened the side of my face and ear. That was the only thing vicious about him, his affection.

"Hey, Bitty. Do you want some?" Mom asked.

God knows I did, that my stomach was raging, but I shook my head.

Mom had a thing for names. Born six weeks premature, I was christened with Bitty as a nickname. *She's such a bitty thing*, someone had said to Mom, and apparently bells went off for her. But Mom also loved her daytime soap operas. When I was little, she'd have them on while she ironed. Somewhere in those wicked, conniving, affair-laden storylines, she'd grown attached to the names Kyle and Trey. It wasn't all bad having an unusual name, but most people expected a boy when they heard the name Kyle. A mild trauma I'd learned to live with.

"Derek called," Mom said, "wanting to know if you were home."

That made my stomach drop to my toes. I didn't think he'd bother to call here.

"Yeah, he fell asleep." I curled my toes inside my black flats. Lying to Mom wasn't my favorite. "Guess he was worn out from the new deck he and his brothers are working on. I just went ahead and left."

My mom gave me that look that said, *You can't fool me*, but she didn't needle me and ask for details.

"I told him you were asleep." She smirked and seemed proud of herself as she stirred her hot chocolate. The spoon made that smooth scraping sound against the ceramic and gave me a homey feel.

"Oh." Hope I remembered that when I talked to Derek tomorrow. If I talked to him tomorrow.

She told me about her showings with the Robinsons and that they put an offer in on a house in Obetz. This would be the fourth house she'd sold this month, if the deal went through. Roger, she said, had taken her out to Ponderosa to celebrate. I updated her on work and school, appreciating the mundane subjects.

We sat at the kitchen table that could only seat two people caddy-corner style. One side of the table was attached to the wall and another side was bordered by the refrigerator. With only the stove light on, the room had a candlelight glow.

"How did it go with Trey and Shelia?"

Maverick returned to Mom's side, hopeful for a piece of crust.

I shrugged. "The cakes tasted funny, like they overdo it with the sugar and flavorings. They picked the white." I thought about Shelia's reaction, and I wondered if my mom had seen Shelia snap like that. But for some reason, it seemed best not bringing it up.

"Did you know there was a guy here today, looking for you?" My heart started pounding so hard I felt the blood rush to my face. There was no gentle way of leading up to the topic of Marty. The cannonball plunge was the best way in.

"Who? An agent or someone wanting to list their house?"

I felt bad, seeing her get excited. "Nothing like that. He said he was with the Columbus Police Department, that they're going to take a fresh look at an old case."

"Oh, so he was here for you? Is this for school?"

"No, Mom." I was so bad at this. "He's looking for you, and he wants information about Marty." I paused and let her absorb the cold water shock Marty's name delivered, but Mom didn't flinch. "You know, *Marty*."

"Yeah, I got it. Heard you twice, once in each ear."

"But do you get what I'm telling you? This guy wants to find Marty's killer."

"Hmph. Who cares about some tramp that's been dead ninety years?" She sipped her frothy hot chocolate noisily.

"This guy is with the police. What if he thinks you did it?"

"I'll set him straight. He won't want to mess with me and get me upset and riled over that trash."

Part of me wanted to scream. Even though I'm an adult, that won't ever matter with Mom. Maybe it's true of all parents, that they wield a leverage over their children that keeps them from bursting forth with what they really want to say. It was a mixture of manners, etiquette, and 'the way things are', I guess.

Handling Mom meant walking a fine line. Whenever I disagreed with her on a topic, my opinion usually didn't matter much to her. A prime example being Mom's fascination with horoscopes. She read her Gemini prediction daily in the *Columbus Dispatch* and never hesitated when *Star* or some other Hollywood rag came out with *'Jeane Dixon Predicts Your New Year'*-type of articles. I repeatedly told her those things were garbage and a waste of her money. She bought the magazines and little rolled-up scrolls beside check-out counters anyway.

But the subject of Marty was different. I knew Mom felt entitled to keep it bottled up because it was hurtful and embarrassing.

"Why can't we just talk about it?" My vinyl chair puffed and squeaked as I shifted. "Just get it all out there and work through it. What's wrong with finding out the truth?" *It's not all about you. A little part of it is about me. Maybe I just need to know.*

Wasn't that how many conversations between parents and adult kids went, always dangling with that last bit that couldn't be spoken?

She shook her head and gave me a mild grin, as if my agitation amused her.

"We've done all right, haven't we?" she asked. "We've made it this far without rattling cages and knocking the dust off what's dead and buried. There's no sense in anyone bothering about that old news. Whatever happened has nothing to do with us. Won't help us none going backwards, because nothing about that matters today."

That was my mother. Flippant, defiant, smart-assy in the face of real problems, and convinced she was Bruce Lee-tough. I knew she felt my frustration, and the fact she dismissed me ruffled me even more. She had all the power to shut down what made her uncomfortable. Her tone told me she was done. Before I forgot myself and let something crass slip, I gave up on the conversation and went to bed.

CHAPTER THREE

The Junkyard Lounge
Summer, 1980

Trey was never home on Saturdays. Mom said it was probably best, and I didn't know why, not until later. Mom always worked, because she said she made good tips on Saturday mornings. I watched *Thundarr* and *Superfriends* or played outside while my dad mowed. Sometimes I saw Nora, our next door neighbor, and she'd invite me over. I'm not sure if she ever combed her hair because it always looked like she just got out of bed, and she wore a housecoat all the time. That's what my mom called it. Nora's voice was shaky and squeaky, just like her hands. She smelled like the stuff Mom rubbed on my chest when I had a cold. I thought Nora was really old, because she had big, round glasses and liked knitting while sitting in a rocking chair. Mom said she was only a few years older than her, but I didn't believe that.

Nora's house was bigger than ours and had a room filled with Barbies and dolls. I didn't care about the dolls. They had weird eyes and puffy dresses with flowers and lace. They looked old. And you couldn't do anything with their hair. Nora didn't let me touch her Barbies or play with them. Most of them were still in their boxes, which didn't seem like any fun. Why would you buy a hundred Barbies and put them on a shelf just to look at?

I played with my Barbies, and I named each one. Morgan and Jackie were my most favorite. They stayed in my room, on the dresser. I also had the Barbie hair salon and the camper. Someday, I'd have my own room of Barbies, and I'd let little girls play with them.

Nora wasn't like other grown-ups. She always gave me tea, even when I didn't ask. I hated tea. A lot. She always hummed and talked to herself. I liked it better when Frank was there. He was Nora's husband. Frank reminded me of Luke Duke from that TV show, since he had really dark hair and wore shirts like Luke. Frank didn't have a big belly like my dad. Whenever I went over there, I didn't stay long. My dad would stand at the fence between our houses and call for me.

We always went to the Junkyard Lounge on Saturdays. It was my dad's favorite place. He said I was too young to stay home by myself, so I got to go. Dad was buddies with Archie, the guy who owned the place. Maybe that was important, because I don't think kids were supposed to be there. I never saw any there besides me.

My mom didn't like it, but Dad didn't think it was wrong taking me there. He said we were spending time together and he wouldn't have to worry about me burning down the house. If I was hungry he'd tell Linda and she'd make me a fish sandwich. I don't know why he never worried about Trey or spent time with him. It was like Trey was invisible.

I liked Archie. It looked like Archie was always squinting, and I wondered if it was because of all of the smoke in the air or because it was kinda dark in there. I'd climb on a bar stool next to my dad and Archie would slide me a pack of Juicy Fruit gum and quarters for pinball and the record machine. Sometimes, he'd tell me not to play The Kendalls. My dad laughed, because I played that one song over and over.

I had to use one of the orange chairs that sat around the tables so I could reach the pinball. Being tiny, which is what people always said about me, was no fun. But I once had the high score on pinball for two weeks. Dad's friends played with me sometimes and I always beat them. But they'd play with a bottle of beer in one hand and a cigarette in the other.

Mom didn't like going there. She said it was *filthy*. The chairs stuck to the floor sometimes because there were sticky spots. Most of the place was dark, except for the light-up signs. The bathroom wasn't like ours at home. It was yuck-brown on the inside and sometimes didn't flush. I only pretended to wash my hands because the water came out yellow-brown. Must've had really dirty pipes.

Next door had a junkyard. That place was a filthy graveyard for junked and wrecked cars. Someone built a fence around it with boards that didn't match and didn't line up like a regular fence. When the boards fell off, they put up chicken wire to cover the hole, or they put a stack of tires there. I only saw it when we drove by to get to the bar and when we were in the parking lot. Sometimes you could hear a dog barking and I was scared it would get through that fence. It gave me the wiggles whenever I looked over, so I kept my eyes shut. I never saw the dog. I'd hold my dad's hand, if he'd let me, and hurry up the steps. Having my dad next to me made me feel safe.

"Marty on tonight?" My dad asked Archie after he started on his first mug of beer.

"Should be in any minute."

I figured Marty was a new friend of my dad's. Archie gave my dad a funny look, almost like he'd said something funny. I don't know why, and my dad got a funny look on his face too. This made me curious about Marty. Maybe he'd play pinball with me later.

Since Archie hadn't said anything about me playing the Kendalls, I hopped off my stool and went to the record machine. I loved the jingle-clank sound the quarters made as they rolled into the slot. I knew the letter-number for my favorite song by heart, but I checked, just to make sure Archie hadn't taken it out.

Minutes later, *Heaven's Just a Sin Away* came twanging into the bar.

Waking up on Saturday with a headache wasn't unusual for me. Saturday was the only day I slept late, and having gone three days without food, my head throbbed like an elephant with a jackhammer. I made it down to the kitchen and the Tylenol, and almost jumped through the ceiling when I saw Derek standing at the sliding doors.

"You scared the crap outta me!" I immediately regretted being quick to snap at him, especially when I had no idea how bad my hair probably looked.

"I've been banging on the door for five minutes."

"Oh. Guess that means my mom must be gone." I glanced around the kitchen for a note but didn't find one. No big deal. Saturdays for her were like Mondays for most people with showings and open houses.

Maverick was busy barking from the utility room downstairs. Mom loved Maverick but wouldn't let him sleep in my bed. Considering the drool Maverick produced, and his bouts of gas, I didn't protest the set-up, but I did keep a healthy supply of rawhides down there for him.

"Did we break up last night?" Derek slid the door shut behind him.

I chewed the inside of my bottom lip, Wishing I could tamp down the rush of blood to my face—or at least undo my bad behavior from last night.

"No." A circus of pain and regret played in my head. Was this a trick question? Had we broken up last night?

"So should I ditch these?" He popped a bouquet of flowers from behind his back. Seeing the flowers only made me feel like more of a jerk. No way I deserved this guy.

"They're beautiful." Breathing in the scent of red roses boosted my mood, and I know I smiled like a bashful idiot. "Thanks."

He kissed me, not in the trashy way most guys do, but with a genuine affection.

"I gotta meet my brothers. We want to finish that deck today. Are we getting together later? Or are you catching up on more sleep?" He glided his fingers through my hair.

Heat dashed to my face again. "I just need to study for finals." That probably ranked high on dumb things to say.

"Do that while I'm working." He kissed my cheek and left.

The kitchen smelled alluring as I cut and arranged the flowers into a vase. My heart swelled, thinking about how Derek made such efforts. Last night was my fault, but he was the one who cared enough to make sure we were okay. I had to shake my head and remind myself not to get in too deep, not to completely fall in love with him. Because sooner or later, I was bound to ruin it.

With the roses done, I downed a couple Tylenol with my morning Coke. Then I snatched my hair into a ponytail and took Maverick for a walk. After we played fetch, I attached his leash to the metal stake in the ground. Maverick had enough length to still roam the yard and plop onto the patio furniture. With his bowls full and a new chew toy, he paid no attention to me going inside.

Mom wasn't home, and I had to take advantage of that.

Meeting Lance yesterday stirred the Marty-memories. Old questions and curiosities had also revived. I drew blanks when it came to the details about her murder. It's not like my parents relived and talked about what happened, at least not to me, and certainly not to each other. Once I got older, I'd never put energy into sorting out what had gone on. That was about to change.

Upstairs in my mom's bedroom, I opened her closet. She only had a few places where she kept old, important papers. The giant box on the top shelf was one of them. I lowered it carefully and sat it on her bed, then dug in.

The contents were familiar. When I was younger and home alone, rummaging through boxes of my parents' private things gave me a secret thrill. Not that there was much inside the box to get excited about. An old portrait of my parents and Trey, before I came along; the hospital band I wore around my wrist as a newborn; various pictures from my grandma that weren't in an album; a fancy pair of cufflinks my dad never wore. A random collection of keepsakes.

One picture that jumped out at me was a Polaroid of a backyard party we'd had. It featured my parents, who weren't standing next to each other, and our old neighbors, Frank and Nora. My mind went back inside their kooky house, to the doll collection and to how gently Frank always treated me and Nora. I understood now that Nora must have suffered from a mental disability. Maybe the dolls made her feel better somehow. The grainy photo captured all four of their smiles and looked like a brief moment of normalcy. Well, as normal as things could be back then. I couldn't remember when they had moved, and I wondered what happened to all those Barbies.

I laid the picture aside and focused on the family album. Tucked in the pages were yellowed newspaper articles and three small envelopes. Postmarked from 1980, the envelopes were addressed to me in scrawled handwriting. They'd each been sliced open neatly and were empty. The envelopes, plain and faded office-white, meant nothing, but the handwriting belonged to my dad. Three pieces of mail postmarked a month apart from one another. No recollections popped into my mind as far as what the envelopes had contained. Because as a kid, getting mail was a thrill. I would've remembered those envelopes—and receiving whatever had been inside.

I turned my attention to the newspaper articles. Obituaries of my dad's brothers; my birth announcement; my grandma being honored for working at the deli for thirty years; cousins playing gigs at the Ramada Inns around Portsmouth. And the articles I knew were there: "Local Barmaid Found Dead" and "No Arrest in Cox Case".

Goosebumps pickled my flesh as I read the details of Marty's death. Found in her home near Lockbourne. Strangled. Police suspect burglary gone wrong. Neighbors reported nothing unusual the night she died.

The second article was equally lame. It recapped the know-nothing events. But it mentioned that her body was found by her husband, Craig Cox. "In light of the circumstances, Cox remained the primary suspect, but no direct evidence could be found against him. Sources claim that Cox and his wife were experiencing marital woes and that papers for a legal separation had been filed."

I never knew Marty was married!

Sure, I'd read the articles before, but it never clicked in my kid-brain that Marty was married. Searching through the snippets of my memory from the Marty-phase, nothing about Craig Cox had stuck. I couldn't say how long it had been since I'd read these articles. Maybe when I was ten or so. Interesting that I skimmed over the detail of a husband. Back then, I didn't care. But now, with the case getting reopened, I cared a lot.

Had Lance visited Craig Cox, assuming the guy was still alive and living in Columbus? What if I looked him up, talked to him myself? If Craig Cox had been the one who found Marty's body, surely he was the one to question.

Did Craig know Marty was having an affair with my dad?

At this rate, I'd need more Tylenol. I put the articles back, closed the album. But when I shifted to return it to the box, more Polaroids tumbled out and onto my mom's bed. I gathered them up and flipped through them. More shots from what seemed like decades ago.

Then I gasped. There was a picture of Marty, exactly the way I remembered her. Blonde hair cut short with soft, sun-kissed curls. Marty Cox was beautiful. She had a glow and shimmer about her, even in a crappy old photo. Pretty teeth, apple-cheekbones. Her lavender blouse had more buttons undone than it should've. She wore the necklace. *How could I have forgotten about that necklace?*

On the snapshot, an arrow had been drawn that started in the bottom border and ended on Marty's forehead. In the white space of the border one word was written in black ink: HIT!

I quickly eliminated any signs of my snooping. Even fought the urge to keep Marty's picture and put it back in the box. A strange nausea strangled my insides. There was so much I'd forgotten. It was probably a hazard of being eight years-old, combined with the fact that no one would've said much to me about Marty's death. I remembered my mom saying something about Marty being dead, something like, "We won't be bothered with that tramp no more." I could hear it in my head. Mom had sounded relieved. Glad.

Did that mean anything? Or was it simply the remark of a belittled wife who was happy that a cheating homewrecker got what she deserved?

And the necklace. Sure, it'd been cheap with a gold chain that would've turned my neck green had I worn it, but that necklace had been my secret treasure. The chain attached on each side of the outstretched wings. Sky blue in the middle that deepened into ocean blue at the edges. Outlined and accented with gold. What had happened to it?

Marty had been like a summer storm. Sudden. Wild. A bit scary, then sweet and refreshing and gone. And after the storm, my dad left us.

Once he'd gone, Trey and I weren't allowed to use his name around the house. Any mention of Dad would make my mom ballistic.

Demoting him to simply Gerald wasn't enough insult. My mom wanted him rebranded and renamed for who he was and what he'd done to us: Greaser. She found it comical, calling him Greaser, a dated reference to guys with bad intentions and loose morals. We'd given her credit for being so clever. Plus, it recognized what he'd done to us. Slipped away without a care in the world.

Finding the picture of Marty, reading the articles about her death I couldn't escape the feeling that I was about to be consumed with knowing the truth. All of it. No matter how ugly it got, how deeply it cut, or what it revealed.

CHAPTER FOUR

I had to go, had to see the old place for myself, and hope that a degree of courage went with me. Since I couldn't focus enough to study, which seemed wrong on a Saturday afternoon anyway, I drove over to the Junkyard Lounge. It was stupid, of course. What did I expect? Billboards in the parking lot that had all the answers and explained everything, including who murdered Marty?

I couldn't say how many times I'd driven by since I'd gotten my license. Maybe I'd done the slow drive by a dozen times, the same way you creep up to and pass an accident. But for the most part it was a 'forbidden' type of landmark that was best avoided. Because after all, what if there was a chance of seeing my dad in the parking lot? Maybe I wouldn't recognize him now. Who knows. My newly sparked curiosity edged me on.

The Junkyard Lounge sat, maybe, six miles from our sliding back door. That'd been convenient for my dad, who stopped in there every evening after work.

I'd decided against taking Maverick with me, knowing he'd bark at anyone he saw in an attempt to make friends. No way I wanted to attract attention.

Not only was the bar still open for business, it hadn't changed much. The blinking arrow marquee, pointing the way for thirsty patrons with its mismatched letters and holes, still sat in the back of a rusted out pick-up truck. I crept my Sunbird closer. Going slow wasn't a problem over here as the bar sat on the other side of dilapidated railroad tracks. Bouncing over them, I prayed my car's undercarriage survived. I eased into the parking lot and took a space on the front side of the building, the side that faced the junkyard. A set of splintered, wooden stairs led to the entrance.

From the outside appearance, maintenance hadn't been a priority. The building needed a facelift from its thin windows to its peeling paint. The parking lot wrapped a dirt circle all the way around. Old railroad ties served as parking space indicators.

When I put my car in park, the absurdity hit me. Here I was in broad daylight sitting in the lot of the old bar my dad frequented. I'd learn nothing sitting there, but I didn't have the guts to go inside. For all I knew, the place was under new ownership. Archie had to be retired and long gone from the place, didn't he? And it was then that I traced through my mind the people who'd been part of my Junkyard world.

Archie, of course. Linda, another barmaid who was there before Marty. Carl, who worked the kitchen and took care of the dishes. What had happened to them?

I kept my eyes on the door, as if I could force someone to come out and talk to me. I was foolishly desperate to see if any of the customers would jog a memory or even remember me.

My dad wouldn't know me. It was a fact that was both depressing and comforting. Depressing because it reminded me, again, of his leaving. I know I'm not the first kid ever abandoned by a parent, but finding a way of living with it and not blaming myself was a psychological battle. I'd done nothing wrong, yet I couldn't escape wondering if I had. Was there something that had triggered an unworthiness to be loved in me? It messed with my head if I thought about it, so just like Mom's box of keepsakes, I put those thoughts away.

Mom had said we were better off when he'd left. Maybe that had been to reassure me. Trey, too. Because when I imagined having my dad around during my teenage years, I cringed. No way I would've had an ounce of self-esteem left, especially when I thought of the way things were between my dad and Trey.

My backyard
Summer, 1978

Dad says I can climb like a squirrel. That's funny. Squirrels are fast, and they can go up higher than people. Mom doesn't like when I climb trees or stand on top of the kitchen counters. I have to if I want to reach the cups and plates. She says I'll break something and get hurt, but I won't because I'm good at climbing, just like Dad says.

I climb in the bathroom, too. They don't know it but I play with Dad's shaving cream. It tastes terrible but I still lick it sometimes. I like the squishy sound it makes when you push the tab. I can make pretend ice cream.

Climbing the trees out back is the best. There are only two I can really climb. The rest are too small. My favorite is the tree by the driveway. And I can get up high enough so that the leaves cover me. It's a good hiding spot and Mom doesn't like it when I go up that high. She thinks I'll fall and break a leg on the concrete. I won't.

One day, I picked three plums off Mr. Frank's tree. The part that hangs in our yard. I don't think that's stealing if it's in our yard. Mr. Frank and Ms. Nora couldn't eat all those plums anyway. I took them fast and put them in my pockets.

The garage door was up. I ran in because Trey and Brian were there.

"What are you doing, pipsqueak?" Trey said. He and Brian were making something with wood and marking it with the hot sticks. "You're not coming in here to play."

I went by Brian. He smiled at me when Trey wasn't looking.

"What are you making?" I asked. Brian had orange hair and pink dots on his face, but he was always nice and smelled like the jean jacket he wore. Sometimes he gave me Now and Laters and he talked a lot about the car he was going to drive when he was allowed. He even said he'd take me for a ride and we'd get ice cream at the Dairy Hut. Why couldn't Brian be my brother?

"It's a picture frame." Brian held up the wooden square. "I'm putting my family's name on the bottom." CARTER was burned in big black letters. I didn't like the smell of the blackened wood.

"It's nice."

"Better get out of here before you get burned," Trey said. "We don't need a baby in here."

"I'm not touching anything!"

"Yeah, well scat!"

Trey never let me stay when Brian was around. Trey only shared things with me when Mom made him.

I wanted to eat my plums so I climbed up my tree. Trey couldn't be mad at me if I was up there. The leaves covered me and I pretended to be invisible. I bit into the plum and juice went all over my mouth. I laughed but Mom wouldn't like my shirt being dirty.

I was going to go in and change my shirt but Dad came out of the house. He walked funny, like he was about to trip. He had a bottle of beer and a cigarette. I thought I heard him say bad words. I stayed still and he sat down in the chair on the patio and smoked. He leaned his head back. More bad words came out. He did that when he got mad at my mom.

Then I heard something fall in the garage.

Dad sat up.

"Wha's going on in there?"

"Nothing," Trey said. He didn't talk to Dad the way he talked to me.

"You boys makin' a mess in there?" He stood and drank from his beer. He walked to the garage but didn't move straight. "I just had that all clean. What is all this?"

"Just my wood burning tools."

"Looks like you got sawdust everywhere." He puffed his cigarette then flicked it into the grass.

"I'll sweep it up."

"You bet you will. What if I wanted to change the oil in the cars today? Did you think of that?"

Trey didn't talk.

"No," Dad said. "Can only think of yourself and your little worthless tools."

I couldn't see everything but I heard clanging, like a toolbox spilled onto the concrete.

"Now look wha' you done. You can't do nothing right. You're worse than your mother. Worthless. You ain't never gonna have a job or amount to anything. No, you're just gonna be here, playin' with toys in the garage all day."

"Dad, I got a job."

Trey did have a job. He worked at Gold Circle opening boxes in the back.

"You ain't workin' now. Just a no-count, worthless bum. Good for nothin'."

Dad said stuff like that to Trey a lot. I never knew what Trey did wrong to get Dad so mad. I didn't like it, and I was glad I couldn't see Trey's face.

"Did you pay the electric bill last month with your job?" Dad got louder. I was careful and slid down some so I could see into the garage. "You think you're some man, but you ain't. You're just a pissy-pant kid. Ain't he, Brian?" Dad finished his beer and tossed the empty bottle at Trey. Trey caught it.

"Oh, does that make you mad, son? You're a big man, right? You want to take a swing at your Old Man, that it?" Dad unbuttoned his sleeves and rolled up both sides while Trey said stuff like *No, Dad, Don't do this! Leave me alone.* "Come on. Let's see if you can take me. Go ahead, I'll give you the first swing."

Trey stood there with a scrunched up look on his face. Brian had picked up some of the tools. I saw his wood frame was now broken.

Dad reached out and pushed Trey's shoulder.

"I wanna see wha' you got."

"No, Dad." Trey didn't say it very loud, and he was looking at the garage floor.

"Don't be no sissy." Dad slapped Trey's cheek. "There. Go with that fire. Come on. I wanna see you swing."

"Stop it!"

Trey put his hands on Dad's shoulders and started pushing him out of the garage. Dad put his hands on Trey, and they looked like two bulls shoving each other. Trey pushed my dad into the grass. Dad fell onto his back and didn't move.

"Leave me alone!"

Trey went back in the garage and told Brian to go home. I wished I could help Trey but his eyes looked red and I knew he would yell at me. Brian took his wood frame pieces and left. I climbed down the tree and looked over at my dad before I jumped out. His eyes were closed. His arms and legs were all over. He looked a giant X. I was scared he was dead, so I jumped down and ran inside to tell Mom. She was in the kitchen standing in front of the sink looking out the window. Her hands covered her mouth. I think she'd been watching. Her eyes were puffy and red.

I told her what happened, but she kept looking out the window.

"Does Dad need an am-blance?" I started crying.

She moved her hands. “No, he’s fine.”

“But he doesn’t lay in the grass.”

“He’ll get up in a minute.” Mom came down to me. “What’s all this?”

I looked at my shorts. They were wet. My plums were all squished.

I cried harder.

My mom picked me up and carried me upstairs to the bathtub.

Memories are a funny thing. They’re fickle. Arbitrary. You can’t make them stay and you can’t erase the ones you don’t want to keep. You can’t sharpen the obscure details and you can’t force them or retrieve them like records in an archive.

I’d sat there in the parking lot of the Junkyard Lounge long enough. Nothing galactic was going to happen. My dad wasn’t going to pull up at any moment. No one from a dozen years ago was going to appear and help fill in my scattered memory banks.

Maybe this was a first step in dealing with the past. I’d never faced it, mainly because I didn’t have to. I accepted what Mom told me and what Trey later repeated. That was it. But this was my history, too. And if my mom was involved in offing my dad’s barmaid mistress, I wanted to know.

I did a quick rake through my purse and found Lance’s card. Giving little consideration to whether or not it was a good idea, I drove to a gas station about a mile away and called him from a payphone. Surprisingly, he answered. I asked him if we could meet, discuss details about the case; he agreed.

I drove to Dan’s Drive-In, a landmark restaurant about ten minutes away. Dan’s was no longer a drive-in where carhops roller skated up to customers’ cars. Like most places on the south side, Dan’s was a weathered and faded version of its glory days but still loved by locals. The inside preserved the 1950s with booths and window trim decked in scarlet, and pictures of Marilyn Monroe and classic cars sprawled against the walls. The table-top jukeboxes were gone but the All-American menu, from home fries to meatloaf, had endured.

I wished I'd been open with Suzette, told her about Lance. No doubt, she could've given me solid advice. And maybe a clue if I was doing the right thing, meeting up with a stranger to talk about my mom's potential guilt.

Making it to the diner first gave me a bit of relief. I preferred having a booth and watching Lance come in. I settled in with a Coke and wondered if Lance expected to eat. My anxiety lurched. Eating sparsely in front of people was one thing; eating sparsely in front of strangers was agony.

Lance made it, greeted me with a wide grin and light embrace, like we were longtime friends. He ordered his own Coke, and we dabbled with chit-chat until our server brought his drink.

He took a sip, then cleared his throat slightly. "Have you had a talk with your mom yet, about Marty?"

"Was I supposed to interrogate her on your behalf?"

"No, but I thought you might get her perspective on what happen that night."

"I told her that you stopped by and that the case was being reviewed." One of my snarky mood swings struck as I folded my arms across my chest. "Told her she was being considered a suspect."

He reared back. "Suspect? Pretty strong word."

"That's why you're here, isn't it, why you're resurrecting the case? You think my mom was involved and you want to pin this on her."

Lance held my stare and didn't look as perturbed as I expected. "I'm only interested in finding the truth." He leaned across the table, flashed his charming smile. "I'm not interested in making this difficult, and no one's being accused. It might be hard right now, since we don't know each other yet, but I want you to trust me." He put his hands on top of the table, as if he was thinking about reaching for my hand but decided against it.

I loosened my arms and slid my clasped hands under the table. "Be straight with me, then. Do you have some piece of evidence that suggests my mom was involved? Because if we're going to trust each other, I need to know what she's up against."

He sighed. "The case file doesn't contain much physical evidence. We're talking 1980 here, and there's not much to go on."

Relief slid through my body. As long as I believed what he was telling me.

"Have you talked to Craig Cox, Marty's husband?" I asked.

"I'm making the rounds." Lance took a long, steady drink from the scarlet tumbler, probably indicating that was all I'd get out of him about Craig.

"Didn't the police claim her death was the result of a burglary gone wrong?" I was glad I'd peeked at those old newspaper articles.

Lance nodded thoughtfully. "That was their public statement, after the case started to go cold. Truth is, Marty's house wasn't too secure. It was in a bad neighborhood and the lock on her back door didn't catch all the way. I think the police wanted people to be cautious and on the lookout."

Our waitress returned for our order, but luckily, we were good with drinks.

"Didn't your mom know where Marty lived?" Lance asked when she left.

A lump formed in my throat. His question unexpectedly took me back to being in the car with my mom and driving through Marty's neighborhood one night. I couldn't remember how we ended up there or how my mom had found Marty's address. She'd mumbled something about snatching Marty bald-headed. But when she discovered that my dad's car wasn't at Marty's, she seemed to calm down. We headed home like we'd made a run for bread and milk but went home empty-handed.

"You mean you think she did it." Anger began sizzling inside of me like Dan's greased grill. I was seconds away from launching my drink in his face. Dan's had tall glasses, so Lance would end up soaked.

"That's not what I'm saying." He held up his hands defensively. "But think about it, Kyle. Your mom and Marty had to be mortal enemies, didn't they? And when the police ask, was there anyone who wanted her dead, I have a feeling Annette Reed came up."

My head buzzed from the racing thoughts. Lance had a point. My mom had a motive. She also had newspaper clippings and a picture of Marty in a keepsake box. On the other hand, he was talking about my mom possibly hurting someone.

"I know it's a lot to think about," Lance said. "I just have a feeling that she knows something, that's all. That she's kept something to herself all these years about what happened. And after all this time," he shrugged, "maybe she's ready to get it off her chest. Could be time for her to open up."

His words cut deep. What if he was right, that Mom knew something? The best revenge for her could've been denying Marty justice. I could see that with Mom. Chills paraded down my back. What would that mean for her?

"Give me a chance to talk to her first, see if I can get her open up." Even as I said it, I didn't quite believe it. Mentioning Marty last night to Mom had gone so well. But could there be more reasons why Mom became snide? She didn't want to talk about it because there was a hidden truth there?

"We'll have to meet up again," Lance said. "Which is fine by me. Only next time, maybe we could make it some place nicer. Even dinner?"

It crossed my mind that Lance Turner was trying to dupe me into something. That bugged me, but so did the fact that I found him mildly attractive. Maybe I *was* interested in having dinner and finding out how far I was willing to trust Lance. That worried me almost as much as what my mom could be hiding.

The Junkyard Lounge
Summer, 1980

It was one of those long nights. We'd been here a long time. I was out of Juicy Fruit and had spent all my quarters on pinball. Dad and Marty were dancing again. I couldn't hear anything they said, because Archie had the record machine up loud, so all I heard was George Jones, Charlie Rich, and Johnny Cash. But Dad and Marty talked the whole time. He had his hands around her waist and her arms were around his neck. Sometimes their foreheads touched. Sometimes they kissed.

My stomach hurt. I didn't know if it was from eating three pieces of the gum or from watching Dad and Marty. Was he supposed to be kissing her? I never saw him kiss Mom like that. But Mom never smiled that much around Dad either.

I lay my head on the bar while my legs dangled. Sitting up on the high stool was always fun, but I was tired of fun and wanted to go home. I wanted Mom.

"You all right, baby?" Linda scratched my head softly as she bent over me.

"Yes." I didn't lift my head.

"You're not getting sick are you?" She set her tray down and came over and put her hand on my forehead. Her hand felt cold, probably from handing out beers. The air conditioner wasn't the best here. Another reason to leave.

"I'm not sick."

Linda didn't hear me, because she turned to my dad, her cold hand now on her hip. "Gerald, you better get over here and take care of this baby. She's not feeling too good."

Dad was running his hands up and down Marty's back. She'd tossed her head back and was laughing like he said something funny. They were the only ones left dancing. Both of them looked over at me.

"She's all right. Ain't you, Bitty?"

I could tell from the way my dad said it how I was supposed to answer.

"I'm fine." I sat up and made a smile for Dad and Linda.

Carl peeked out from the kitchen. He had shiny black hair like a vampire and his apron was always dirty. His eyes went big every time he stared at Marty. I don't think anyone saw him do that but me.

"That's a good girl." Dad rubbed his face against Marty's neck and she giggled.

I didn't feel like a good girl, because I wanted to yell at him to stop dancing with Marty and to take me home. But when we got home I didn't want him saying those mean words to Mom.

"It's getting awful late, Gerald." Linda cracked her chewing gum. "Might be time to put this baby in bed."

"Just a little while longer," Dad said.

When I heard that I almost cried. There was no such thing as a little while.

"Linda, why don't you get us a shot of Black Velvet?"

Dad and Marty were holding hands when they came over to the bar. Marty ran her fingers through my hair. I didn't like that. Only Mom was allowed to do that because she did it the best. I wasn't listening to what she said. I jumped from the stool and went to one of the tables while they tossed their heads back and drank from the tiny glasses. I pushed four orange chairs together and lied down all curled up like it was a bed. I squeezed my eyes shut, hard, wishing I could make every bit of everything go away. I wanted Marty to go away the most.

CHAPTER FIVE

When it came to compartmentalizing, I was a master. I could switch gears from perfect student to responsible office clerk to model daughter to loving girlfriend effortlessly, all while stuffing away the things that bothered me. Being able to bottle most of my emotions felt like a gift, one that set me apart from most girls. Starving from emotional expression was probably a good thing, and it hardened that protective shield I kept around myself, not letting any one person get too close to me.

I didn't know what to think about Lance. He didn't act like the cops I'd met through working at the law office. Maybe it was because he was younger, and if a detective was going to sift through people's pasts and till the dirt of buried skeletons and buried secrets, then coming across as personable and gentle was probably wise. Being young and appearing unassuming also helped him, I guess.

Of course, I was distracted by whether or not he was genuinely attracted to me. My experience in playing the field was fairly nil. I'd spent most of my time on the bench. If he was planning on using me for information and sex, he could forget it. On both counts.

Back home, with still no sign of Mom, I called Derek. He said he was waiting for me at his place. Hearing his voice comforted me. A much better sensation than what I got from time with Lance.

After taking care of Maverick, I made it to Derek's apartment. Lance got stuffed into in his newfound box in my mind. Now wasn't the time to play with the details of our conversation. Shelving Lance came easy, especially when I walked in and realized that Derek had set the mood for a romantic at-home dinner.

He'd set up a card table in the middle of the living space, complete with a tablecloth and candles. A modest bouquet of flowers, in a tall glass, occupied the center. Folded paper towels served as napkins while two plain white plates awaited the main course.

No one had ever done anything like this for me. Being the center of attention wasn't for me, neither was giving a cutesy reaction.

Derek came out of the kitchen carrying a bowl.

"You did all this?" My smallish voice gave away my glee.

"I thought we'd hang out here tonight."

His strut and deepened voice were meant as a tease. This was Derek proving me wrong about what I'd said, that he never planned anything special for us. Glancing at his table setting, I liked being wrong. He was more than capable of taking charge and putting creativity into an evening together.

"I see." My smiled made my cheeks tingle. "What are we having?"

"Spaghetti with extra crispy garlic bread and hamburger instead of meatballs. House specialty."

I laughed and kissed him appreciatively after he sat the bowl on our charming table. It didn't matter that spaghetti wasn't one of my favorites or that I hardly ate hamburger. I'd pay for this meal later with stomach cramps and an uncomfortable trip to the bathroom, but I knew it'd be worth it. That came with the territory of not eating and then overindulging. Tonight, I didn't care. I'd soak this evening up for what it was: a night of my boyfriend lavishing me with tenderness and attention. Nothing could be better.

Being with Derek felt good, almost too good. What could this guy possibly see in someone like me? I was lousy at relationships because I was always afraid of getting too serious, of having sex with the wrong guy, and of messing up my life like my mom had by marrying a guy like my dad. Moments like this with Derek confused me. Where were we really headed as a couple? Were we bound to run out of things to talk about and argue over? And was he serious about saving sex for marriage? What if I changed my mind and didn't want to wait, would that be the end of our relationship for him?

None of that mattered now. We enjoyed our little dinner, extra crispy garlic bread and all.

I called and left a message on the answering machine for Mom, though I wondered how she still wasn't home. I thought again of the keepsake box and Marty's picture with "HIT!" written on it. All those fragments to the past had me shaken, edgy, suspicious of every little thing. Because otherwise, I would've enjoyed missing out on her disappointment that her daughter was *sleeping* at her boyfriend's house.

But on the other hand, maybe she was keeping busy and staying away on purpose. Avoiding me, so she could safeguard her secrets and keep me at bay.

My evening turned out as I predicted with me spending more time in the bathroom than cuddling on the couch with Derek. Having worked for twelve hours, Derek conked out on the couch while I was occupied. Not unusual. We made an interesting couple.

I helped myself to Derek's bed, wondering if this was a slice of what married life was like. At the same time, I had trouble sleeping. Tomorrow was Sunday and Mom's designated family dinner day. No matter what the rest of the week was like Mom devoted Sundays to cooking and making us sit around the dining room table for one meal. Deep down, she wanted us to be like the Waltons. Sunday dinner became a tradition after Greaser gave us the slip.

Considering the events of the last couple days, I knew I wouldn't sleep. I'd lie there, alone, mentally mulling through the newspaper articles and conversations with Lance, and knowing I needed to make an effort to talk to my mom before Lance came calling again. But how? How did I bring up what had to be the most painful aspect of her past and convince her that purging the truth would be good for all of us?

Derek was perfect for this. Being around family was his element. Not hard to understand since he was the youngest of four and had enough cousins and relatives to stretch the length of the Ohio River. More impressive was that they saw each other regularly with cookouts and get-togethers for every imaginable milestone. His mother actually owned a picnic basket and knew how to make pie crust from scratch. I wasn't sure I could make it in his world as an overly self-conscious introvert.

A dinner of six people was nothing for Derek. He could be comfortable in a crowd or at my mom's caddy-corner table. I envied his conversation skills and that way he had of making everyone around him feel good. Relationships scared me. Probably because my parents' example had been an epic disaster.

Since our late night chat, I hadn't talked to my mom. Watching her buzz around the kitchen now, I knew there no chance of rehashing Dad and Marty details. Not that there ever would be an ideal moment, but I had a feeling Mom would make sure of it.

Maverick was Mom's biggest fan when it came to her cooking, but Mom couldn't handle drool drips on the floor while she worked, and in the small space, she often stepped on his paw. So Maverick was relegated to the utility room while we ate, which always made Derek snicker.

"I need you to take care of the rolls," she said, apparently irked by my standing around.

I set the oven and readied two packages of dinner rolls. Thankfully, I wasn't trusted with much else for these meals. Trey, Shelia, and Derek occupied the rec room downstairs. I kept my jealousy in check each time a burst of laughter or happy ruckus lilted to the kitchen. Mom had an unspoken commandment that I belonged in the kitchen on Sundays. That jealousy tag-teamed with resentment while I did the dishes afterward. Shelia brought dessert each week because she wanted to. Mom marveled over them, but I never touched her brownies or cookies or triple chocolate cake.

If that wasn't enough, dread built inside me, not only for having to eat in front of others, but also because there was no escaping my mom's hillbilly cooking. Although I'd convinced her that she was the only fan of chicken livers (which wasn't true; Derek ate whatever was on his plate), she still whipped up culinary nightmares—open-faced roast beef, broiled turkey necks, and fried bologna, which she called Kentucky round steak. Her adoration for Bisquick and Crisco ran deep, although her 'secret ingredient' of choice came from a container she kept in the fridge, bacon grease.

"Holler down and tell everyone we're ready," Mom said.

I slid the tray of rolls into the oven. "Aren't we waiting for Roger?"

"He'll be here soon."

We couldn't do things like family dinners when Greaser lived here because he preferred being drunk over being with people. Toward the end of our time as a dysfunctional family, he also proved unreliable. We never knew when he'd bother to come home from the bar. The longer he stayed meant the worst shape he'd be in, but there were also nights when he didn't come home at all. Of course later on, we found out he'd been with Marty. I was grateful my mom didn't have to tolerate that humiliation anymore, along with the cruel things he used to say to her.

"Are you nailed to the floor?" Mom asked.

My memories had hampered me.

I called up the others and returned to roll duty. Mom was right about Roger. By the time we were filling our plates with chicken and dumplings, Roger had arrived and joined us. As usual, he greeted Mom with a peck on the cheek. Another positive habit she'd grown used to.

Roger Coughlin was as opposite to my dad as a man could get. Capped with snow-white hair that he styled like Pat Sajack's from *Wheel of Fortune*, Roger wasn't much taller than Mom, had a baritone voice that could rumble leaves off trees, and turquoise-blue eyes that seemed ripe with good intentions when he smiled. He loved his German Shepherd, Mac and his silver Jaguar. Two things that most attracted my mom to Roger were his upbringing and his business savvy. Raised in the hills of West Virginia, Roger came from a long line of coal miners and never knew a day in his life without hard work. Mom could relate to that, as well as to leaving behind what she knew and making a life elsewhere. In the five years they'd worked together, Mom credited Roger with making her a better real estate agent. He'd lost his wife four years ago to cancer and his grown daughters lived in Chicago and Cincinnati, which meant he could devote most of his time to work and to courting my mom.

"Got those rolls ready, Kyle?" Roger teased. Aside from the standard chit-chat, we didn't interact much. Not that I made a real effort. He was interested in Mom and that was fine, especially if it made her happy and distracted her from nit-picking me.

"They're waiting on you." I sat the basketful on the table, next to my empty plate. I showed off the vase I'd filled with Derek's roses and used it as a centerpiece. Placing it off center, I hoped it would block Mom and Roger's view of my plate and discourage any comments.

Then I positioned my can of Coke strategically, further blocking sightlines. Roger had once been the nosy one who mentioned how little I ate and no wonder I was *skinny as a string bean in a drought*. Nothing like being uncomfortable in your own home.

"Do you think you can get to the yard next week?" Mom asked Derek as we settled in.

My fork slapped my plate. "Mom! You can't keep asking Derek to mow the lawn."

"Why not? He's capable, and I feed him."

Derek laughed.

Mom did this, made her passive-aggressive demands on people in front of others. Derek didn't understand her tactics like I did. Plus, I hated how Mom never made Trey mow the lawn. But in her mind Derek was supposed to, like a penitence he had to endure for fornicating with her daughter. Which wasn't happening. Drove me crazy.

"Yeah, I don't mind." Derek shrugged. Then to Mom, "I'll take care of it. Oh, hey, I saw your neighbors put their house up for sale. How come they didn't list with you?"

If he changed the subject because he noticed I was tense or simply because it was worth mentioning, I couldn't say.

"Ah, never cared much for the Whittiers anyway. Not like the homes in the Meadows go for much these days, maybe eighty or ninety. Not enough meat on them bones."

"Frank's old house is on the market again?" Trey plopped into his seat after returning from the bathroom. "How long's it been since he had Nora committed?"

"A good number of years." Mom tilted her head slightly. "Best thing for her. Poor Frank. All he went through, taking care of her."

"He put Nora away?" I asked.

"She's at the psychiatric hospital, just outside of Columbus," Mom added. "Frank couldn't handle her on his own anymore."

I didn't know what that meant exactly and now didn't feel like the right time to ask, since Roger and Derek probably didn't know who Frank and Nora were. But it irked me. Another example of details I'd missed, thanks to being ten or so when they moved out.

Mom and Trey shared a little history about Frank, Nora, and the dolls while I stewed over the old-news revelation. Shelia, who didn't seem interested in hearing about our former kooky neighbors and their problems, reached for a catalogue she'd laid on the buffet.

"Kyle, you have to tell me what you think of this for the bridesmaid dresses." She flipped to a dog-eared page and handed me the *Modern Brides* magazine.

I had no hope of matching her zeal but I mustered up some enthusiasm. It was an honor being asked to be in the wedding party, or so I thought at first. In fact, it saddled me with responsibilities: hosting a shower and planning a bachelorette party. These required a people-person skill set I didn't possess. And looking at a picture of the bright lemon-colored dress Shelia was excited about made me want to crawl under the table.

"That says summer wedding," was all I could think to say.

"Do you think the ruffles are too much?"

All around the bodice? "No."

"If you're lucky," Roger continued, "maybe you'll get to wear that dress twice."

I glanced at the photo. "Not sure where else I could wear it since it's pretty formal."

"How 'bout to another weddin'?" The more time Roger spent around Mom, the more his accent became pronounced. Same thing happened when Mom visited her family in Kentucky. An Appalachian drawl probably didn't help sell real estate but it was part of them.

Was it the thickening of the accent that dulled my senses? Maybe. Because I wasn't sure how to reply to Roger's comment until I glimpsed my mom's face. I'd never seen her eyes that big before, and

I realized that Roger was hinting at his own wedding to my mom. Interesting how Mom didn't mind putting Derek on the spot but squirmed when the tables turned.

Roger reached into his back pocket and with his hand quivering put a small velvet box on the table.

"Well, Ann, should we make it official?" He put his hand on top of Mom's, probably to calm his nerves and to show his love.

Bewilderment and delight collided onto Mom's face. She stared at the box with her jaw open.

"Go ahead." Roger nudged her softly with his elbow. "See what you think."

Trey and Shelia leaned in as Mom went for it. Now her hands trembled as she pried the edges apart. When Mom had first mentioned Roger's proposal, there hadn't been a ring. Maybe that's why she'd cast it aside and treated it casually. One velvety box and a squeak later, that changed.

Inside was one of the most beautiful rings I'd ever seen. Bewilderment took a turn on me, knowing how stingy Roger was. He'd often leave the table when it came time to pay the check at a restaurant, leaving me, Derek, or Trey to pick up the tab.

Of the material things in life, Annette Reed loved jewelry most. Her commission checks split three ways: bills, savings, jewelry fund. As her success as a realtor grew, so did the rings on her fingers. Trey once cautioned that she had the beginnings of a Mr. T starter set, but she happily flopped a bedazzled hand at him and ignored him.

"Let's see it on," Roger said, when Mom did nothing but stare at the ring and hold it up, as if she was examining a rare artifact.

"If you try it on that means you accept," Trey said before she'd made a move.

"That's an old wives' tale." But Mom put the ring on her index finger, on her right hand, and admired its sparkle.

We laughed, Trey and I in particular, because we knew she wouldn't be told what to do, not after what she'd endured with Greaser, and because Roger couldn't have looked more uncertain and helpless if he tried.

A lot could be said for my mom's character and integrity. She never passed a panhandling Vet without warm thanks, a donation, and an interest in his story. During my elementary and middle school days, she volunteered whenever parents were needed, and she chatted with the lunch ladies and janitor as much as she did other parents and the teachers. She valued hard work over a pretty face and a healthy bank account over modern conveniences. Like a dishwasher. After Sunday dinners became tradition, I considered this a character flaw, especially since I became the dishwasher.

"Mom, why can't we get this thing fixed or at least get a new one?" I slapped the top of our butcher-block dishwasher, which, in my lifetime had never cleaned a load of dishes. Mom used the inside of the dishwasher like a filing cabinet, complete with fat manila envelopes containing real estate deals, tax receipts, and other useless paperwork.

Roger had left soon after dinner. Not because he wanted to but because my mom ushered him out, said she needed time to think before making any big decisions. After Roger was out of sight, she took the ring out of its box and busied herself with posing and admiring the rock, while also ignoring my question.

Shelia and the guys were back with the TV while the womenfolk of the house took care of clean up. All I needed was a bonnet and a full-bodied apron. Oh, and a washtub for those pesky dishes. Maverick was enjoying yard time, after finishing the plate Mom had fixed for him.

"Do you even like Roger?" I folded my arms and leaned against the dishwasher relic.

Mom turned to me. "What makes you say that?"

"Seems like most women cry and gasp and fall into the arms of the man they love as they accept the proposal. Not you."

"Well, it wasn't a fancy proposal, and we've both been married before."

"True, but you act like you'd rather string Roger along than commit. Are you afraid to get married again?" I'd never tampered too much with the subject before. After Greaser left, she seemed set on being independent and self-sufficient.

"Oh, I'm afraid, but there'd be no mixing of my money with his." Mom was on dish-drying and put-away duty.

I took that in. "That's your main concern, money?"

"Sure as Hell's fires! I've worked hard for every cent." She rubbed the last dish with such fervor, I though the glaze would be removed.

"You're not in love with him?"

She stopped and held the dish to her chest. "Love doesn't do you much good in life. Doesn't pay the bills or buy you diamonds like this." She wiggled her fingers, making the diamonds glisten in the light.

"Does Roger know you feel this way?"

"Of course! I already told him that if he wanted me to take him serious he'd have to give me a ring and pay for the kitchen remodel. I'd keep my name. Oh, and there'd be no living together."

My head was spinning. "What? That doesn't make any sense."

"Sure it does. Neither of us wants to sell our house, and that way when his girls are here they have a place to stay, and he can stay with them."

"Then why get married at all?"

"He promised me half of what he's worth, and I promised to take care of him if he got sick. Losing Bev scared him. He thinks he'll go the same way, that he probably picked up some disease from serving in the Korean War years back. Plus, he's got a good twelve years on me, so he's likely to go first."

I sank onto the puffy vinyl seat at the caddy-corner table. Her practicality didn't surprise me but the coldness of how this arrangement sounded did. I wondered if this was all true, if Roger genuinely agreed to such terms. Would there be any sex in that marriage? I shuddered all over, hoping to shake that last thought from my mind.

"Sounds like you two have it all figured out." Deadpan was the best way to describe my voice.

"We'll see. I still haven't made up my mind. You never know if something better is gonna come along."

My thoughts shifted to Derek. What would he think of a woman marrying only for money, and would he be worried that I was the same way? Mom had a point about love, that it wasn't useful. I understood that. Falling for someone was dangerous, maybe led to mistakes. I was finding it harder and harder to resist Derek physically. Did that mean I was falling in love with him, that being intimate would deepen, solidify my feelings for him? I didn't know how it worked. And with Lance showing up out of nowhere, I questioned if there was something wrong with me, finding even a slight attraction towards someone who thought my mom was possibly guilty of murder.

After the dishes, we made the mistake of playing Monopoly. It drew the guys away from the TV but Mom was merciless. More frustration did wonders for my mood. Trey and Shelia escaped when the slaughter was over. Trey hadn't said anything to me about the subject of Marty and the re-opening of the case. Not that we had a chance for a real conversation with everyone around. But how could he say nothing? Wasn't he the least little bit worried that Mom could've been involved?

"It's getting pretty late," Mom said not long after Trey and Shelia were gone.

I got the hint. Here was Mom shifting into old-fashioned country girl. Boys didn't stay late because the neighbors might talk. Although Mrs. Davis only had nice things to say about Derek and the house on the other side sat empty.

"Nine o'clock is late if you're Amish," I said. "We're going to watch the Sunday Night Movie." Maybe I'd turn the tables on her, let her know that I wanted some alone time in the rec room with my boyfriend.

"Oh, well, I wanted to see that special on 20/20."

Having only one TV in the house created conflict, but not enough for any of us to splurge on getting another one.

"Oh. Well, we can just go to Derek's place—"

"No, that's fine. I'll catch it later." She packed up the remaining pieces of the game and took it with her as she left the room.

Mom might dominate at board games, but she could learn a few things about relationships and expectations. I didn't notice her telling Trey and Shelia not to have sex when they got back to their apartment, so why the double-standard when it came to me?

We invited Mom to watch with us, but she said she had paperwork to catch up on. Derek and I shared the couch and didn't say much while the show was on. Since Derek made sure there wasn't enough room for Maverick to join us, my pup napped on the carpet. I finally felt relaxed. I sat sideways with my legs in Derek's lap. He caressed my bare skin gingerly as I raked my fingers through his hair. It took a lot for me to feel this comfortable around a guy. I knew then I was an idiot for thinking life could instantly be this easy with someone like Lance.

I let my guard down.

"I love you." I'd said it plenty of times, but this was a moment where I was letting myself go, like taking a swan dive over the edge of the walls I'd built around myself, hoping Derek was the one meant to catch me.

Derek flashed a half-smile and kissed me. "Love you, too."

Mom was wrong, picking money over love. That wouldn't be me. In fact, I was still peeved about how the day had gone with her, so much so that I decided not to bring up Lance or his suspicions. What was the point of trying to talk to her when I was the only one who had any interest or urgency? No, I'd let her cling to her stubbornness and let the new investigator track her down, hound her with questions, and see if he had better luck prying out her side of the story than I'd had.

CHAPTER SIX

Mondays are pure evil, especially with finals looming overhead that I hadn't studied for. Between time spent with Derek, fussing with Mom, wasting time on Lance, and even venturing to the Junkyard Lounge, I'd kept putting it off. I crammed, best I could with two hours. That bloated feeling left over from Sunday's dinner didn't help.

After my exam, I headed to the law office, planning to spend the rest of the day sulking and ear-deep in paperwork.

"That's it?" Suzette greeted me when I looked in on her. "That's how you come in looking after the weekend? Didn't you spend any time with that stud-muffin boyfriend of yours?"

Another reason to love Derek: he made me look good.

"Yeah, we hung out."

Suzette glanced at me sideways as if she knew I'd been naughty.

"But…." I hesitated.

"What?" Suzette straightened. "Are you pregnant? Because, babe, I will ring you out if so."

"No, nothing like that, but I do have a problem."

"Sit." Suzette pointed to the seat in front of her desk. As I lowered myself onto the high-back leather chair, she laced her fingers together, having transitioned from funny and free-spirited to serious lawyer lady. "Now spill."

I told her about Lance showing up at my house on Friday, intent on finding Marty's killer. Oh, then I had to explain who Marty was, and that my mom was being considered a person of interest. I felt like a magician pulling a dozen handkerchiefs out of my mouth. Suzette scribbled notes on a legal pad but suddenly flattened out her hands and looked at me.

"Is this for real? Are you kidding me? You sure you didn't steal this from an episode of *Guiding Light*? Am I on a hidden camera show?"

I bit my bottom lip and shook my head. Hearing myself tell the story was surreal. Embarrassing. Suzette took off on a rant about how thoughtless and irresponsible my dad was for taking a child to a bar—and then exposing me to his affair.

"I've heard a ton of crap," she said, "being in the business of family and marriage disintegration, but this is a mess." She reared back in her chair and caught her breath before switching gears. "This guy Lance, he's Columbus PD?"

I nodded.

"He show you his badge?"

"No." My scalp prickled. I'd taken Lance at face value. What kind of legal professional does that?

"Was he in a cruiser?"

"No."

Suzette considered that. "Said he's with a new division?"

"Yeah, he said it's where detectives take a fresh look at an unsolved case. Cold case or something like that. He said the case file didn't contain much evidence or interviews, but he thinks my mom might be able to remember something that could help." Back to more lip chewing.

Suzette looked pensive a moment, then asked, "What are you not telling me?"

I sat as if I had a stomachache, hunched and knees almost to my chest. Cringing, wondering if there was a chance my mom had hurt Marty. "I went through some of my mom's keepsakes and found two articles about Marty's death, then I found a picture of Marty with the word 'HIT!' written on it. It doesn't prove anything but—"

"Could look bad. I get what you're thinking. Hmm. You could be right. What does your mom say about it?"

"She won't talk about it, won't take it serious."

"You think she's hiding something from you?"

"Yes." I realized I believed it. Suzette had a point. Mom sidetracked our conversation because there had to be something she didn't want me to know. Just like with Frank and Nora, she'd never mentioned Nora's hospitalization, but she knew.

"Want my advice?" Suzette asked. "Talk to your brother. He's older and had a better understanding of what was going on. I bet he has to know something."

The only thing worse than talking to my mom about Marty was talking to Trey about Marty. For Trey, having information I wasn't privy to was like having a toy he didn't have to share. It also meant he had a closeness with Mom that I didn't. A secret club I wasn't allowed in.

Considering his reaction was, *I can't believe it's taken this long*, when I mentioned the case was getting a new investigation told me plenty. He held the same calloused attitude toward Marty as our mom. The more I replayed our brief conversation in my head, the more convinced I became that Suzette was right. He had to know something. Maybe he knew what Mom was hiding.

Suzette let me skip out of work before lunch so I could catch Trey at his downtown office. Not calling ahead was best. That way, even if he wanted rid of me, he'd have to talk to me. Her grand idea. Not mine.

It was sad that I really didn't know what Trey did. Sure, I knew the name of the company he worked for and that he was a computer analyst. Beyond that, I was clueless.

Luckily, I maneuvered downtown enough to know where I could park. I'd still have a short walk but it gave me time to practice what I'd say. I checked in with the receptionist and she buzzed Trey. Instead of getting the go-ahead to take the elevator up to his office, Trey met me in the lobby.

"Are the phones broke in your office? What are you doing showing up like this?"

"Glad to see you, too." I'd never shown up at his office uninvited. My heart seemed lodged in my throat, beating like a jackrabbit on fire. Even when you're family, there are lines you don't cross. I hoped my impulsiveness conveyed that I needed his attention. Needed his help.

He glanced around at the flow of people traffic in the building, as if he was embarrassed being seen with me. After a curt nod for the receptionist, he took me by the arm and led us outside. I wondered if he was planning on taking me back to my car, but we strolled over to a hot dog vendor. My stomach curled at the thought of a Jumbo Dog. I said I'd already had lunch and would stick with a Coke. Trey ordered a Volcanic Dog with the works. That included a hot sauce laced with habanero peppers. Poor Shelia.

Our order in hand, we walked over to the Statehouse and sat on the steps.

"Sorry for not calling first. I don't mean to make you mad." The best I could do, trying to soften him up.

Trey didn't look at me. He gave a half-shrug and focused on unwrapping his lunch.

"We haven't had a real chance to talk. I know Marty isn't your favorite subject, but if the police are revisiting her case, shouldn't we all talk about it?" Who was I kidding? Softening up Trey wasn't possible. I went with bluntness instead.

"So some guy comes around asking questions and now you're *Magnum P.I.*?"

"I thought we could come together on this, be a united front for when the police show up and start asking questions. Especially if you and mom know something about who murdered Marty." I bit my straw and took a fizzy sip, fearful I'd pushed too far.

"This is all about you." Trey bit into his chili dog and managed not to wreck his dress shirt with dripping sauce or a stray onion. "Always got to have the attention."

My jaw went slack. If my brother had any special talents, it was the art of turning every situation into being my fault. When I was younger, I usually fell for it, but now, I was tired of the runaround from my own family.

"Marty getting murdered is hardly about me."

He ignored me. "And the timing of all this couldn't be better. I really want to dig up the past with my wedding six weeks away. I don't have enough to stress about."

He worked on his meal while I silently recovered from the verbal jabs. Why had I bothered to come?

"Fine." I said it as tersely as I could.

"None of this makes sense. Why get into the Marty debacle now, after all this time? You really think Mom could bust someone's skull? Come on, Kyle. Don't go stirring up ghosts." Despite his rupture of chatter, he said it in a manner of calm I didn't know he was capable of. Then he turned to me. "Don't do that to Mom."

"I just want to find out what happened and for you and Mom to stop treating me like a kid. Like I'm not part of the family." That was the real issue for me. Being shut out. That familiar claw of rejection swelled in my chest. Because it wasn't enough that my dad walked out on me; my mom and brother kept me at arms-length emotionally. I couldn't deal with that now and scarfed a deep breath to tamp it down.

Trey gave a mild shrug and looked away. For a while we were quiet, me sipping my drink, him managing those bites.

"You're the lawyer in training. If you need to play detective, check out that guy she was married to. Makes the most sense that he did it. Leave Mom out of it."

"Don't you think the police exhausted that lead?" I asked.

Trey crinkled the paper remnants from his grub and tossed them in the nearest trash can. He dug his hands into his slacks and shrugged. "He's gotta know more than anybody."

"What about Dad?" Saying Dad out loud made my insides quiver, like the first time your parent hears you cuss. "Should I track him down too?" Where that came from, I couldn't say.

Trey started walking back to the entrance of his office building. Before he went in, he glanced over his shoulder and gave me that expression that only rarely passed between us. The look that reminded me that we had our own secrets.

"You always were his favorite. Bet he'd love to see you."

He left me in the bustle of Broad Street. A shiver chased away the afternoon warmth. Not because I feared being alone on the city streets, but because I knew that resolving Marty's case meant seeing my dad. Even though twelve years had passed since Gerald "Greaser" Reed abandoned his family, I knew right where he was.

I walked over to City Center mall and to the food court on the lower level where the payphones were. I pressed the numbers for the law office, even though I knew Suzette was at a meeting elsewhere. She'd check messages later. If there was anyone I could genuinely trust in this endeavor, it was her. I waited for the answering machine beep.

"Hey, Suzette, I met up with Trey but it didn't go anywhere. However, a name came up that I need you to check out for me please. A guy named Craig Cox." I spelled it. "And if you can, check on another guy for me, Frank Biser. I'll explain when I see you."

My backyard
1979

We had one of the biggest backyards in our neighborhood, and that was good and bad. Good because lots of people could come over and play. Bad because my dad said cuss words when he had to mow in the summer.

When the neighbors came Dad made hamburgers on the grill. Sometimes I helped. Dad poured the black rocks in, squeezed something wet onto them, and tossed in a lit match. I didn't like the smell. Dad would jump back and yell, "Whoa!" when the fireball came at him, even though it happened every time. The hamburgers were good, and I could have all the ketchup I wanted.

Mom liked when it was our turn to have people over. She made her fruit salad with Miracle Whip, which was my favorite. She cut up cantaloupe and made stinky coleslaw. Our neighbors brought gross stuff, like baked beans and macaroni covered in weird stuff. At least there were potato chips, so I could make my plate full.

Mom liked our neighbors and talked to them on the phone or when she was in the yard. When Mr. and Mrs. Davis were gone on vacation, Mom took care of their newspapers and mail, and when Mrs. Cunion slipped and broke her leg in three places one winter, Mom made casseroles and sent Trey to shovel her driveway every time it snowed.

Dad didn't say much to people. He talked to Frank and Brian's dad, Curtis. When new people came he would shake hands and be nice but always end up around Frank. Mom spent time with everyone, except Dad.

A lot of the grown-ups talked about Buckeye Steel. They worked there. So did my dad. They kept their voices low and hung their heads, so it must've been a bad place. Dad said he was worried about being laid off, but I didn't know what that meant.

"We need some more beers," Dad said it to Mom as she sat a new pitcher of lemonade on the picnic table. "Better get another case out of the garage."

"There isn't anymore." She didn't look at him. "You've had the last of it."

"You knew we were having people over, why wouldn't you stock up at the store, get more than usual?"

People started turning their heads and looking at us.

"I did," she said, "and now we're out."

"Not too bright, is she?" Dad said it to everyone. He had a smile on his face and made it sound like he was joking, but my stomach started pinching.

"It's all right, Ger." Mr. Davis came over and patted Dad on the shoulder. "We've all probably had enough. Nothing to get upset about."

"Sure there is." It came out like *shore*, like his tongue slipped. "You got ol' Margie there, Bill, you ain't gotta put up with a dumbass." He gave Mom that wrinkled-grumpy face, which meant he was just getting started with the meanness.

"Bout time we all shuffled home," Mr. Curtis said. He took his wife by the hand and started down the driveway. Others did the same while calling out goodbyes.

Thank you, Annette.

Everything was delicious.

Take care, Gerald.

These were the things people said as they left, but I wanted to scream, *"NO!"* I wanted to grab them all and tell them not to go, that it was going to get bad, that my mom needed help. Dad would say those awful words. Mom would do the dishes or pack his lunch for the next day and pretend she didn't hear him. Then Dad would get in her face and tell her she was doing something wrong or that her hair looked terrible or he didn't know why he married her. She would yell something back and they would keep going. I would hide in my room, like Trey did. I wanted someone to stop it tonight.

Tears came to my eyes, but I couldn't let anyone see. Mom would be embarrassed. She said crying was for babies and I was a big girl. I didn't feel big.

The Davises stayed behind, along with Frank and Nora, who was playing with her hair and humming.

"Here," Mrs. Davis said, "why don't we help you straighten up." She took a trash bag from the box on the picnic table and shook it open. Mom gathered used paper plates and slid them inside.

"Naw." Dad stepped over to them and almost fell. He swiped the bag from Mrs. Davis. "Don't be helping her. Let her clean up since she ruined everything." He threw the bag at Mom. Plates and bits of food tumbled out. Some of that white macaroni stuff stuck to Mom's arm. It was so gross but she acted like it wasn't there. "Good for nothin'."

Mom turned her head as bits of his spit came her way.

"Can't buy beer like she's 'spose to. Can't make coleslaw a starvin' dog would eat."

He picked up the bowl with what was left of the coleslaw and dumped it by Mom's feet. Mrs. Davis gasped and went to her husband's side. Mr. Davis had that look that grown-ups get when they don't know what to do or say.

"That's enough, Gerald," Frank said. "Party's over for tonight. Annette didn't do anything wrong. There was plenty to drink tonight."

"Yes, everyone had a nice time," Mrs. Davis added. Mr. Davis nodded.

"Let's clean up and head on in." Frank went to get a new trash bag, but Dad pushed him away.

"It's my house and I said she can clean it up," Dad said. "You best get on the other side of that fence, Frank."

Frank stood there, like he wasn't going to move. I'd never seen that look on his face before. He usually smiled a lot, but now he looked the way a parent or teacher does before they give a spanking.

"Why don't you go on in, Ger, and sleep it off." Frank looked at my mom. "Leave Annette alone. We'll take care of out here."

Dad stepped so close to Frank that their noses almost touched.

"You ain't standin' on my property tellin' me wha' to do." He pushed his chest into Frank, and that's when Frank pushed back. Dad fell backwards onto the picnic table then rolled off into the grass, taking everything on the table with him and kicking over the grill. The racket caused a few neighborhood dogs to bark. I was glad there weren't many people there to see, because I saw Mom's face and knew she was embarrassed.

It was dark now and we only had one patio light, so I couldn't see Dad for a second. I thought he was knocked out again, like when Trey pushed him into the yard. The Davises and Mom stepped over to check on Dad, but he swiped his arm at them like an angry cat, so we all stayed back.

He worked to get up. I heard him grunt. When he was on his feet and faced us, there was a line of blood down his forehead that went to his cheek. Mrs. Davis gasped and covered her mouth. Everyone else stood there staring but Dad didn't look at anyone. I wondered if he knew he was bleeding.

It looked like it was hard for him to blink and stand straight. His walk had a wobble, but he made it into the house and didn't saying a word.

Mom, Frank, and the Davises started picking up. Nora was in our patio rocker, gazing at the stars. Mrs. Davis put her arm around Mom and said something to her that I couldn't hear. Mom said, "It's fine. I'm all right," and I could tell she'd wanted to cry but didn't.

I helped but knew it was best not to say anything. Mom had said it was all right, that meant I better act like everything was all right. I wasn't sure how, since I didn't remember anyone else falling down like in a fight scene from *Starsky and Hutch* at any other gatherings.

"It's getting late," Mom said to me when the clean-up was almost done. "Why don't you get ready for bed. I'll be up soon."

I nodded.

"Good thing we had you here to help, otherwise we'd be out here all night." Frank's smile was back, and that made me feel better.

I didn't want to go in the house by myself but had to. Good thing I knew how to slide the door open and move around without making noise. That way I could see what my dad was doing and stay out of his way. Lights were on but I didn't hear anything. I went to the top of the stairs and peeked around the wall, keeping my eyes even with the carpet so I could find my dad's feet. No feet standing in the bathroom and the door to his bedroom was open. From my safe spot I couldn't tell if he was in bed because I didn't turn on the hall light.

But then I heard it. Dad's snoring. He'd gone to bed. That's what he usually did when words were hard for him. It was like fussing with Mom was too hard, so he went to sleep. I don't know why he fussed at Mom anyway.

I let out my breath and wondered if Trey was in his room. The door was shut and was always shut when Trey was in there. I tried looking under the bottom of the door to see if I could tell anything, but it was too dark. And Trey didn't snore.

He probably already knew what happened. Either Mr. Curtis told him, or he was watching from somewhere. Trey couldn't climb trees like me, but he had hiding spots. And he never told me where they were. Being invisible was a better trick than climbing trees.

I could get ready for bed without any light. When I slid under the covers I decided I was going to wait for Mom. She would come into my room at night and run her fingers through my hair after I lied down. That helped me fall asleep. After tonight, I needed help falling asleep.

But after a long time, after I thought about everything and Dad falling over the picnic table again and again, Mom didn't come. I got scared and had to check on her.

Leaving my room was even scarier. My chest felt like someone was playing with that red rubber ball and wooden paddle game. If Mom saw me, she might get upset. If Dad woke up, he'd really get upset. Going downstairs without making a sound was harder than going up the stairs, but I did it. All the lights were off in the house, and I'd heard Dad's bear-snores on my way down.

Standing in the dark kitchen, I figured she must've gone to bed and forgotten about me. That was okay, but I still wasn't sure I could sleep. I was about to go back to bed, but that's when I heard something coming from outside. Above the kitchen sink I saw the windows were still open, which was how I heard the talking.

Like a squirrel, I climbed on top of the counters and leaned in close to the windows. Mom and Frank were sitting on the patio, smoking cigarettes in the dark.

"I don't think you should wait, Annette." Frank took a puff on his smoke. "Seems like he's gotten a lot worse. Can't be good for kids to be around him."

Mom didn't say anything at first.

"I can't leave. I don't have anyplace to go and I don't have enough money. Once I get my license I can make changes. For now, we'll just have to get by."

Frank sighed. "I'm not sure I can take watching this much longer."

"You can't afford to worry about us. You've got Nora to look after."

I didn't see Nora on the patio. Maybe Frank left when the Davises went home and came back after putting Nora to bed.

They were quiet for a while, just smoking.

"Well, if he acts up again like he did tonight, you call me," Frank said. "I'll hop that fence or tear it down if needed. I'll keep my rifle ready, 'cause I ain't afraid to use it if I have to."

Mom laughed a little. "I hear ya."

I didn't know grown-ups stayed up late talking when the house was dark and quiet. I liked that Mom and Frank were friends and that he wanted to help her. Maybe I could get Frank if my dad started with the cussing and yelling. When I thought about Frank bringing a rifle, it made me feel cold all over.

CHAPTER SEVEN

With her palms spread on her desktop, eyes wide, Suzette greeted me with, "So, what happened? How'd it go?"

I sighed. My shoulders drooped as much as my frown. "Nothing from Trey. He's just like my mom. Won't say a thing about Marty's death." I'd picked up a fresh box of Buckeye Donuts on my way back and slid the box across Suzette's desk. A carton of fresh brewed coffee, too. Nothing like a severe sugar rush for the back end of the afternoon.

"Sorry, babe."

I shrugged, conceding defeat on the subject. "Did you get my message?"

A corner of her lips curled into a devilish grin. "So I work for you now?"

I plopped onto the high-back leather chair, my expression matching hers. "Hardly. You know I'm in desperate need of your wisdom, and your connections with CPD."

"True." Suzette punched the air with a pointed finger. "At least Warren is a better cop than he was a husband. Plus, the station was on my way back to the office. Lucky for you I adore your skinny behind."

Suzette made an incredible lawyer and, by her own admission, a lousy wife. Twice divorced and a frequenter of Victory's, a downtown bar known as the place to go for one-night stands, Suzette's personal life worried me. I kept that to myself, though.

"Did you find out anything?"

“Nothing on your boy Frank, but we hit the jackpot with Craig Cox.” She pulled a thick file from her attaché case and laid it down in front of me. “I haven’t been through all of it, but I got the gist. Seems he’s been in and out of jail for years. Want to guess what for?”

“Murder?” It sounded stupid after I said it, but it had popped out of my mouth like a reflex response.

“What’s that, wishful thinking? No, babe. Assault and battery. He beat up his girlfriend a few times.”

I took the folder and started flipping pages. Craig Cox stared back at me in his mug shot. It was dated ten years ago. I couldn’t say Craig looked familiar as I tried racking my brain for a memory of him. Nothing came to me.

But I would say that Craig was better looking than my dad had been back then. According to the file info, Craig was taller and thinner than my dad. And he had a full head of dark blonde hair. What had Marty seen in my dad that was an upgrade from her husband?

“Any chance you’re coming back to earth soon?” Suzette asked.

“Sorry.”

“The arrests were in ’82 and ’86, so he’s kept his nose clean for a while now. He lived with his wife’s sister after getting out, then got a job at a body shop. Been there ever since.”

“If he went to jail in 1982 that means it wasn’t for beating up Marty.” I said it more to myself than to Suzette.

“Hard to do if the woman has been dead for two years.” She said it with that sarcastic flair of hers and a bite of jelly donut in her mouth. It smelled so good. Donuts and coffee had no hold over me, though. The tastes, for me, never measured up to the smells.

“But just because he didn’t go to jail for it doesn’t mean he didn’t rough Marty up a few times,” I noted. My mind drifted to my dad. As far as I knew, he never hit my mom, but there were so many times—too many times—when I feared he would. Threats and name-calling were his weapons of choice. “Maybe Marty never called the police?”

For ages, men got away with beating their wives simply because they were wives, mere property. Police often didn't get involved in domestic disputes until women ended up dead after years of being victimized by crazed husbands. Laws had changed, thankfully, but even back in the 70's and early 80's, calling the police could make life worse for an abused woman. She had to press charges and take action on her own. Husbands played nice for a while or threatened the wife with what he'd do to her if she got the police involved. Maybe that was what Marty's life looked like back then.

Suzette pointed a finger at me. "Now you're thinking. Yeah, I'd say two trips to the birdcage shows he had a problem. Guess you'd have to find old neighbors or maybe even the sister to see if he ever beat up Marty."

That sounded impossible.

"Can I keep this?" I asked, my fingers splayed across the file pages.

"How 'bout you go through it, take notes, do what you want, but we keep it in the office?"

"Sure. It's probably not a good idea to take it home anyway." I briefly imagined my mom coming across the file. She would blanch, just reading his name on the file's tab.

"So you going to tell me about this Frank guy? Who's he and how does he fit into this drama?"

I kept details about Frank simple, told Suzette that he was our neighbor and a nice guy. Maybe I was only interested in him because of his situation with Nora. Although I did recall Frank mentioning that he was willing to use his rifle on my dad if needed. Could that account for anything? And the more I ran that late-night patio conversation between Mom and Frank through my head, the more I became certain that Frank had deeper feelings for my mom than just being a 'good neighbor'. Not that it mattered now.

"Like I said, CPD has nothing on Frank." Suzette finished her donut and wiped her mouth. "You want me to check public records?"

"No, I guess not." Frank Biser wasn't going to give me answers about Marty's death. "Craig is the one we need to focus on."

"Fair enough. Oh, and just so you know, I asked Warren to check out your boy Lance and his connection to the investigation."

I nodded my appreciation and got up to leave. Suzette cleared her throat.

"Just one more thing." She gave me that over the glasses glare. "Promise me you're not going to do anything stupid. We're not *Cagney and Lacey* here. You know what I mean?"

"Yeah, I got it. All I'm doing is reading up on my new friend here." I held up the file like a newly won prize.

"I'm warning you," there came the pointy finger again, "behave."

I made a cross my heart motion over my chest and topped it with my hands held together, as if I were praying. Prayers might be needed, because I knew I'd have trouble staying true to that promise.

Part of that promise went downhill after work, when I convinced Derek to come with me to a new, special place I had in mind.

"You sure this is a good idea?"

No.

"Are you afraid?" I asked.

"I just don't think we should be doing this."

Suzette should've been more specific when she made me promise not to do anything stupid. This wasn't stupid. Dumb and unwise, maybe, but not stupid.

Derek was earning more awesome-boyfriend points. He just went with my nudging without asking too many questions. I was sure he'd make up for that later.

"So why are we here again?" he asked.

"I kinda wanted to see the place, wanted you to see where I spent some of my childhood." Okay, that had to sound pathetic. Why did he put up with me? Besides the fact that I had saved him some of the donuts I delivered to Suzette.

"Okay, I get it, but why now? Why the urgency?"

I couldn't answer that without bringing up the issue of Lance. Since I wasn't in the mood to get into that subject, I simply shrugged.

We eased over the railroad tracks and into the parking lot of the Junkyard Lounge. A strange sense of familiarity hit me, like I was reviving the improbable bond I had with the place. If that was possible.

After he parked and shut off the engine, Derek looked up at the entrance. "I've never been inside a bar."

That didn't surprise me. More virgin territory for Derek. And vaguely, though the timing was terrible, I wondered if we'd lose our virginity to each other.

"Come on." The only reason I had an ounce of courage to get out of the truck was because Derek was with me. What made me feel suddenly anxious to return to the place where my dad had started his affair with Marty?

"You know we can't drink." Derek had reached the legal drinking age but my birthday was a few months away. He had no interest in drinking, though, because of his faith and because he said it wasn't good for his body. Both reasons only made him more attractive to me.

"Right." Drinking wasn't an option for me either. Age aside, I saw what it did to my dad, knew how it made him treat my mom. Maybe most people could handle a beer or two, but I wasn't interested in even trying.

The closer we got to the entrance, the more we could hear the music from inside. No way it could still be flowing from that old jukebox I'd once played with. We scaled the chipped concrete steps. No barking came from the junkyard. I took a deep breath as Derek moved to open the door.

Inside was nothing like I remembered. Sure, there was that blue-tinged cloud of smoke floating like a familiar ghost and the floor was probably still sticky and *filthy*, but the inside wasn't cave-dark. Dim lighting from the ceiling gave a strange, cozy glow to the entire room. The pinball machine was gone, as was the jukebox. So were the orange chairs. A platform featured instruments but no players. Country music filtered in from a sound system and mingled with the scent of cheap air freshner. Other than my childhood memories, I didn't have anything to compare it to and didn't know what other bars were like, but all things considered, the place had seen a few updates.

Two guys, not much older than me and Derek played pool and glanced our way. A handful of others littered the space.

I quickly slid atop a stool at the far end of the bar, nearest the door. Derek followed my lead.

"Your dad really brought you here?"

I was glad he kept his voice low.

"Yeah." I knew that didn't make sense. Who took their kid to a bar? Or more precisely, who took their eight year old to a bar in the ghetto? My dad.

Memories bombarded me. I could still picture the Junkyard Lounge as it had been twelve years ago, complete with the glow of the jukebox and the roll-clang-ping sounds of the pinball. I could smell the beer nuts and even taste a fresh stick of Juicy Fruit.

"What can I get you?"

I snapped form my recollections and found myself staring at Archie. All this time and he was still here.

"Archie." I said it without thinking. It was then I realized I hadn't planned anything past getting in the door. What could I say to people I recognized from so long ago?

His surprise matched mine. Then he blinked and squinted and stared at me as the wheels in his head must've started churning.

"Don't tell me it's you. Kyle, Gerald's little girl?"

How on earth had he remembered me?

"Yes." It sounded like someone had punched it out of me. Weak and breathy.

"How you been, sugar? Awful good to see you."

He reached across the bar and hugged me. That happened frequently, right? I had a feeling the other patrons were staring at us now. Thinking about it made me jittery, which I didn't need.

"Thanks, you too." I was at a loss for words since I hadn't expected to be having this conversation. What *had* I expected? I introduced Archie and Derek, hoping for a brilliant transition into Marty, but I had to go with, "How've you been?"

"Growin' old here," he chuckled. Although his hair was now a mixture of white and gray and his cheeks and middle were puffier, he still looked the same.

Derek sat there and took it all in, I guess.

"Say, how's your mom doing?"

"Good." I'd forgotten that Archie knew her. Truth was, my dad once encouraged my mom to work there as a barmaid. That was before Marty started. Dad got Mom inside the Junkyard Lounge twice, I think. It had been her way of trying, but a bar wasn't her scene. She never drank, and sitting there watching her husband drink himself to intoxication wasn't her idea of fun.

"So what about Linda and Carl, are they still here?" If Archie was still manning the bar, then it was possible the whole crew was still around.

Friendly and sincere, Linda had been all smiles and curves. She always wore a crisp-white button down shirt that strained across her cleavage, and she resembled *Dynasty*'s Linda Evans with her dishwater blonde hair and feathery bangs.

Carl had been the cook and dishwasher. In contrast to Linda, he was quiet and wore a dingy apron that rarely saw the wash. His hair hung down in his eyes when he didn't finger comb it to the side. Carl used to give me the creeps. I swore he never blinked, and his dark brown eyes penetrated without him saying a word. Carl wasn't all bad though. He left a bowl of milk out back every night for the stray cats that prowled the area.

"No, Linda died of cancer a few years back," Archie said. "And Carl, he's my nephew. Don't know if you ever knew that or not, but he's doing all right. Works over at the Wonder Bread factory."

It was a lot to take in. A merry-go-round of emotions swirled through me.

"Wow, I'm so sorry. Linda was so great." There were no words good enough for when you abruptly learn of someone's passing. Archie had cared about her, and Linda had been good to me. She never let me touch my fish sandwich without washing my hands first and she kept me to a two-Coke limit.

Archie put his elbow on the bar and leaned in to me and Derek.

"Whatever happened with your dad? I heard he up and left."

I glanced at Derek. "You mean he hasn't been here? He didn't keep coming?"

Archie shook his head. "After Marty was gone he never came back. The police came around looking for him, asking questions, but we didn't see him no more. I figured he felt pretty bad about the way Marty died."

"What do you mean?" My scalp prickled.

"I knowed your dad was with your mom and all, but he had it real bad for Marty. Loved her. There wasn't much they could do about being together, but he didn't like how Marty's husband was treatin' her. There wasn't much he could do about that neither, I reckon, and after that fight in the parking lot—"

"Wait. What fight?"

Archie tilted his head sideways. "Don't you 'member that? Hmm. Maybe you weren't here that time your dad and Marty's husband got into a brawl."

Had I been there? I pushed and rattled the boxes of memories in my mind but couldn't recall my dad getting into a rumble in a parking lot. Surely that would've stuck out, had I been there.

"I guess I missed it," I said. "Why were they fighting?"

"Over Marty, a'course. We all knew she had it rough with her husband and she wanted to leave him. He found out about her and your dad, and well, one night he showed up here all blasted out of his mind. Irene, that sister of hers, was with him. Guess she drove him because he couldn't hardly stand. I think she was trying to look out for him, discourage him and all that, but he gets here and starts hollerin' from outside, calling Marty all kinds of names. A bunch of us go out there, including Marty and your dad. He stood out there and threatened to kill Marty if she didn't end the affair. Marty didn't know what to do so she says she'll go home with him. I think that was her way of trying to calm him down, but your dad wouldn't hear of it. He pulled Marty away from him and told her to go back inside. Then those two started cussing at each other. Good thing you weren't here. Wasn't long before your dad laid into him, licked him good and put him out flat. Irene ended up taking him back home."

Several ironies slapped me in the head. To hear Archie talk, I almost pictured my dad as a hero, defending Marty from her abusive husband. But how could that be? He yelled and swore at my mom when he was drunk. Even when he was sober he wasn't a good husband. He always treated her inferior and criticized her out of the side of his mouth. Mom took it, never provoked him. I didn't understand until I was older that she'd probably done that for my sake and to keep what peace there was. I couldn't help but wonder what Archie would think of Gerald Reed if he really knew him.

Listening to Archie's tale of forbidden love nauseated me. What kind of crap did Greaser feed them about Mom? Was she an endless nag? Was she the one driving him to drink, pushing him into Marty's arms?

Anger simmered inside me. That's how it was. Dad cared more about the drunks and barmaids at the Junkyard Lounge than he did his family. We could be ridiculed, belittled, abused, and embarrassed while he risked a beating to defend his mistress.

Despite everything, I'd never hated my dad. I hated what happened to my mom and Trey. I hated having to predict my dad's mood when I was younger and usually end up having it wrong. But now, hearing how devoted he was to Marty, finding out that he was capable of chivalry and love, just not toward my mom, I hated him.

"A'course that might've been the only time that feller was drunker than your dad." Archie chuckled, but Derek and I couldn't find the humor in his remark.

I slid from the stool, unable to stomach anymore. Derek followed my lead without any prompting.

"You takin' off? Already?"

"It's been great seeing you, Archie, but we should go."

"Next time you come in, little lady," he winked, "beer's on me."

Derek and I didn't say much during the drive back to his place. It was farther than going back to my house, but I couldn't risk seeing Mom.

With my luck she'd probably detect the scent of stale beer and Camels on me when I walked in and know where I'd been.

I slumped onto Derek's couch and rubbed my head, hoping I could erase the ache. How was it possible to feel numb and over stimulated at the same time? Maybe Archie had a point, that now would be a good time for me to take up drinking. My mind felt like perfectly-racked pool balls after that first hit from the cue ball. Thoughts were rolling in a mad-panic direction. Archie might've been the only person, besides Marty, who viewed my dad as a nice guy. I could've educated Archie, told him that Gerald Reed never bought his wife a birthday present or complimented her when she got her hair done at the Fiesta Salon. Could've told him about the conversation I'd heard while hiding under my parents' bed....

Mom and Dad's bedroom
Late Friday Night, 1979

Only Dad played hide and seek with me. He'd found me three times already, but he was getting slow. I waited a long time for him to find me in the cabinet under the kitchen sink. So I picked an easier spot and slid under the bed. I heard footsteps on the stairs and put my hand over my mouth so I wouldn't laugh. But the tickles in my stomach left when I saw both my parents' feet. They were talking. That meant Dad wasn't looking for me.

"I got laid off."

Mom didn't say anything.

"Well, ain't you gonna gripe and yell?" Dad asked.

"We knew it was coming," she said. "That's why I've been picking up doubles."

"Oh, cause I can't provide."

She sighed. "No, because it helps. We'll be all right for a while."

"No, I'm just worthless, ain't that what you wanna say? I'm not good enough for you."

"There's nothing to fuss about. We'll figure something out."

"Cause it's all my fault, right? Bet you can't wait to tell Frank and ol' Clara Davis 'bout how Gerald can't keep a job, how lazy he is."

Mom didn't say anything again.

"Just go downstairs and get a knife." A second later, Dad flopped onto the bed. Every part of my skin felt like it was being poked with needles. The bed was so noisy I thought it was going to smash on top of me. Why was he talking about a knife?

"Go get your knife and stab it right in the center of my chest. That way you can collect the life insurance. You'll be done with me and have plenty of money. You don't care about me none anyway so it should be easy for you."

"Oh, hush up, Gerald. Stop acting so foolish. Kyle'll hear you."

"Don't matter none. You hate me, she probably hates me too." His voice sounded funny. "I'm no good. Let's just get it over with."

Mom went into the bathroom and locked the door behind her. Dad stayed on the bed. There was some shaking. I don't know if Dad was crying, because I was shaking too and making myself stay real quiet….

Derek joined me on the couch but didn't touch me. Unusual for him, but I was glad. I wanted distance but I wanted him to read my mind and hold me and tell me everything would be all right. It had been stupid, going back to the Junkyard Lounge. Trey was right, I shouldn't have stirred things up. Now I was reliving past hurts and opening old wounds. Questions and confusion twirled in my head like a carousel out of control.

"You didn't mention all that stuff about your dad."

"It's not exactly great conversation material for a date." Despite the chaos in my head, my defensive reflexes remained sharp.

"Yeah, but we've been together for a while now. Why wouldn't you tell me your dad had an affair?"

My insides bristled. It was excruciating, admitting to this guy who'd known nothing but two loving parents his whole church-going life that my parents were not only divorced but that my dad had walked out and never looked back. At the time, Derek had left it alone. Either he was mulling that scene over, or he was too shocked by the freakish nature of the issue to press any further. Since then, I'd waited for the day when I thought his parents would tell him that a girl like me wasn't good enough for a near-perfect guy like him.

"So Archie said that Marty died," Derek said. "When did that happen?"

I'd forgotten that Derek didn't have the whole picture yet, that he didn't know about Marty's murder. In a breath of a second, I had to decide if I wanted to trust Derek with everything and let him in on my past.

"She was killed a few weeks after my dad moved out." I'd said it.

"Does that mean your dad was a suspect?"

"As far as I know, both my parents were." I told him that when my Dad left, he didn't go and live with Marty, and I wasn't sure why he hadn't. "It's pretty messed up."

"Yeah, sounds like it."

"Now's your chance to run," I said, with the lackluster it deserved.

He looked at me and laughed. "You think that scares me off or something?"

I didn't know what to say.

He draped his arm around me. "Can you make me a promise?"

Another promise? First Suzette and now Derek.

"Maybe." I let myself ease into him.

"Don't go back to that place," he said. "It's not good for you, and there's no point in looking back. You can't change any of that stuff. Let it all go and just move on."

It was worth a thought. Tonight hadn't been good for me, and trying to submerge myself into those murky waters of past memories proved draining and frightening. Maybe it was a good thing Mom and Trey had kept quiet about Marty all those years.

But the best response I could give Derek was a nod. I agreed with him. Mostly. I closed my eyes and felt Derek breathe, welcomed the sound of his heartbeat thumping steadily in my ears. Soothing as this moment was, I couldn't explain to Derek that the past wasn't going away, that a need-to-know ache was growing inside me—and promised not to be satisfied until I knew who killed Marty Cox.

CHAPTER EIGHT

I accidentally spent the night at Derek's. The topic of my dad and Marty was too raw for us to dwell on for long. I'd left a message at home saying I probably wouldn't be late. So much for that. The movie we'd picked up from Blockbuster had been a dud, and we both fell asleep. I was surprised Mom didn't call around midnight or so, checking up on me and egging me to come home.

Derek popped awake before six in the morning. His alert, cheerful disposition chased me off, which was fine since I had another final and work.

At home, Mom was in the kitchen, working on her coffee consumption. I'd hoped I could sneak in and somehow make it seem as though I'd been there and had just gotten home late last night. No such luck.

"Thought you were coming home?" she asked.

"I'm home." I held out my arms ta-da style and put forth an overly cheery smile. Might as well try being humorous, I thought. Maverick came bounding toward me. I sat and welcomed his kisses to my chin and rubbed his ears.

Mom shook her head and returned the creamer to the fridge. The door required two yanks to open these days. Silence was Mom's best weapon for inducing guilt. I knew what she was thinking. *Looks trashy to be spending the night somewhere and dragging in the next day.*

"When are they starting the remodel?" Maybe she'd let me change the subject.

"When I get the money." Her crabby retort was her way of letting me know she was irritated. She wouldn't confront me about staying at Derek's directly, but she'd grumble about how broke she was, how she worked so hard and no one appreciated her, how she did everything around the house and busted her hump…

Instead of fueling the tirade with my presence, I grabbed a Coke and made an escape upstairs, mad that my day was already off to a touchy start. I immediately prepped a dozen snarky remarks in case she added a jab about a daughter who stays out all night, figuring she wouldn't let me slip away that easily.

Sure enough, she told me while I was hitting the stairs, "Some guy named Lance called for you last night, wants you to call him back."

I paused on the steps long enough to let her words register.

"Oh. Okay. Thanks." I tried not to rush the words or attach an emotion. Before Mom launched her questions, I ducked into my room and closed the door, knowing that had to burn.

I leaned against my closed bedroom door and let that shot of adrenaline run its course. Apparently, I hadn't mentioned Lance by name, just referred to him as the investigator. I didn't feel like filling her in.

But Lance had my mom on the phone. He could've dug in, fired away with questions. Not that Mom would've been cooperative, but he could've made the effort. What had stopped him? Part of me wanted to think it was a courtesy and that he was waiting to hear back from me first.

I didn't want to think about Lance. I already regretted how I just treated my mom. I didn't like the growing distance between us or the festering secrets. Mom didn't know I'd been to the Junkyard Lounge, talked to Archie, or went snooping through her things. Each one of those revelations might hurt her, no matter how I explained it.

Don't do that to Mom. Trey's words echoed in my head.

I pressed my forehead against the door and eased out a long breath. Was justice for Marty worth jeopardizing my relationship with my mom? The easy answer was no.

Lying wasn't my thing. I was never good at it, especially when I was little. Since I got busted and spanked when I lied about Trey breaking Mom's favorite angel figurine (the glued-on wing fell off) and about how my brand new coat ended up covered in thick mud when I was seven (playing along a creek bed, where I wasn't supposed to be), I gave up lying.

With my last final completed—and good riddance, Statistics—I was free for the rest of the spring and summer to work full-time with Suzette at the office. But before I plunged into transcribing depositions and bankruptcy paperwork for the next twelve weeks, I had to make a pit stop. And further bend that promise about not doing anything stupid.

I'd called Lance back from the student center at school and agreed to meet him at Cardo's Pizza, which wasn't far from the office. I could exercise my two-squares of pizza eating, if needed, since it was only day two.

"Thanks for calling me back," Lance said as he slid into the opposite side of the booth.

I hated how my pulse quickened when he came around. The guy had nothing on Derek in the looks department and might be the type some would describe as scrawny. Yet I didn't understand why I wanted him to like me. Like me in a burning-desire kind of way.

"I'm probably wasting your time here. I could've told you this over the phone." *But I wanted you to want to see me*. "My mom isn't going to get into it. For her it's buried in the past and done. There's not much I can do."

Lance sighed. "I'm not surprised. It's what I expected you'd say all along. No one really wants to talk about a murder, especially if she's a suspect."

I almost launched myself from the crackled red vinyl seat. "You're wrong about that! There's no way—"

"Take it easy! I don't think your mom did anything."

It took me a few seconds to realize I'd almost stood. Lance stared at me and waited for me to sit again.

"I'm sorry," he said. "I didn't mean to get you upset."

I scowled at him. "You didn't think suggesting my mom could be a killer would get a reaction?"

"You're right. I'm an idiot." He sighed. "I never thought your mom had anything to do with Marty's death."

"That's not the impression you gave me a few days ago."

Lance held up his hands. "Just hear me out. Don't get it twisted. Back when it happened, your mom was probably a suspect. She doesn't want to get into it now because she's worried about getting scrutinized again." He paused and looked at me hard. "You wouldn't have listened to me if I'd told you the truth."

"What truth?"

"If I would've told you the truth from the start, you wouldn't have been interested in helping me."

My gaze narrowed. "Are you playing some sort of game here, Lance? Because—"

"Your dad killed Marty."

We both froze. Each studying the other. I searched his eyes, desperately wishing for a sign that he was telling the truth.

"Like I told you," Lance said, "there isn't much evidence in this case, but I think it's obvious your dad is responsible."

"You think he killed her, based on what?"

"Because of their affair. Marty wanted out of her marriage and she wanted to be with your dad. She pressured him to leave your mom, but your dad kept stringing her along. He'd been laid off from Buckeye Steel like a lot of people. Right?"

My insides turned to ice. Lance didn't play fair. He brought up pieces of my family's history when it suited him. Not the ideal way to build trust.

"Here's how I think it went down," he continued. "He went to Marty's that night, probably drunk. Maybe he reassured her that he would leave but needed more time with money being tight. Maybe that wasn't enough for Marty, and they got into a fight about the whole thing...and it ended badly."

My mind suddenly reeled back to a strange moment. I was in the kitchen with my parents when the phone rang. We'd been getting prank calls. My mom would answer but the caller would hang up and call back. It repeated until my mom took the phone off the hook. But this night, my dad answered. He stood there for the longest time, listening. I could hear a voice on the other end practically shouting but I couldn't make out the words. After a few minutes, my dad glanced at my mom then spoke to the caller, *"I don't have a choice."*

That remark sparked my mom's fuse and set her off. Maybe she heard what was being said. Or she just knew. She yelled at my dad like I'd never heard. *"Don't have a choice? What do you mean? Ain't no one here nailing you down. You can leave anytime you want."* On it went, for ages it seemed. Then, Mom took the phone. *"You want him, Marty? You can have him! He's all yours, you piece of trash!"*

Obscenities followed and flowed until my dad snatched the phone and hung it up.

"How do you know this?" I asked, when I broke from the memory.

"From interviews in the case file."

"I'd like to see them. Do you have copies?"

"Not with me," Lance said. "But I can have some made."

Sitting there, I suddenly felt at a painful disadvantage. It was as though he'd dipped into my head and ripped out an embarrassing scene from my childhood. My dad had actually said those words with my mom right there. I wondered if Archie knew about that, or if it was part of the poor-Gerald façade he probably crafted for his buddies at the bar.

"Why didn't you mention this before, about my dad?"

"I didn't think you'd care, since he ended up leaving you and your mom. Figured you might have some hostility toward him."

"You've got the case file, all the facts, why are you here, Lance? What do you need me for?" I couldn't let Lance know how unnerved I was. How could he act like it was normal, tossing out information about my parents that way?

"There has to be something, somewhere, that proves he was involved. That's why I need you. You're close to this thing."

He put his hand on top of mine, without a hesitation this time. Ordinarily, I would've flinched, pulled away, but I forced myself to appear steadfast and unshaken.

"Kyle, I need you to help me prove your dad is guilty."

Minutes later, I bolted, politely as I could, without giving him a response to his 'need' for help. How could Lance know those things from my family's past? Did those interviews contain that much detail?

Before parting, I'd emphatically told Lance I wanted to see that case file. He promised. But I wasn't sure how much faith I had in promises now. Nothing made sense, and I couldn't help feeling like a dog chasing its tail.

I'd been studying Criminology long enough, and had watched enough reruns of *Matlock*, to understand that most killers made mistakes. When it came to crimes of passion, crimes committed in the heat of the moment, like Lance believed, then there could be even more mistakes, since the killer hadn't planned on covering up a felony. My dad wasn't clever and he wasn't lucky. He wasn't the kind of guy who got away with murder. But where was the evidence against him?

It was easier believing my mom had been involved because she had a conniving streak when necessary.

I arrived at the law office and put my compartmentalizing skills to work. Time to put the murder investigation away and focus on custody battles. Bob, Ed and Crystal were occupied with a deposition, and Suzette was in full-on lawyer mode. We didn't get into the Marty case much, other than Suzette asking if I was done reading Craig's record. I said I was still working on it, then made sure to slip from her radar before she got wise and sensed I'd been up to something. I wanted to tell her about the Junkyard Lounge visit and my meeting with Lance but I needed to rehash it over in my brain first.

I appreciated days like this, when I could submerge myself in work and forget real-life messes for a while. But during the ride home, I considered what Lance had said about there being little evidence. I wouldn't find a confession letter among Mom's papers, but there was another place I could poke around. If I was right, there could be something useful waiting for me in the dishwasher. Getting it wouldn't be a problem, but slipping it from underneath Mom's nose could be a challenge.

When I pulled in the driveway, my plan for snooping derailed. A car I didn't recognize was parked in my way. Not unusual. Mom could be meeting a client and having someone sign paperwork.

But my jaw dropped when I saw Frank Biser come down the driveway and meet me. Clearly, Frank was the type who aged well, since I would've known him anywhere. His eyes still radiated kindness. I greeted him with a hug.

"What are you doing here?" I asked with an exasperated breath.

"A little birdy told me the house was up for sale again. Thought I'd stop by, visit a bit, and maybe take a look at the old place. I went around the back and knocked, but no one answered."

Guess Mom wasn't home.

"How's Nora?" I wasn't sure if it was taboo to ask, considering Nora's condition, but how could I not?

Frank hesitated. "She's not doing so good."

"Oh, I'm sorry." I had no idea what to say.

"Well, here and there she has a good day, but...." He glanced at the house next door. "She misses the old place."

"A lot of memories here." My gaze drifted to the corner window on the second floor, where the doll room had been.

"Yep. Boy, if that fence could talk."

I thought about that. All the times my parents and Frank had traded vegetables from their gardens. My dad calling me home. Frank telling my mom he was just on the other side.

"Do you ever see my dad, Frank?" It felt strange, asking. But lately I was more acquainted with strange than I thought possible.

Frank looked at me as if I'd asked him a trick question. "No, I haven't seen him for a good long stretch. Can't say I'm sorry about that, though, after all he put your family through."

I nodded. "It got pretty ugly there for a while."

"Sure did."

"I probably never told you, but I'm glad you were there for my mom that night of the backyard picnic, when Dad went a little crazy."

He hooked his thumbs into the belt loops on his jeans. "I was glad it turned out okay. Could'a been a lot worse."

We hesitated, probably each caught up in a moment of imagining the grim possibilities. I wondered if he remembered sitting on the patio, smoking and talking with Mom in the middle of the night.

"Have you seen your dad any?"

"No, but a lot of things have resurfaced lately. There's been a lot of talk about that woman he was seeing."

"She got killed." Frank said it with a flat, detached tone.

"They never caught who did it."

"Yeah, I remember that."

I wished I could've asked what else he remembered, what the situation had been like from his side of the fence.

"Do you think my dad could've done something like that?" It was a harsh question to drop on someone I hadn't seen in years, but Frank had been there. He knew my parents in ways I didn't. And unlike Mom, he seemed willing to talk about the past.

Frank's eyes narrowed, and he gave me that same solid cold stare he'd given my dad that night before toppling him over the picnic table.

"It was only a matter of time. Your dad was like a ticking time bomb, bound to hurt someone."

Until that afternoon, when Lance had suggested it, I hadn't thought of my dad being capable of murder. But when I considered how he treated Trey and how he threatened my mom, the idea didn't seem far-fetched. What if Lance was right and my dad killed Marty in a fit of rage?

"Tell you the truth," Frank said, "there were many nights I stayed up, just listening and ready in case your mom needed help, because I was always afraid he was gonna kill your mom."

CHAPTER NINE

Frank couldn't hang around until dinner, which struck me with a blend of disappointment and relief. He gave me his business card and took down our phone number on the back of another one. The number had been the same all these years, but Frank probably never called, just came over. He said he'd try calling Mom and catching up with her another time. Watching him leave was hard, because I didn't know if he'd come back, and I had dozens of questions tumbling in my mind like Bingo balls ripe for plucking.

With Frank gone it was just me and Maverick. After taking him around the block and tossing him some bacon from the stash Mom kept for him, I reverted back to my original plan of snooping through Mom's papers. The dishwasher-file cabinet came about because Mom didn't believe in waste. She claimed it used up too much water and electricity and wasn't worth running for only three people. So it became handy for her to stash a variety of paperwork in there as her real estate career flourished. She'd since bought another filing cabinet, a real one, but she still kept older items in the dishwasher. My fingertips walked along the labeled tabs and edges until I found what I wanted, the one titled "Vinny".

But I almost died and melted into the floor when the sliding door flew open. Being anxious and occupied, I hadn't heard anyone drive up.

"Have you seen Trey?" It was Shelia bursting in.

I folded the dishwasher door back into place, maybe a little too swiftly. Maverick barked and hopped over to her, happy to see her, but Shelia had her reservations about pit bulls and flinched. I called him off and he came back to me. “Uh, no, I don’t think so. Why? What’s wrong?”

“I was worried about him. He hurt his head.”

“What happened?” I thought about our impromptu lunch yesterday and how he ushered me out the door. Sympathy for his head didn’t surface quickly.

Shelia walked through the kitchen to the bottom of the stairs and glanced up, then poked her head down into the rec room. I’d never seen Shelia that unsettled.

“Oh, that stupid medicine chest in our bathroom. The hinge has been loose on that door for ages. It slipped and the edge cut into his forehead.” Back in the kitchen now, she wrung her hands. “I told him to fix that stupid thing a hundred times.”

“Sounds kinda painful.” Although I wasn’t sure why a thump to the head would prompt Trey to come here, unless there was an emergency repair-your-forehead kit here that I didn’t know about. Wouldn’t surprise me at this point. “Sorry, but I haven’t seen him.” Mentioning our brief lunch seemed pointless.

“I’d better go home then.” After a quick embrace Shelia rushed out door, much the same way she’d come in.

It wasn’t until after she’d left that I felt my heart pounding like an Olympic sprinter’s. I thought I’d been caught going through Mom’s things. Sneaking a peek into buried files, or even a tucked-away keepsake box, violated Mom’s privacy and didn’t make me feel good about myself. But since she wasn’t willing to talk about it, what else could I do? At the same time, there was an unexpected thrill of filling in mental blanks and fleshing out specifics that other people already knew.

But as I held the Vinny file to my chest, a mild panic simmered. What would it mean to discover the truth? If I found out that Mom, or my dad, was involved in a murder and a cover up, what then? I couldn't turn her in, but could I find a way to live with it?

Before I opened the Vinny file, I took precautions. I locked the sliding door and pulled the curtains across the opening. The kitchen windows were open, allowing in that spring evening breeze and sound warnings of a car in the driveway. This time, I knew to be alert. Maverick stuck to my side, sniffing the air, the file, and giving me that curious expression with his head tilted.

Vinny referred to Vincent A. Fox, a private detective Mom hired two years after Greaser ran off. She wanted to go through with a divorce but needed to find Greaser.

I never met Vinny, but I remembered Mom and Trey talking about him and that Vinny had tracked down Greaser.

I unclasped the manila-colored packet and paused. If I dumped the contents onto the dining room table, beside the sliding doors, there was no way I could clean up the contents and place it back in the dishwasher in time. Shelia's whirlwind visit being proof.

No, the best thing was to take it to the law office and copy everything. Then I could put the file back and take my time reading the contents. Plus, I could get Suzette's point of view on whatever I found out.

Perhaps it was cliché, but I hid the file under my bed. Wasn't that where all good secrets were kept?

Being sneaky and manipulative proved draining. I headed to the bathroom, intent on taking a hot bath, until I glanced into the sink. A streak of dried blood stained the basin. Scanning the vanity and floor,

I didn't see any more blood, but the wastebasket held discarded tissues tainted crimson.

"Trey?" Maybe Trey had taken a serious wallop to the head. No wonder Shelia had been frantic and concerned. But why would he come here to clean up?

The sight of blood chased me from the bathroom and down to the kitchen with Maverick at my heels.

I screamed when I saw Trey standing with the fridge door open. Maverick barked but his ears dropped and his tail thrashed happily when he realized it was Trey.

"You trying to scare me to death?" he asked while stashing the milk container back in. He'd spilled droplets onto the front of his shirt, thanks in part to his reaction of getting caught drinking from the jug and in part from my scream.

The sliding door was still locked and covered.

"How'd you get in?" I asked.

"Still got a key to the basement door." He tussled with my dog and Maverick loved it, to my chagrin.

So much for me being alert. I hadn't heard anything. Luckily, I hadn't emptied the Vinny file onto my bedroom floor.

"Thanks for leaving a bloody trail." I pointed upstairs, as if that would easily reference his handiwork. Trey said nothing, so I tried again. "Shelia was here a little while ago looking for you."

"Was she?" He wiped his mouth with the back of his hand. "What did she say?" Above his right eyebrow, two butterfly band-aids bridged the thick, blood-red gash. It was then I noticed the scarlet-colored splatters on his shirt and that his hair was wrecked.

"She said you got hurt in the bathroom, that the medicine chest attacked."

He gave a hmph-laugh.

I stood there, looking at my brother not looking at me and wondered what was going on. Why was it near-impossible to get answers? A strange sense of embarrassment burned in me, as if I didn't belong in my own house and Trey did. Moments like this made me question if my brother even liked me.

"Where've you been?" Shocking how much I sounded like Mom.

"Brian's."

Trey and Brian Carter had maintained their friendship, despite the humiliation my dad served up. Brian's parents had a loft apartment above their detached garage that came in handy during their teen years for partying and antics of their own. When he was between girlfriends or living arrangements, Brian lived there.

"So you got clocked in the head, came over here to clean up, then went to Brian's?"

Trey shrugged. "Something like that." He rummaged through the cabinets, making noises and talking to Maverick, and was apparently uninterested in telling me his story.

"What about Shelia? She's looking for you."

With a bag of Cheez-Doodles and Coke in hand, he brushed past me and said, "Let her look," as he headed down to the rec room, Maverick prancing at his side.

Although it was silent and behind Trey's back, I threw my hands up in the air in a *What does that mean?* kind of way. What I wouldn't give for some truth serum to serve Mom and Trey right now.

Guilt needled me, knowing I'd taken my mom's file and stashed it under my bed. Combining that with the silent treatment from Trey, and Maverick's all-about-Trey mood, I had an intense desire to get out of the house. Especially before Mom got home.

I went to Derek's and hung out in front of his TV. He'd gone to his parent's house for dinner. Tonight was his mom's household-famous, as she called it, Hamburger Helper casserole. Derek wanted me to go along, but I took a pass. Having Derek's place, and the remote, to myself for an evening was bliss.

Although I'd had a crush on Mark Harmon since watching *The Deliberate Stranger*, a movie about serial killer Ted Bundy—weird, I know—and I enjoyed watching him play a tough cop on *Reasonable Doubts*, the peacefulness of being alone lulled me to sleep.

Trey and Brian stood in the dark beside the grill, flames flickering up, each holding a beer. Neither one looked at me. From the light of the flames, I saw Dad, slumped in the patio chair, a beer in his hand and his eyes staring blankly. Had Frank shoved him too hard?

I kept moving but my feet were heavy and slow. I followed a sound, a familiar rhythmic hum. It came from next door. Frank's house. I went in the front door and upstairs. There was Nora, seated at her sewing machine, crafting clothes for her dolls. When she pressed the foot pedal of the machine, it made that rhythmic hum.

Nora hummed too and held a cigarette. It made her task of guiding the fabric more difficult but she seemed not to notice. An audience of dolls sat watching, the moonlight flooding in, lighting their faces. It was the only light Nora had. Ash at the end of her cigarette defied gravity. But then it fell. I knew it would! Right onto the dress she was making. She scrambled, brushed the ashes away while holding the cigarette between her teeth. The fabric was okay? She returned to humming and sewing.

I moved downstairs, leaving Nora to her dolls. Now, I followed the voices. Out back, on the screened-in porch of Frank's house, sat Frank. Mom was there too. Each occupied a folding patio chair. They held hands across the space between them. Smoldering cigarettes occupied their other hands. Slowly, Frank turned his head toward Mom.

"I'll keep my rifle ready, 'cause I ain't afraid to use it if I have to."

"Frank..."

I startled awake on Derek's couch. Mark Harmon and Marlee Matlin were still on TV, making me realize I'd nodded off. It took a minute for the dream fog to clear. When I replayed the dream back through my head, I gasped.

Frank! A sickening thought took hold. What if Frank had been involved? Had he killed Marty as a favor to my mom?

I didn't stay at Derek's that night. I didn't even stay until he got back. That dream had me rattled. So did my new theory.

At home, I found Trey sleeping on the couch in the rec room, the TV still on and Maverick piled beside him, snoring. I heard Mom puttering around upstairs. I silently prayed she hadn't come home and fulfilled an inexplicable urge to vacuum under my bed. I headed up to my room.

"Oh!" Mom, sitting on the edge of her bed, jolted when she saw me at the top of the stairs. Seems that reaction was going around. "I didn't hear you come in, Bitty."

"Sorry." I joined her in her bedroom.

We traded chit-chat about our day and about Trey and Maverick. She seemed uptight and distracted. I figured she wouldn't give me an honest answer if I asked why, so I forged a gentle grin.

"Hey, Frank Biser stopped by this afternoon." I fished his business card from my jeans pocket and handed it to her, then shared the gist of my conversation with him.

Mom stared at the card. No doubt a swarm of memories bombarded her.

"I always liked Frank. He's a good man."

I wondered if she'd ever showed Roger such tenderness. Thinking of Roger, I glanced at Mom's hand and noticed the engagement ring wasn't present. I wasn't sure if she'd worn it outside of the house yet. Maybe she just didn't wear it to bed.

"Did you call Lance back?"

Her question caught me off guard. I'd forgotten she'd spoken to him.

"Yeah, I took care of it." I stood and faked a few stretches, said I needed to get to bed. Early day and all.

"Do you know Lance from school?" A grin tickled the corner of Mom's lips.

"Um, no."

This was one of those Mom-games she played, like calling Derek's when it was time for her little girl to come home. Now, she wanted to be cute and act like we were good girlfriends, talking boys.

"Does Derek have some competition?"

I repressed the burst of laughter that threatened. She thought she was so clever.

"About as much competition as Roger has with Frank."

Sleeping with a smug look on my face must've agreed with me, or at least helped motivate me out of bed early on Wednesday and into the office. With the Vinny file safely in tow, I felt especially victorious. Though over what, I couldn't say.

By the time I finished copying every document, picture, and piece of scrap paper in the file, Suzette arrived. A box from Fourbakers Bakery was cradled in her forearm, the aroma of fresh-baked éclairs wafting throughout the small building. Bob and Ed lit up, while Crystal and I traded we-know-better glances.

Suzette was about to make camp in the conference room next to her office.

"Can I ask a huge favor?" I said as she arranged her coffee and confections.

"You knocked over a mini-mart last night and you're on the lam?"

I held up the Vinny file. "Ever heard of a guy named Vinny Fox?"

Suzette flashed three shades of red and almost toppled her coffee mug over the box of baked goods.

"Maybe. How do you know Vinny?"

As best I could, I gave her a recap of how my mom found him a decade ago in the Yellow Pages and hired him to follow her estranged husband, post the murder investigation of his dead mistress.

Suzette dropped a few expletives. She abandoned the stack of files she'd planned to work on in favor of the Vinny booty. We spent the next hour going through all of it. Black-and-white photos of my dad, always alone. A copy of a bank statement, receipts, an application for employment at the 76 gas station, even a copy of his tax return. How Vinny managed it, I didn't know.

"Are you catching what I am?" Suzette asked. "All these records have an address for Mr. Reed—the same address."

"Yeah." I said it without an ounce of enthusiasm.

"So you've known about this?"

I nodded. One of the secrets Trey and I shared was that we'd driven by that address years ago. Mom had told Trey where Greaser lived. Both of them were shocked, because he'd set up in a duplex in a small town about thirteen miles from our house. From time to time, Trey and I had driven by. I think Trey liked keeping tabs on Greaser, liked knowing he still had the same car, and so forth. I had liked being included in the adventure—and keeping it from Mom. But we hadn't stolen away for one of those road trips in ages. There was a chance Greaser had moved by now, but I doubted it. Something told me that Trey was still keeping watch.

"What about this?" Suzette handed me another paper. This one was from a yellow legal pad and included a handwritten list.

--No pension, NO ALIMONY

--No child support, braces, D.C. trip funds, college

--In exchange for FULL, irrevocable custody, sole ownership of all property

I didn't know why the sheet was in Vinny's file. Seemed like it belonged with Mom's legal paperwork on the divorce. Maybe Vinny gave her the idea, told her if she wanted full custody she'd have to give up her rights to child support. It wasn't in my mom's handwriting. If my parents divorced when I was ten, custody only applied to me. Trey was eighteen by then or close enough.

"Looks like your dad got off pretty easy," Suzette said. "That's a lot for your mom to give up."

I agreed. "It's too bad. If she would've had a good lawyer she could've had everything on this list."

"You mean if she would've had *me* for a lawyer, she would've gotten everything."

The thought of Suzette ripping my dad and his lawyer in court made me smile, although I had no idea what the proceedings had been like.

"Are you upset, seeing that your mom didn't fight more?"

"No. My mom is practical and understands survival. Custody of me and ownership of the house meant my dad had nothing to come back to. That's my guess anyway." Still, I bet she looked over her shoulder plenty, wondering if he'd come back to taunt her or to take the house for himself. By then, she didn't have Frank next door anymore waiting with his rifle.

This paper also reminded me what a smart lady Annette Reed was, hillbilly bred or not. She knew the best way to get rid of my dad was to absolve him of any financial responsibility. It's what he wanted all along. Giving up any claims to money also required her to work two, sometimes three, jobs for several years before getting her real estate license. She made sure I had braces, a college education, and a trip to D.C., all without my dad. Pride swelled in me. So did an ache, because I wanted my mom loved and taken care of and worry-free. If Roger was the one who could do that, I hope she'd learn to let down her guard and love him.

When we finished scrutinizing every scrap, I sighed to myself. "Seems like we're getting nowhere fast." My loose theory about Frank wasn't worth bringing up. Not without any evidence.

"It takes time, babe."

We started gathering the file contents when I cocked my head and asked, "So, how do you know Vinny?"

Suzette tapped the stack of papers against the table until all the pages lined up. "Three words: college, tequila, Halloween weekend."

"That's four words."

"Yeah, that's what I told Vinny, but the rest is history."

I didn't quite understand, but before I could say anything else, Crystal tapped on the door.

"There's someone here to see you." She looked at both of us. "She doesn't have an appointment but wants to talk to you anyway."

"Who?" Suzette asked.

"She said her name is Irene Slater and that she knows who killed Marty Cox."

CHAPTER TEN

From the looks of Irene Slater, life had not been kind to her. She had a mass of thick black hair that probably hadn't seen a salon in decades. If I had to guess, Boy George took care of her make-up, which was dark blue eye shadow, black mascara and dried-blood-red lipstick. I could say she was a badly weathered version of Elvira, but that didn't capture the tarnish of defeat that cloaked this woman. And it was an insult to Elvira.

"Please, Ms. Slater, have a seat." Suzette held out a hand, welcoming her and inviting her to take a seat in the conference room. We'd cleared a spot at the table for her, having tucked away contents of the Vinny file. "Can I get you a coffee or donut?"

"Why not?" She sat her giant black purse on the tabletop.

Suzette and I traded stares. Being the underdog clerk, maybe I was supposed to serve our unexpected guest, but Suzette was closest to the goodies. I shifted my glance to the donut box and Suzette slid it across the table to Irene. With the coffee pot behind me, and having forgotten about the fresh coffee in the carton, I poured a cup and set it before Irene. Fine waitresses Suzette and I were not.

"So, Ms. Slater, we understand that you have information regarding an unsolved murder." Suzette eased into the chair next to Irene, attempting to make eye contact with the woman, but Irene was busy making googly-eyes at the donuts. She dangled her fingers above the treats before plucking out her donut of choice.

"Yes, ma'am." Irene bit into the donut.

"If you don't mind me asking, what's your connection to Marty Cox?" Suzette asked.

I'd taken the chair at the end of table and armed myself with pen and legal pad.

"She was my sister."

Irene cast a glance to the floor while Suzette and I passed a glimpse between us. I was pretty sure my heart skipped a beat. If Suzette was expecting any recognition from me, I couldn't help. I had no memories of Irene, but after talking with Archie, I knew she had a meaningful part in Marty's life. And hadn't Archie mentioned that Irene was with Craig on the night of the parking lot brawl?

"I'm terribly sorry for your loss," Suzette said.

"It's been real hard," Irene said with a mouthful of donut.

"I can only imagine. What brought you to us?"

Exactly what I wanted to know but felt too paralyzed to ask.

"Got a contact down at the station. He checks in with me sometimes, let's me know if there's anything new where Marty's concerned. He called the other day, said Craig's file was getting some attention." Irene shrugged. "Don't know if he knew you or not, but he gave me your name and all. So I'm here to help." She ended that with a self-satisfied nod.

Suzette let the info sink in. No doubt she was running the possibilities in her head of who could've been the one to tip off Irene. I had a feeling Warren was high on her list.

"We're not detectives," Suzette said, "you should take this to your contact at the Columbus Police Department—"

"Been doin' that for years. Never got me anywhere."

Suzette's stare returned to me. For a moment I wondered if Irene had stumped her.

"Look!" Irene snapped, "I'm offering you information. Are you interested or not?"

“Of course.” Suzette kept her professional demeanor intact, but I had a feeling she was getting annoyed.

After licking her lips and fingers alike, Irene reached for her black bag, poked a hand inside, then slammed items onto the table.

“What is this?” Suzette asked, a tinge of disgust in her voice and her eyes darting back and forth from the tabletop to Irene.

“Nothing much. Just some pictures of my sister having the living daylights beat out of her.”

I reached across the table for one of the items, a Polaroid snapshot. My breath caught as my eyes absorbed the image. Not only was the woman in the photo bloodied and bruised, she was also familiar. Chills blanketed me, and my mouth hung open. I looked to Suzette.

“It’s Marty.”

We needed a moment to regroup, each of us reeling for different reasons. Suzette suggested we start over. I made a fresh pot of coffee, though I wasn’t sure I did it right, while Suzette gathered the scattered pictures and looked them over. Irene helped herself to another donut.

As I fiddled with the pieces to the coffee maker, I studied Irene and searched my mind for any traces of her. Had she been there, in the background of the Junkyard Lounge and in the midst of my dad’s affair with Marty? No flashbacks were triggered.

“So did you take these pictures?” Suzette rifled through the Polaroids.

“Most of ’em. These were two times her husband beat her up.”

“Craig Cox.” Suzette peered over her glasses.

"Only husband she ever had."

Suzette ignored the snark in Irene's comment. "Did Marty ever go to the hospital for her injuries?"

"Are you kidding me? You know what that would've cost? Where we come from, there ain't no such thing as a hospital unless your leg meets a chainsaw."

"That leads me to believe then that she never reported these incidents to the police, either."

"Calling the police never helped. By the time they got there, Craig was gone or passed out or he and Marty were made up. They always told her she'd have to press charges, do a bunch of paperwork, and all it would mean was a few days in jail. That wasn't worth it, wouldn't change what was going on."

Irene was right. Fortunately, laws were changing, and abused women didn't have to live in shame and fear—or retaliate in a *Burning Bed* type of way. More help and resources were available, but more strides were needed.

There were over two dozen snapshots of Marty, but Irene said those only captured two incidents of abuse at Craig's hand. Irene had photographed Marty from multiple angles. In one set, Marty's left eye was swollen shut. In the other, she had a busted lip and blood on her clothes.

"There are no dates on any of these," Suzette noted.

"Does that matter?"

"Maybe not now, but if you're taking these to the police as evidence against Craig, there isn't much they can do. The pictures only prove Marty was hurt. They don't prove murder."

"But I was there! She called me yelling and crying to come help. I tore him off her before, then he'd go stumbling out of the house while I stayed and took care of her."

"I understand." Suzette kept her tone steady and sympathetic. "In a court of law, though, all this is circumstantial evidence. On their own, the pictures don't prove anything, other than the fact that Marty was mistreated. That's probably why you haven't had much attention from CPD."

Irene ran her fingers into her hair. "There's no justice in this world. Here I thought there'd finally be someone on my side, after all this time, someone who could help put that creep away for what he'd done." She started gathering the snapshots into a pile. I cringed, since I wanted to go through each of them.

"I know this is difficult, Irene, but can you tell us what you think happened the night Marty died?"

She plopped her back against the chair, took turns looking at both of us. "What good is that gonna do?"

"Honestly, I don't know, but it's a place to start."

"You might remember something that can help." Maybe it wasn't my place to interject, as both women turned to me with expressions of mild dismay. Being Marty's sister, she had to have a unique insight. Wasn't that what Lance kept saying? My cheeks burned at the idea of parroting Lance.

"Well, all right." Irene kept her posture ramrod straight. "I can't say I approved of everything my sister ever did, but I thought Craig was good for her, at first. Thought she'd settle down. She had a thing for chasing married men and stirring up trouble, but she loved Craig, fell for him hard. Marty had a good job as a receptionist and Craig worked nights at the adhesive factory. They did well for a couple years, got along and all. Then Marty wanted kids, probably because I had my first around then." Irene chuckled and lingered on the memory.

"I guess it wasn't meant to be," she continued, "They never had kids. So that started them bickering. Marty got restless and started going back to her old ways. Had an affair with her boss. That set Craig to drinking, hard, because she talked about leaving him for her boss. But her boss ended up firing her. This sorta thing went on for years, the whole time they were married. She went through a couple more jobs before she ended up as a barmaid."

"At the Junkyard Lounge?" I asked.

"Yeah. She got on real well, then started another affair with a married guy. Big difference was, this guy was in to making promises, told her all the stuff she wanted to hear, about how he was going to leave his family for her and make her the happiest woman ever."

Archie had pretty much said the same thing, but once again hearing about my dad's romantic side, while knowing how he treated Mom, was a dichotomy I couldn't reconcile in my head.

"Was it this guy?" Suzette held up a Polaroid shot I hadn't seen. It included Marty cuddling up to someone. Part of the picture was blurred at the corner, where someone's thumb had gotten in the way while taking the photo. My stomach clenched when I recognized my dad.

Irene pointed a finger. "That's the one. Said he'd protect Marty, never let nothing happen to her, but Craig would rather see her dead than happy. He made sure of it too."

There were three of them. Candid pictures of my dad and Marty. I became fixated. Here was a guy being playful and affectionate with a woman who wasn't his wife, wasn't the mother of his children. My mom deserved better. She gave him everything a wife could give, yet that wasn't good enough for him. As far as I knew, there were no pictures of my parents embracing and hamming it up for the camera. Not like that. It was a good thing my insides were empty.

What had been so special about Marty Cox? Maybe she was prettier than Mom, but to hear Irene talk, Marty wasn't a woman worth getting involved with.

"Did you ever meet him?" Suzette asked. "The one making Marty all the promises?"

"Couple times. Wasn't nothing special about Gerald." Revulsion flashed across Irene's face. "Another loser, if you ask me."

"Do you think there's any chance he could've hurt Marty?"

Goosebumps prickled my arms as the same question slid through my mind.

"No." Irene rolled her eyes. "Gerald was a mostly a coward."

I waited for her to mention the Gerald-Craig rumble outside the bar, but she didn't say anymore. Irene wasn't wrong, calling my dad a coward, but hearing it still stung.

"So what are you ladies going to do now?" Irene finished the donut on her napkin. If I'd counted correctly, that made three she'd scarfed down with her retelling of events.

Suzette cleaned then replaced her glasses. "There isn't much we can do. Like I said before, we're not directly involved with the investigation."

"But I know you're on to Craig," Irene said. "You wouldn't be bothering with his file if you didn't think there was something worth looking into. You gotta have a lead or something that means *something*."

I knew Suzette would have a hard time arguing against that logic.

"Tell you what, Ms. Slater, let's make sure we have each other's numbers and let's stay in touch."

After Irene and her black bag had gone, I needed time to myself in the bathroom. Irene had left some of the photos, because Suzette told her we'd create a file and save her info. Maybe Suzette sensed my need to scrutinize every grainy detail, because she'd picked out one of my dad and Marty together. I took it into the bathroom with me to obsess over.

They were close, cuddling cheek to cheek, so they'd both make it into the frame. Their carefree smiles made my chest hurt. How could they be so happy, knowing they were destroying a family and hurting people they once claimed to have loved?

This was one of those days where I didn't have to psych myself into not eating. The day's events had caused enough gut-wrenching anxiety that I couldn't eat if I tried.

I patted my face with cold water. One thing I didn't understand—if my dad was so crazy about Marty, why didn't he move in with her when he left us? What had kept him from setting up house with his lover? Was he afraid of Craig, even though he had thrashed him in the parking lot? It didn't add up for me.

I understood why Irene was dead-set against Craig. The Polaroids capturing Marty's injuries were damning. If a man could raise a fist against his wife, he wasn't too far from murdering her. Craig made the perfect suspect but was never arrested. It made me wonder what information Lance was still withholding from me.

Back in the conference room, Suzette was organizing info into the promised folder. I slid the photo across the table to her.

"So our new gal-pal Irene seems to have her hooks in someone down at CPD." She glimpsed each of the photos again before dropping them into the manila envelope. "Not sure how lifting a file turns us into *Charlie's Angels* though."

"Yeah, me neither." I said it absentmindedly but couldn't deny a creepy feeling, knowing someone was keeping tabs.

"Hey, I know this wasn't easy on you. How you holding up?"

"I'm fine." Embarrassed to my bone marrow was the proper response, but there was no need to do that to Suzette. I hated inconveniencing people with my feelings, and being the center of attention for my boss's pity only deepened my humiliation.

"I'll say one thing for Irene, she makes a decent case for Craig as the culprit. In cases like this, it usually is the husband."

“So what’s next?” It had been pretty heavy duty for a Wednesday morning.

Suzette dropped her head back and groaned. “I’m gonna have to call Warren. Because at this point, we need to get a look at the case file and see if we can figure out why CPD didn’t solve this case years ago.”

Suzette realized I was going to be useless for a while, so she suggested I take a long lunch and clear my head. I appreciated that and told her so. Having a chance to escape did me good. I wanted to shake those images of Marty from my mind. All of them. It would take more than springtime sun on my face and a drive with the windows down, but it was a start.

I thought I’d try going home, since it wasn’t far, and I could return the Vinny file to the dishwasher.

But when I pulled into the driveway, I saw Mom’s car sitting in the opened garage. At least I could stash the file under my seat until later. Seeing Mom wouldn’t be easy. Not after Irene’s visit, topped off with snapshots of my dad and Marty canoodling.

Maverick was enjoying the yard on his leash. After I gave him some belly rubs, I left him to bask in the sun. Then I took a deep breath, headed inside to see Mom.

“Hey.” I decided it was best to sound upbeat, considering our last few conversations had gone a bit sour. “Home for lunch?”

“Just got in.” She fluffed her hair. I felt bad right then for having thought Marty was a tad prettier. After all, where were my loyalties? “I can whip us up some BLT sandwiches.”

Why is food a parental tool, used equally for good and bad purposes? And offering up a BLT sandwich wasn't playing fair. My stomach flipped at the thought. I had no defense. Plus, I was tired of feeling hollow. I wanted that comfort of being with my mom and knowing what it felt like being warm again on the inside.

It was day two of no food. That's when the stomach cramps and rumbles were the worst. By day three that usually settled. Day four often meant a headache, but I usually didn't make it that far without eating something.

"Sure. Sounds good," I said.

Mom went to work. She said she'd had a cancellation for the afternoon, which explained why she was home. Roger had offered to take her to lunch, but she told him she had too much paperwork to catch up on. I noticed the engagement ring was still MIA.

I told her about my finals and rehashed my chat with Frank. For the first time this week, I felt a sense of normalcy return. I'd been on edge with Mom and had a hard time being around her. This was what it was supposed to be like, the two of us, busy working women, enjoying each other's company over lunch.

"Did you talk to Trey this morning?" I asked after a few bites, delicious food rolling around my mouth and a pickle to boot.

She nodded. "He didn't look too good. Said he might have his head checked out."

"Did he call Shelia?"

"Not that I know of."

"Why did he stay here last night anyway?"

Mom arched her left eyebrow almost as well as Lee Majors. There it was. A perfect example of how random memories could be. I hadn't watched *The Six Million Dollar Man* since I was a kid, but that particular facial expression—an image of rebuilt Steve Austin running in a red tracksuit with that permanently poised eyebrow—had found a home in my brain.

"I didn't ask him," Mom said. "He was already asleep on the couch when I got home, and I left him alone. This morning," she shrugged, "it didn't seem to matter."

That left me perplexed, since sleepovers weren't routine for Trey. "He's been acting weird."

"It's the wedding. Tests a person's mettle."

"Do you think they should get married?" I'd never had any doubts about them, until I saw Shelia panicky and Trey hiding out with a bandaged gash.

"Probably not for me to say."

I stopped mid-chew, fearing I might suddenly choke. When it came to me and Derek, she had plenty to say. There were times I wondered if parenting stopped or expired at a certain age. Was Trey too old to listen to his mother? Not that a thing like that would stop Annette Reed from sounding off. Opinions on other people's lives was one of her specialties. Or maybe it only worked that way with girls. Was the mother-daughter bond one that entitled her to a lifetime of interjecting her *wisdom*?

I nudged my plate away, having lost my appetite for the other half of my sandwich.

"But if something's wrong, shouldn't we do or say something?"

She shook her head. "It'll either work itself out or it won't. Best to let sleeping dogs lie. No need for us to get in the way."

I couldn't have disagreed more. Wasn't that how people ended up in shipwrecked relationships, stranded with each other, a mortgage and two kids when it was too late, because no one would speak up, say they noticed the signs that the union was doomed? Wasn't that how a woman ended up with an abusive spouse?

The phone rang. I jumped up and answered, grateful for the distraction.

"Oh, hey," Lance said from the other end. "I wasn't expecting to catch you at home. Thought I'd be leaving a message."

I didn't want to say much with Mom close by, so I kept my responses to one word. Oh. Hmm.

"I just wanted to see if you had time to get together." A hesitation hitched in Lance's voice. Maybe he would've preferred talking to the answering machine.

"I've got a little time left on my lunch break. I can meet in ten minutes?" It was sloppy, but my burning frustrations with my mom kept me from thinking straight.

Lance agreed and we chose a spot.

Before Mom could interfere with questions about why I was running off so fast, I thanked her for lunch and dashed out the door without even looking at her.

CHAPTER ELEVEN

I met Lance in the parking lot of my old high school, someplace where I didn't have to bother with food. School was letting out for the day, and I liked wading into the hustle and bustle. The lack of privacy also worked for me. What we could have to talk about since our meeting at Cardo's, I couldn't say.

I parked in the teachers' side of the lot, away from the main traffic, and got out of my car. Lance arrived soon after and joined me.

He surprised me with flowers.

"Wh-what are these for?" I didn't do well with gifts, always worried that my reaction wasn't sufficient. Plus, Lance and I were barely friends. He had no business giving me flowers.

"I'm sorry I came off like a creep yesterday. Honestly, I didn't even think you'd want to see me again."

No need to tell him I only came to escape an argument with my mom.

"They're nice." I inhaled the bouquet, thinking that move was required. "Thank you."

A football zoomed over our heads as teenagers made their way to their cars. Funny how I'd been one of them only two years ago. Now, I was, what? More mature? More accomplished? More certain of who I was and where I was going in life?

"I know I made a mess of things." Lance shook his head. "When I got into this, I wasn't expecting to meet someone like you. And I didn't plan on getting distracted."

What was he talking about?

"Don't get me wrong, I still want to find Marty's killer, but…I also want to get to know you, apart from all this. I was probably stupid, coming at you the way I did, saying a bunch of crazy stuff about your parents."

I didn't know what to say. I wasn't the kind of girl that guys fell for all the time. I was quiet, moody when I wasn't quiet, and not exactly a Cindy Crawford-type beauty. I was skinny, awkward, smart, and strangely good at all three. Usually, the kind of guys I was attracted to paid no attention to me. Maybe that worked. Kept me virginal and out of trouble. Until Derek.

Derek.

Naturally, I hadn't mentioned having a boyfriend. Why would I? Lance had shown up in my driveway practically accusing my mom of murder, then my dad. Somehow, that didn't say love connection or have anything to do with Derek.

"I'm not sure what to say, Lance."

"I know. This hasn't been the ideal start, but I think you're beautiful, and maybe we could see where it goes."

He'd found my weak spot, calling me beautiful. Skinny, awkward, smart girls didn't hear that often. At the same time, his words made me feel as if I was under a microscope. What did he find beautiful about me? And at what point would I turn him off?

This was ridiculous.

"Yeah, it's been weird, and I don't know Lance. I have to go back to work."

"Then why don't you call me? Maybe we can find a place and just talk, if you want."

"Yeah, maybe. I'll think about it."

Would I? What was there to think about?

I sank into my car, cradling the flowers, then funneled into the remnants of student traffic. This was the first time since meeting Lance that his primary focus hadn't been Marty.

As I drove away, with Lance somewhere behind me, I couldn't ignore a nagging thought: was Lance using me and setting me up for something? Despite the flowers and the floaty-dreamy feeling I had from being desired, I had to remind myself of a universal truth, especially when it came to men—TANSTAAFL, *There ain't no such thing as a free lunch.*

I finished the rest of the afternoon by putting in solid time at work. Since Suzette had more going on than just my father's dead mistress case, there was plenty to focus on and catch up, if I wanted to keep getting a paycheck. Compartmentalizing came through for me again. I wanted to break down, tell Suzette all about Lance and the crazy feelings stirring inside. Should I take a chance on him? Or was it bound to end up with me getting hurt? And why was I thinking about Lance like he had boyfriend potential, or that he was a better catch than Derek? Where was my loyalty to basically the best guy I'd ever met?

I worried that I had an in-bred character flaw. Thinking of my dad and what he'd done, was I doomed to repeat the same mistakes? To ruin good relationships? If I wasn't good enough for Derek anyway, was this the best way to let him down and move on, with someone new already waiting on the side?

No. There was no way this was how love worked.

By the end of the workday, the bombardment of my thoughts hadn't eased. I thought about poking my head into Suzette's office, asking if she could talk. Second thoughts got the best of me, though.

At home, I liberated Maverick from the utility room and played tennis ball fetch in the yard. After, I showered and changed, having made plans with Derek. I ditched the flowers from Lance. If my mom saw them, I'd have to tell her they were from Derek, but if Derek came over and saw them…well, I didn't want to keep track of too many lies. My head was already about to burst.

I also had a chance to slip the Vinny file back into its place in the dishwasher since Mom was out.

Feeling like a dutiful daughter, I put in a load of clothes before cleaning up dishes in the sink and leaving a note for Mom that I was out with Derek. Good girl marks for the day.

Derek was almost ready when I got there. His parents were having a cookout and he wanted to go, primarily because he had this thing about who among his brothers could eat the most of his dad's hamburgers. And with spring warming up, his family enjoyed evenings outside. I would think they'd get sick of each other, working together all day, then getting together for dinner. Didn't these people need space? Their own lives?

"You seem quiet," Derek said on the drive to his parents'. He ran his hand over my leg, lovingly, then held my hand. There were no expectations at the end of his fingertips. Meaning, he was touching me just for the feel of *me* and to express his affection. I loved that.

"Long day at work." It was the easiest response. I wasn't ready to tell him about the pictures of Marty and my dad. He'd be kind about it, but it felt like another fossil from my past to be ashamed of.

"Does working there ever make you think about doing something else?" he asked.

"What do you mean?"

"Are you sure you want to be a lawyer? Won't it be hard to deal with that depressing stuff all day and still have time for your family?"

I considered that. Bob and Ed put in serious hours, missed dinnertimes and occasionally tucking kids in at night. Suzette didn't even have that kind of life outside the office to miss. She had a string of divorces and dead plants. There was also school to think about. I still had a year of undergrad then law school. My professional life wouldn't officially start for half a decade at least. Where did a family fit into that plan?

"You just want me to be like your mom." I don't know why I said it or why I said it with such vinegar, but I did. That wasn't enough, though. "Staying at home and raising a boatload of kids isn't my dream. I don't want to cook and clean all day and wait for you to get home."

"Who said anything about that? I was just wondering if you were really happy with your job. Seems like it wears you down and stresses you out."

"Yeah, right. Be real. You want a little wife who's all about crock pot meals and sewing curtains. That can't be me." I slipped my hand from his, not because I was mad at him but because I felt that heaviness of unworthiness descend. I'd never really fit into Derek's family. His mom was boisterous and homey in ways I never could be. Even his brothers' wives stayed at home with their kids and spent their time talking about side dishes, crafting, and playdates. I had no idea how to create a home and build a world around chili recipes and family. This relationship had to be doomed.

"I just asked a question," Derek said, his tone still even. "Why are you jumping to conclusions? Did something happen today?"

That hurt. Just when I thought I had something to be mad about, he went and proved that he did know me, that he could tell if I was bickering because something else was picking at me. I couldn't tell him what was going on. I couldn't mention Lance, or the pictures I'd seen, or meeting Irene.

I sighed. "Just a bad day. Sorry for being a brat." Was I? Yes, I was sorry. I didn't have a way to work through my frustrations, even though that was my own doing.

At his parents', we fell into our routine. Him with his dad and brothers. Me with his mom and sisters-in-law. They were good people, each of them, and a genuine camaraderie dominated. I was secretly jealous. It was the kind of family they presented in Hallmark commercials, or that one coffee commercial where the son comes home for Christmas, wakes everyone up with a freshly brewed pot. How could this many people get together and life be so good and simple?

By the time we left, Derek had put away six burgers, tying with his second-oldest brother, and I'd suffered through a hot dog and chips. His parents hugged me like I was one of their own. I told myself to ignore that pull, that yearning of wanting to belong. I was too broken and imperfect to play a permanent role here.

"You feeling better?" Derek asked when we were in his truck again. His hand was back on mine, and I couldn't deny the energy he gained from being around his family. The same way Superman thrived off sunlight.

"Yeah, I'm good." Time with his family felt easier than being with mine.

"My dad was on me a little, wanting to know what my intentions are with you."

I tensed.

"He said it's about time I quit stringing you along, that a pretty girl like you won't wait forever." With that he kissed the back of my hand. "Have you thought about it, us being together, making it official?"

"I don't know. I mean, marriage…?" The word knotted in my throat.

"Yeah. I love you," he looked over at me when he said it, "and I can see myself spending the rest of my life with you."

It was a good thing I was sitting, because his words would've knocked me over. Sure, we traded I love yous, affections, and had feelings for each other. But was this it? Were we meant to ride off into the sunset together and build a happily ever after? When did two people figure that out?

"It's a big step," I said. "It should be right, for both of us. I mean, are you sure you've dated enough? And what about the sex?"

That brought a huge smile to his face. "The sex will be awesome."

"But you still want to wait until we're married?"

"We've waited this long. It'll be a bonus. And just think, how many people nowadays can say they waited until they got married to have sex? We'll get to tell our kids and grandkids that."

My head started spinning. Did he say grandkids?

"So what do you think, maybe in the fall, have a wedding outside?"

"Wait, fall as in three or four months from now?"

"Why not?"

"What if I'm not ready?" That sounded awful. Worse were all the things running through my head. What if I want to date Lance? Maybe I want to date a few other guys—maybe have sex—before getting tied down. What if I'm not meant to be married?

"We love each other. I was thinking maybe it's time for the next step."

"Just stop! Why are you pushing me into something I'm not ready for?"

Right then, he looked at me as if he didn't know who I was. I coiled slightly in my seat, both from the shame rippling through me and from the tears that threatened.

I didn't go inside Derek's apartment when we got back. Neither one of us wanted to deal with the other. How had we gone from talking marriage to needing space and time away from each other? Tears spilled down my cheeks as I drove home. Just enough so I could get by Mom, get to my room and hunker down for a good cry. I'd ruined everything.

At home, Mom was on the phone and Trey was sorting laundry. Maverick snoozed on the couch.

"Back again?" I said to Trey.

"Looks like it." As usual, he glanced over me like I wasn't there. "You the one who left clothes in the washer? Nice move, lawyer lady."

"Aren't you the one getting married in a month?"

He paused.

"Shouldn't you be doing laundry at your apartment, you know, the one you share with Shelia? Or maybe fixing that medicine cabinet?"

"Like you know anything about it." Trey delivered a glare meant to cut me down to the size of a Smurf.

Maverick's eyes peeled open and he beat the couch with his tail. I rubbed his ears and kissed his head, thankful that someone was happy to see me.

"What's the fuss about?" Mom asked, apparently done with her call.

"Your daughter's playing Little Miss Know It All," Trey said.

"Just trying to figure out why my big brother is doing laundry at Mommy's house and avoiding his fiancée."

"Kyle!" Mom stepped in front of Trey, like she had to shield him from my words.

"What? Why do we always have to pretend with him? I'm sick of it!"

"It's none of your business!" Trey said.

"Yeah, why would my family be any of my business? Why can't we ever act like normal people and just talk?"

They looked at me, like a united front, and said nothing.

I'd had enough. No way I was going to stand there and wait for Mom to start chiding me for being inconsiderate to Trey. I stormed out of my house wishing like never before that I could slam that pitiful sliding door.

My dramatic exit left me with a problem. Nowhere to go and sulk. I wished I'd brought Maverick with me. I thought about going to Derek's, crying and apologizing, telling him that I did love him and that I didn't want it to be over between us. But I couldn't. Fear gripped me, told me that he'd turn me away after I poured out my heart. No way I'd risk that kind of rejection.

I lied and convinced myself that there was only one person who could make this night any better. I called Lance from a gas station and asked if he wanted to meet up and talk. He was game, so I gave him the address for Suzette's office. It was the only place where we could be alone. Being alone with the guy who thought I was beautiful made perfect, reckless sense.

Ten minutes later, regret stirred inside me. Inviting Lance to the office for a rendezvous was a breach of Suzette's trust. And at this point, she was one of the few people I hadn't upset.

As I waited for Lance in the empty parking lot, I considered leaving. It was late, closing in on eleven o'clock, and meeting up with a guy I hardly knew made no sense.

That was true for most of my life at the moment.

Lance pulled into the gravel lot before I changed my mind. With every move, from getting out of the car, forcing a smile, walking over to him, I wanted to forget the whole thing, forget that I even knew Lance Turner.

The other businesses in the area had already closed. A few streetlights gave off a damp light while moths and other nighttime bugs played chaperone.

"I'm glad you called." Lance slid his arms around my waist and embraced me.

My face and body flushed. "I know it's kind of late."

This was a mistake. I'd set myself up for becoming the kind of girl I despised.

"So this is where you work?" He looked over the building, best he could in the low light.

"Yeah, I work for a lawyer."

His eyebrows jumped. "That's pretty impressive."

"Is it?" I fumbled the key in the door, then nudged it open. I'd worked late with Suzette a few times but hadn't entered the place in pitch black darkness. Luckily, I managed to flip on the lights without crashing into a table or chair.

Now what?

"Um, thirsty?" In my head I was frantically searching for a way to backpedal this scenario.

"Sure."

I checked the mini-fridge behind Crystal's desk. She kept a healthy supply of Diet Cokes there, but Bob also stashed regular Cokes. I took a couple. We sat on the couch, an ocean of awkwardness between us.

"I really don't know much about you, Lance."

"Not a lot to tell. Just a guy from a busted up family, grew up in a poor part of town, graduated high school, been trying to get into law enforcement."

The similarities we shared came as a surprise. One sentence and I learned more about Lance than I had in our previous encounters. But it didn't ease my regret of inviting him here.

"My dad wasn't around much," Lance continued. "Only when it was convenient for him or sometimes not at all. Mom struggled to keep everything together."

Lance didn't make my heart flutter the way Derek did, but I knew what it was like, growing up in a broken home. Maybe it showed on my face, that I understood.

He set down his Coke and inched closer to me.

"Can I be honest with you?"

"Yeah, sure." My pulse hammered.

"Ever since that first day I saw you, I kept thinking about what it would be like to kiss you." He slid his fingertips along my bare arm, giving me instant goosebumps. I did my best not to flinch or let on that my body temperature had probably shot up a hundred degrees.

I let him move in even closer as I held my breath.

"Ahhem!!"

We both jumped up.

"Suzette! What are you doing here?"

Her hair was loose and wavy in a wrangled sort of way. With her eyeliner smeared, she resembled a raccoon. Despite her disheveled look, I'd never felt so intimidated.

"I think that's my question." She planted a hand on her hip. "Who's this?"

"Lance. He's just a friend." I always had to make it worse.

Her face stern, she nodded. "A friend who's leaving."

Lance took the hint and made a hasty exit, skipping proper introductions. I was glad he didn't mention calling or seeing me later.

"What the hell was that?" Suzette pointed toward the door.

I sighed deeply. "A mistake."

"A few minutes later and it could've been a huge mistake."

"Yeah, maybe." I sank back down onto the couch. Suzette came and joined me.

"Come on, Kyle, you're smarter than this. You don't need to be sneaking around with a guy who looks like a bad version of Eric Stoltz and still wears Hush Puppies."

We laughed and she put her arm around me. I leaned into her. It felt as though she was catching me from a fall. I liked that.

"What are you doing with that loser? Where's that hunk of yours?"

I wasn't sure how to answer. So much had happened in the space of a few days.

"Long story."

She shrugged. "I got cold pizza upstairs and all night to listen."

"Really?"

"Really."

I gave in, started for the stairs, because at this point I needed to jump from the train of self-destruction.

"So why are you sleeping at the office, and where's your car?"

"Makes you wonder about me, doesn't it?" Suzette gave my shoulders a faux massage. "Good grief girl, you need to eat."

CHAPTER TWELVE

After I told Suzette about my blow up with Mom and Trey, she made me call home. I felt like a scolded child, but she swore my mom would be worried and would want to hear my voice, no matter how late it was.

She was right.

Mom answered after half a ring, apologized profusely, and wanted to know when I'd be home. I said not long.

Suzette let me finish explaining about Lance. Everything about Lance. She didn't have solutions, and at this hour, I didn't need any. I only needed to let it out, like a hot air balloon being deflated.

We cleaned up our pizza mess, though we didn't eat. She hugged me, hard. The kind of hug that you feel in your soul that reminds you that you're valued and have a place in this world. I needed that, too.

At home, Mom was waiting in the kitchen. We didn't say much, but she hugged me too. Trey's car was still there but I didn't mention it. Maverick whimpered and nudged me. I buried my face in his and welcomed every slobbery kiss.

I can't say I slept well that night, but it felt better getting up on Thursday than it had in a while. Trey and I muttered sorrys to each other and I guess that was more progress than I'd believed possible. I still didn't know why he was suddenly staying here, but after hearing an apology from him, it was best not to push too hard. The worst part was not knowing how much damage I'd done to my relationship with Derek and if it was salvageable. I couldn't call him since he was at work. He deserved my groveling in person, which would have to wait till later.

Suzette was already in the office when I got there. Who knows if she'd even left? We kept it professional and normal but didn't treat each other like nothing had happened. If I needed to pull her aside to talk, I knew I could. I liked that she left it up to me and that she gave me space.

It took three Cokes to get through the day, and even though it was May and pleasingly warm outside, Suzette kept our area of the office frigid, which probably helped me stay awake too. At least I knew to wear a jacket to work.

I second-guessed my decision not to call Derek about twenty times but didn't. It would've meant talking to his answering machine, but at least he'd know I was thinking about him. About us. Desperation toyed with me, because I didn't know what move to make. Another headache flared.

Suzette ducked out later in the afternoon and said I could leave early for the day. Having a couple free hours added to my day gave me a much-needed lift—and sparked a crazy idea.

Out in the office parking lot, with no one looking, I found a sizable rock. Not hard to do out there. Hard would be the next part, busting my taillight. It took a few smacks, requiring more force than I imagined, but when it was done I picked up the broken plastic pieces and took them with me as I set off for the biggest risk I'd ever taken.

Getting off work early helped ensure that the body shop would be open still, but it didn't guarantee who'd be there, available for repairs.

Streamline Auto Body was down the road from Westland Mall. Although the mall had once been a thriving center with anchor stores and over fifty shops, its business and traffic was now threadbare. Two major stores hung on, but the area also suffered from a drastic rise in crime, which chased customers away to Northland or Eastland Malls.

I parked in front of the body shop. The building needed a fresh coat of paint and a sign that wasn't busted. Good thing I'd stopped by in broad daylight.

A man came out of the building, wiping his hands with a filthy blue rag.

"Hey, there," he said, smiling, his dark blonde hair flapping in the breeze. "Can I help you?"

I knew the instant I saw him, it was Craig Cox. The oval-shaped name patch stitched into his shirt confirmed it.

"Hi. Yeah, I got a problem here with my taillight." I walked around to the back of the car to show him. He joined me and barely glanced at the broken pieces. In fact, he spent more time glancing at me than my car. As stupid as it sounds, I hadn't considered the chance that he might recognize me. What if he'd seen me at the bar with my dad? But was it possible he could recognize me from when I was eight? I held my breath and hoped my face wasn't giving away my anxiety.

"Taillight, huh? You sure you want me to fix that? I bet your dad could pop on a new one in ten minutes. Save you some money."

A bit of relief hit me, but I needed to think fast.

"Well, it's my dad's car. I accidentally backed into a dumpster and wanted to get it fixed before he saw it." I cringed inwardly at my fumbling lies. Did that even sound believable? Was he on the verge of throwing me off the property?

His smile broadened. "Oh, I see. Come on in then." He waved for me to follow him.

Inside the building I met Vikki, the office manager. She handed me a clipboard with a paper to fill out.

"If you want, you can wait over here in my office. It ain't much but the seats are comfy. Won't take me long though." More of that smile. It drew me in, and I couldn't find anything disingenuous about it.

What also amazed me was that I didn't feel creeped out, standing next to the guy who'd beaten Marty—and according to Irene, maybe even killed her. Like a gentleman, he ushered me to his office, which was basically a cubicle, not a walled-in, private office.

"Help yourself to anything," he said before ducking out with a wave.

Since I knew I didn't have much time, and because Vikki was waiting on the form, I went to work, jotting down info. Having near déjà vu from when I dropped in at the Junkyard Lounge, I wasn't sure what I planned to accomplish, showing up where Craig Cox worked. Getting here had taken enough bravado and flimsy strategy. I peeled off my jacket since I'd gone from freezing to having my nerves set ablaze. I had to get something out of this venture. But what?

After I'd filled out the sheet, I surveyed Craig's desk from my seat. The usuals were present, paperwork, pens, mug, a phone smeared with grease. I wanted to get into the drawers.

I hated body shops. Everything smelled like rubber and grease and made my head throb to near explosion. If this crazy spy mission was going to be fruitful, I needed to do something.

I stood, shaking my pen, maybe too dramatically, in an effort to convey it wasn't working. An act, solely for Vikki, who glanced and smiled my way. I scanned Craig's desktop, pretending to search for another pen. Nothing jumped out. I pulled open the top drawer and did a casual pawing around, all while my eyes frantically searched for...something. I could feel Vikki's eyes on me and I didn't want to rile her suspicions, so I stuck with the desktop, picked a new pen and tried it out. As I was playing out my ruse, I noticed the framed pictures. One featured a dog. Another showed Craig and Marty and a young boy. My throat went dry. I couldn't resist picking it up for further inspection. Craig's hair was blonder and Marty looked happy. So did the boy in her lap. And around her neck was the butterfly necklace.

"All done."

Craig startled me, although I'm not sure how long I'd been standing there, holding that picture.

"You're right," I said, too exasperated, "that was fast."

He noticed the frame in my hand.

"Oh, sorry." I put it back, and when I did, I noticed another photograph that almost knocked me off my feet. "Nice picture of your family. Your little boy is cute." I felt as if I was talking with a wad of bubblegum in my mouth. My words stuttered a tad as I fought the impact of an emotional tailspin.

"He's my nephew, but that's my wife. Well, was. She died years ago."

I watched as the memory came over him. Somberness clouded his features.

"Sorry to hear that," I said. "It's hard losing someone you love."

He looked at me and after a long second broke out that charming smile.

"You're right about that. Not a day goes by I don't think about her, miss her. Why don't we get you settled up here and you can be on your way?"

I submitted the paper and paid for the repair. Craig even gave me a discount, said he felt bad a 'little girl' like me having to pay for that to keep her daddy from getting mad.

By the time I was back behind the wheel of my car and pulling out, I was convinced that not only were people wrong about Craig, but that I'd also been made a complete fool of.

What a liar! I screamed it in my head over and over and wished I could pummel my dashboard into pulp.

Next to the family picture in Craig's office had been another, one where Craig stood proud and had his arm around that same little boy. Only, the little boy had grown up and was graduating high school—and happened to be Lance Turner.

Maybe there was little chance of recognizing Lance in the picture with Marty, since he had been around ten, but there was no denying it was him in the graduation picture, which wasn't as old.

So Lance wasn't just investigating Marty's case. He had an emotional attachment. A personal connection, which he'd failed to mention. Although I guess he was too busy calling me beautiful and trying to swoon me out of my underwear.

But why had he used me? Why come to me, when I knew practically nothing about the details of Marty's death. Why me?

I couldn't think straight and nothing made sense.

I went home, not knowing where else I could go.

But arriving home only stupefied me even more. There was Derek, mowing the lawn. Shirtless.

I'd forgotten that he'd agreed to play landscaper this week for Mom. Seeing him, I took it as a good sign, but I tried not to let my excitement show. What if he planned to fulfill his commitment then never see me or speak to me again?

After I put my car in the garage I went up to him, feeling the shake in my knees. He released the safety lever and the roar of the mower died. Then came his lukewarm grin.

"Hey, I didn't know you'd be here," I said.

"Yeah, I thought you'd be at work." Slivers of grass clung to his chest.

"Got off a bit early."

"Me too."

Already, I could feel us stall. It was hard for us to look at each other.

"I'm sorry." It felt good, saying it first and meaning it. "I was a total jerk last night and you were nothing but amazing. The truth is, I'm scared. I never thought I'd meet anyone who could love me the way you do, and I'm scared every day that you're gonna wake up and realize you've made a mistake or something and move on. And maybe you don't know it because I've been too scared to show you, but I love you, more than I thought possible and more than I've ever loved anyone in my life. If I hurt you, I'm sorry. Any girl in the world would be lucky to have you, and if you never want to talk to me again, I'll understand."

I didn't get the last part out completely before he pulled me into his sweaty goodness and kissed me.

There was no telling how long we stayed like that. Luckily, we were in the backyard, or Mom would've heard about our scene from old Mrs. Davis or Mrs. Cunion. Finally, we broke and came up for air.

"You think too much," Derek said. "You were right, I probably pushed it too much last night. It's just that I love you, and I see how happy my brothers are."

"Yeah, I get it. I just don't want to disappoint you."

"Not possible."

He moved in for another kiss, but we were interrupted.

"Hey, can you two horny toads take it someplace else? Can't you go five minutes without being all over each other?"

Trey wasn't brave enough to come out of the house. The best he could do was yell at us through the opened kitchen window.

"He's just jealous." And Derek helped himself to that kiss.

After such a tender moment, I needed a shower for more reasons than one. Trey was off his game as far as his teasing remarks went, but I didn't mind for a change. Not much could've spoiled my mood. I walked Maverick, then showered and changed quickly so Derek could have the bathroom. Trey and I hung out in the kitchen, talking like regular adults. He mentioned that Mom was showing a house on the east side. I asked if he'd seen any sign of the engagement ring or had any news on her answer to the proposal, but he was as clueless as me. Trey didn't bring up Shelia, so I followed his lead. He whipped up a chipped beef sandwich for himself, making my inner child drool, while I made ham sandwiches for Derek. Maverick exercised his perfect-catch skills as Trey and I took turns tossing him bites of meat. After we tidied the kitchen, Trey handed me a message.

"It's from Suzette. She said to tell you she got the file, whatever that means. Oh, and some guy named Lance called." Trey looked at me and did a poor job of imitating Mom's high-arching brow. "Lance?"

I thanked him, crumpled the note, and shot it in the garbage can for two points. Right where Lance and anything concerning him belonged.

As I waited for Derek, I was disappointed my venture into Craig's world revealed little except that he still loved Marty—and that he was Lance's uncle.

Wait a minute! Was I missing the obvious here? Was Lance part of the investigation as an attempt to save his uncle? If Craig had been the primary suspect all those years ago but was never arrested, maybe Lance was trying to clear his uncle from suspicion. *And he'd known who I was and about my parents all along!* Maybe Craig filled him in. Would that explain how Lance knew such details about my family's past?

"Ready," Derek said when he joined me in the kitchen. "Where are we off to?"

I had to put my speculations on hold.

"Well, it's a surprise," I said.

Derek shot me a playful look that told me he was unsure but willing to go along.

We told Trey we were off but didn't mention where to. A good thing, because Derek wasn't thrilled when I told him, once we were in his truck, that I wanted to go back to the Junkyard Lounge.

"I thought we agreed to stay away from that place?"

I had a lot of explaining to do, more than I could manage in the short drive there, but I begged sweetly and reminded Derek how much I loved him. He caved. As he chomped down the sandwiches I'd made him, I shared about finding Craig, Marty's ex, and how I was convinced he wasn't the killer. That I needed to poke around more, come up with something new. Before Derek could get carried away with questions, we were parking and making our way inside. Like we were regulars.

The fear of running into my dad had faded. With the updates that had been done, the bar hardly reminded me of my childhood visits here. It was as though the Junkyard Lounge became two different places.

Archie greeted us with a smile and a wave when we walked in. Patrons glimpsed our way but quickly returned to their drinks and buffalo wings.

"I's wonderin' if you'd make it back," Arche said, as Derek and I each straddled onto a stool. "You took off here so fast I thought I'd done chased you off with talkin' too much."

"Sorry about that. It was a lot of memories to take in." I looked to Derek as he slipped my hand into his, underneath the bar. A deep breath later, I forged ahead. "No one's ever really talked to me about Marty and all the things that happened back then. I want to sort through it now, see if I can understand everything." I didn't want to share about the investigation, not knowing if it would ruffle Archie, make him skittish and clam up. “You seemed pretty sure about Craig, that he was the one who hurt Marty.”

“Makes the most sense. He had anger issues and drinkin’ issues, put that in with a wife who’s foolin’ around and a man like that’s likely to do anything.”

My interaction with Craig had been brief, but I still had trouble seeing him as a killer.

“But the way things was between your dad and Marty, ain’t no tellin’ what really happened, which is probably why the police ain’t never figured it out.”

“What do you mean?”

“Well, Linda said that Marty was tired of waitin’ on your dad to leave your mom, tired of waitin’ on him to make good on his promises. Said Marty started seein’ another fella. Someone younger than her.”

“Are you saying that Marty was cheating on my dad?”

Derek sniggered. Couldn’t say I blamed him.

“It sure sounded like it. Linda saw ’em together, said that fella was awful young.”

“Did she ever say what his name was?”

“Naw, not that I can recollect. I never saw him neither. That was all part of their women talk. Marty never said nothin’ ’bout it to me, but Linda never kept quiet. Don’t think that woman could’a kept a secret for two seconds.”

“Did my dad know about this younger guy?”

“I ain’t sure if he did.”

For a moment, I enjoyed the thought of Marty pulling one over on my dad. I couldn’t say for certain, but I imagined a woman stepping out on him, especially for someone younger, had to stick in his craw, as the saying went.

But that made me wonder, would it make him mad enough to kill Marty? Not that I’d admit it, but Lance’s theory replayed in my head. *Maybe they got into a fight…and it ended badly*. The more I thought about my dad being two-timed by Marty—and outraged by it—the more I could picture him losing his temper with her. And what if Marty's abusive history with her husband helped muddy Gerald Reed as a suspect? Frank believed my dad had it in him, to kill someone. That it was only a matter of time. What if Marty ended up the victim, instead of my mom?

Derek and I sipped Cokes and kept Archie talking, but more revelations didn't manifest. Except for Marty's new boyfriend, nothing new came to light. Archie and I traded memories for a while, with him giving me the evolution of Linda's sickness and death and the struggles he'd had keeping the place open for so long. He was planning to retire in a few years and *Let the place finally go to the junkyard*, he said jokingly, hooking his thumb toward the dilapidated establishment place next door.

Soon after, Derek and I made our exit, and during the drive home, we switched roles and Derek played detective.

"So on the way over, you told me you found this guy Craig."

"Yeah." I drug the word out, curious and unsure what Derek was thinking.

"Wasn't that kind of dangerous? I mean, what if he would've remembered you?"

Funny that Derek had the same stray thought as me.

"Then he probably wouldn't have fixed my taillight. I don't know. Couldn't have been too dangerous, showing up during the day where he works." Because it seemed absurd now, being afraid of Craig, who'd been kinder to me than my own father.

"Okay, but was it worth it? Were you able to find out anything?"

I found out about Lance, but I couldn't explain Lance as easily as I'd explained finding Craig. I knew I'd have to come clean on the subject, but I was so in love with the euphoria of where things stood with Derek. Even the thought of Lance invigorated that heaviness—that fear—in my chest of losing Derek. *If he found out Lance and I were alone…* No, for the moment I'd forget about Lance and bask in my fairytale romance a little while longer.

Lance had been right, though. Talking to Archie had revived his memories and unearthed information that might've been overlooked during the original investigation. Archie seemed unphased when he mentioned Marty's new boyfriend. As if it wasn't worth bringing up. Maybe Archie didn't care that Marty was murdered, since she'd stepped out on his buddy. Who knew how the friends-at-the-bar code worked? But if there had been another guy—and Gerald Reed was on the verge of being replaced—this 'new boyfriend' might be the key to everything.

CHAPTER THIRTEEN

I hadn't put much thought into Suzette's message about the case file last night. I'd been absorbed in relief knowing Derek wasn't upset anymore, and I wasn't quite sure what case file she meant. Could've been for the Drumms or another case she was working.

Derek didn't stay long after our return from the Junkyard Lounge. Since I hadn't slept much the night before, I didn't mind. Food, I could do without. Sleep was a different matter. So a solid night's rest had me feeling sharp the next morning when I got into the office.

"Okay, I might've lied a little," Suzette said.

"About the case file?"

She nodded. I waited.

"I don't exactly have it, but I know where it is." She did a little dance from her chair.

"Which case file?"

She slapped her hands on the desk. "Marty Cox, you numbskull."

"Oh. I wasn't sure how far you were willing to take things."

"Are you serious? After I let Ms. Fritz the Nite Owl eat all my donuts? Oh, I'm in this thing till the end, babe. But we have to go to the file." She popped up from her chair, smile set, and reached for her purse and keys. "You ready?"

"Where we headed?"

"Downtown. Got a few surprises lined up for you."

"I don't like surprises."

"Suffer through it, babe."

Few experiences compared to riding shotgun with Suzette Worley. She maneuvered downtown traffic like a drunk stunt driver and used her horn unashamedly. It also wasn't unusual for her to be searching through her attaché case or checking her lipstick in her rearview mirror while driving. How we made it anywhere in one piece, I couldn't say, but Suzette always managed it.

When we arrived at the Columbus Police Station, I was grateful to plant my feet on blacktop. Walking into the building, I stood a little taller and strutted with purpose. The sharp smell of authority and being surrounded by men in uniforms had that effect. Most girls probably loved the mall or salon the way I loved the police station.

After signing in as visitors and receiving badges, we were greeted by a portly officer with slicked back hair.

"Kyle, I want you to meet a friend of mine, Warren Worley."

I smiled and introduced myself, then turned to Suzette. "As in *your* mister Worley?"

"Formerly." She said it out of the side of her mouth and placed enough emphasis on that one word to indicate her regret of the union.

Warren, looking anything but displeased, flashed a smile. Then he glanced at Suzette and gave her a wink. Either he hadn't heard her remark or he enjoyed the revulsion he inspired.

"Suzette told me you two are involved in an old case." Warren began walking and led us to the elevators.

"Not sure involved is the right word," I said, hoping I didn't sound off-putting. "Interested might be a better choice."

He nodded and said that older, unsolved cases were kept in the basement.

"That reminds me," Suzette said, "Could you please repeat to Kyle what you told me about your cold case unit? You know, a little about the team leading the investigations."

Warren looked at me. "Cold case is a fairly new term. It basically refers to an unsolved case or one that hasn't had any activity or new leads in a while. Recently, the department gave the go-ahead to three men to form a unit with the specific purpose of reviewing such cases in the hope of generating new leads or finding new evidence. They can take their time, go through the evidence and for the most part, just give an old case a fresh set of eyes."

"Do you happen to know if one of those investigators is named Lance Turner?" I asked, although I had a feeling I already knew the answer.

"No, sorry. Mark, John, and Allen. They're all retired from different areas of law enforcement. Mark spent thirty years as a beat cop; John worked homicide, and Allen was a supervisor at the crime lab."

I caught the expression on Suzette's face that was a mix of *sorry* and *told ya so*. If I had to guess, that was one of the surprises she'd intended for me. I couldn't deny there was a sting and a feeling of being duped, like I'd suspected. At least I hadn't made a total fool of myself with Lance. Small consolation that it was.

We left the elevator and any traces of natural light behind. Warren led us into a room that shocked my eyes with its stark white walls and floor when he flicked on the fluorescent lights.

"Here's how it works," Warren said. "You're free to look through the contents of the file, including any physical evidence that pertains to the case. However, gloves must be worn at all times, and no items may be removed from plastic bags. We can make copies of interviews, photographs, lab reports, so forth, but the file stays here. Are we clear?"

"Yes, thank you," I said.

“Suzette already took care of the paperwork. There will also be an officer in the room with you at all times.”

“Understandable.” CPD had to have measures of protecting evidence, especially if the case ever went to trial.

Warren’s glance lingered on Suzette until she gave him a stern expression.

“Let me check on Ralph. He’s supposed to be down here.” Warren left the room but ducked his head back in a second later. “Oh, and Buchanan is on his way.”

Suzette gave a pleased nod.

I plucked a pair of latex gloves from a tissue-like box and stretched them on. Two six foot long utility tables were pushed together, making one large workspace. Suzette readied notepads and pens. Minutes later, Officer Ralph entered, cradling the banker’s box with MARTY COX written on the ends in bold, black permanent marker.

My pulse amped knowing I was about to get into the meat of this case. I steeled myself, did a quick inner pep talk that I could handle the information inside that box. I’d finally know what happened on the night of Marty’s murder, and I’d reveal a new side of my parents, one I wouldn’t be able to rewrap and tuck away ever again.

My brain devoured and overloaded on the details of the case. One of the first items I came across was the crime scene photos. All in black and white, they showed Marty, face down on a rug by her entryway. Then there were pictures from the county coroner and the autopsy. According to the report, Marty had suffered blunt force trauma to the back of her head and cerebellum. A small amount of blood stained the rug. Bruising around Marty's neck was noted but *did not contribute to her death*.

I wrote and circled strangled on my notepad, recalling that one of the newspaper articles from Mom's keepsake box claimed Marty had been strangled. Why the discrepancy? Another thought rumbled around in my brain but wouldn't come to the surface. Too much to process.

Statements from officers on the scene said that there were no signs of a struggle at the home, but an end table had been found overturned and a photo album on the floor. Interviewed neighbors heard and saw nothing.

Those were the basics. Then came the pay dirt.

Fingerprints. Police had lifted several prints from the side door to Marty's garage. The door had been found ajar but with the glass panes intact, suggesting there hadn't been a break-in. The prints were primarily on the inside knob and on an outside pane of glass.

"I never knew they had a set of unidentified fingerprints." I heard the exasperation in my own voice. "Did they check my dad for a match?"

Suzette flipped through papers. "Says here all known suspects were compared with prints from the scene. No known match."

Fingerprints on a door that led to the outside could've come from neighbors or kids in the area. Maybe even a delivery boy. Or, they could've been left by a murderer, fleeing the scene.

"Must be why they never made an arrest," I said.

Suzette shrugged. "It's possible. A defense attorney worth his salt would've used that to cast reasonable doubt."

I poured over the interviews with Craig, word for word. He described finding Marty late that night and said no one else was in the house. Notes in the margins indicated he was emotional. He admitted that they were having marital problems and that they weren't living together presently. He often stayed with Marty's sister. Craig even discussed the altercation he had with Gerald Reed in the parking lot of the Junkyard Lounge, but said that he didn't kill his wife.

Chills slithered over me as I envisioned my dad at the scene, standing over Marty's body.

Next, I gave the same treatment to my dad's statement. Funny how it sounded like him, only on paper. Gruff, short answers. Skimpy details, especially when asked about the affair. He made it sound like they'd hardly spent any time together, like the two of them enjoyed a short fling and he didn't know her that well. No mention of their plans to abandon their families and head into the sunset together. No doubt he was thinking of himself and of covering his own rear. When it came to questions about his marriage, he replied that they got along but had the same issues any marriage faces. There was no mention of the fact that he and my mom were already separated by that point. As always, Greaser's number one priority was himself.

"Have you seen this?" Suzette handed me a report.

Annette Reed Interview. When Det. Buchanan questioned Ms. Reed about her whereabouts on the night of Ms. Cox's murder, Ms. Reed claimed she was working at the Western Pancake House, 344 South High St., Columbus. However, when Buchanan checked with the management, he found that Ms. Reed's timecard had been falsified on the date specified. When questioned further, Ms. Reed had no explanation for the error and maintained her claim that she was not at or near the deceased's residence.

I met Suzette's stare. "A falsified time card? What does that mean?"

Suzette gave a shrug-twitch. "Almost sounds like she had something to hide."

I flipped to the next page and saw Mom's name, written in bold red letters and circled. I held it up for Suzette to see.

"Looks like that detective thinks she did it."

"My mom fudged her timecard on the night Marty was killed?" I ran it through my mind, not believing my own words.

"Either she did or someone changed it for her." Suzette scanned over the report again before handing it to me. "Doesn't say which."

I read through it and laid it aside. I went back to the sheet with my mom's name on it and turned it over. On the back was a list of bullet points:

--was seen driving by victim's home a month prior
--endured trouble, possible abuse in her own marriage
--falsified timecard, lied
--slender & petite, capable of blow to the head ?

Blow to the head? Where had I heard that reference?

I suddenly felt as though I had creepy crawlies trapped underneath my skin and scampering all over me. Clearly, this investigator had his sights set on Mom as the guilty suspect. I read the list until the words blurred and my eyes hurt.

"Come on, what are you doing? Give me that." Suzette examined the paper for herself. Within seconds, she understood my inner turmoil. She gave me a stern look and shook her head. "You've got to stay focused." She tapped the paper with her finger. "This is one cop's thinking, that's all. It doesn't prove anything, except that he's doing his job."

She was right. I had to keep my head on straight and distance myself from my feelings for my parents, if I hoped to get anywhere with the information.

Just then, the door opened and in walked a tall, lean man. His face was a mixture of gentle wrinkles and stoicism, in my opinion. A full head of gray hair and wearing a nicely tailored gray suit, he looked like the sort of guy who would date my mom. He greeted us with a mild grin and could've passed as a Humphrey Bogart look-alike.

"Good morning ladies. I'm Harlan Buchanan." He instantly filled the room with a respect-worthy presence and an old-school flair. Nestled between his fingers was a cigarette.

The name resonated.

"Detective Buchanan?" I asked.

"Retired," he added.

"Detective," said Officer Ralph, "sorry but there's no smoking in the building."

"Right." Buchanan snuffed out his cigarette in a nearby ashtray. "The rules keep changing." He flicked it into the trash. "To answer your question, miss," he said to me, "yes."

We all shook hands and traded intros. I purposely omitted my last name but no one cared or noticed.

"Warren tells me you ladies are looking into the Cox file." Buchanan took a seat at the table and helped himself to the strewn papers.

Most of what was there had to look familiar, since he'd been the lead detective. I sat nearby and absorbed his every move, his every eye glance. He'd been there, at Marty's house, saw her bruised and dead, and he'd suspected that my mom had something do with that.

I wondered what he would think of me, the suspect's daughter, being here. Would he mind or see it as some kind of conflict of interest?

Buchanan flipped through the paperwork, mentioning how it bothered him the case went unsolved.

"Nothing grates on a cop like an unsolved case," he said as he stacked the pages back together. "If you don't mind my asking, why the interest? Have you ladies found something new?"

"Not exactly," Suzette said. "The victim's sister approached us, actually."

I appreciated that Suzette threw in a bit of bended truth and wasn't exposing our true connection. At least not yet.

"Irene? Was that her name? Interesting lady." Buchanan darted a side glance our way. "What did she have to say?"

"She's convinced the husband did it. She brought us a collection of the husband's handiwork in rearranging Marty's face."

"Yeah, I remember the guy." Buchanan shook his head. "Ruled him out early."

"How come?" I tried to sound like I belonged in the conversation.

"Well, I shouldn't say ruled him out, but we didn't have a case against him." He picked up a photograph, one that showed Marty face down on the floor in her home. "Marty was struck from behind. One blow to the head. She also had those marks around her neck, if I recall. All that was too tame compared to what the husband put her through, and if he would've wanted to strangle her, he would've succeeded in no time. Massive hands on that guy."

My mind flashed back to Craig wiping his dirty hands with the equally dirty rag he'd used at the body shop. Buchanan was right. Craig didn't have hands made for handling delicates. Maybe that's why he made a good fit working in automotive.

"So the blow to the head, strangulation marks," Buchanan went on, "to me, kind of suggested a fight. Someone tried strangling her but she fought them off. Considering her size, it had to be someone small, like her."

You mean slender and petite, like my mom?

"But according to the pictures," Suzette said, "nothing's broken, the house isn't wrecked." She checked notes. "A side table was knocked over that had a photo album on it, but that's it."

"I think it was a quick confrontation," he glanced from Suzette then to me, "a ladies' quarrel."

His words felt like fire in my lap, but I couldn't react.

"The suspect shows up, gets let in because Marty knows him or her—for the sake of our scenario. They get into a verbal altercation. Suspect tried strangling Marty, pushed her into the living room where she bumped into the end table, broke free from the hold. Maybe Marty hits back then tried to get away. Got struck in the head."

"And that's part of the reason you suspected Annette Reed," I said.

He nodded. "That, and the fact she lied about work. Plus, after talking with her and her husband, it was easy to tell things weren't rosy at home."

"So why didn't you charge her?"

"Came close. We had motive: Marty was having an affair with her husband. We had witnesses who put her at Marty's house a few weeks before the murder. And the timecard. But at the end of the day, it wasn't enough. Too many loose ends. We also didn't have the weapon used to strike Marty. That looks weak to a jury and a good defense attorney would've poked holes through what we had."

I rubbed the back of my neck and squirmed in my seat, hating the idea of my mom being under arrest or in the defendant's chair in court.

"What about the other guy Marty started dating, the younger guy?" I asked.

"Other guy?" Buchanan asked.

"What younger guy?" Suzette echoed. The two looked at each other before their stares landed on me, and I realized I had a lot of explaining to do.

In a weird way, I had an instant crush on Detective Buchanan. His sharp mind and knack for details were exciting. I could overlook the fact his eyebrows needed tamed. He had a sense of style but lacked arrogance, and despite a career of dealing with unsavory types and people who lied to him, he seemed genuine and compassionate, even when he took to questioning me.

I admitted that I'd been to the Junkyard Lounge recently and talked to Archie, the owner, who shared about Marty's new love interest. Suzette and Buchanan treated the info like the discovery of King Tut's tomb. I understood their enthusiasm, but I doubted there was any hope of finding loverboy.

"This almost makes sense," Buchanan said. "If we've got another player, that could be our guy. Marty's tired of her husband, tired of the affair, she moves on to someone new. New guy shows up at her place, no forced entry needed. Something goes wrong, she upsets him. He tries strangling her, so on and so forth."

"Then he leaves through the side door to the garage," I said.

"And leaves his fingerprints." Suzette slips the report in front of Buchanan about the unidentified fingerprints, probably in case he'd forgotten that detail.

Buchanan shrugged. "It's a new possibility."

"But after all this time," I said, "there's not much hope in finding this guy."

Buchanan seemed to appreciate the observation. "In my experience I always found there was somebody who knew something. You just have to start poking in the bushes, see what jumps out."

CHAPTER FOURTEEN

Maybe I'd done it, I'd proven Mom wasn't guilty of killing Marty. Finding out that Marty had started seeing someone else before her death opened the door for plenty of reasonable doubt. That might explain the unidentified prints on the side door and the reason why the case was never solved.

Suzette and I finished going over the file and packed up. We thanked Detective Buchanan repeatedly. He gave us his card and encouraged us to keep him informed of any new developments. I think he wanted to get involved in the case again but there wasn't much he could do. Of course, I could say the same for me and Suzette, but we had bushes we could poke into, as Buchanan had suggested.

We spoke with an officer who took down a report about our new information on Marty's case. He assured us it would be added to the file. Whatever that meant. Would on-duty detectives be given an alert about our new tip? Would said-detective head out to the Junkyard Lounge and basically repeat my interview with Archie? Or would the case get handed over to the cold case team with a new urgency attached? I didn't know how it worked.

Plus, I wondered who was serving as Irene's *contact*. Would he or she let Irene know there was a new development?

I wished I could've ripped out the sheet with Mom's name on it and the reasons she was under suspicion. Just like I wished I would've told Buchanan who I was in connection to Marty's case, so he would know I was there to help clear any doubt surrounding my mother. The most important thing was knowing for certain that Mom wasn't guilty.

Even so, I couldn't get that nagging timecard out of my head.

Warren escorted us to the door. Suzette was pleasant and appreciative but made a grimace once we were outside.

"Nice of you to give me a heads-up back there, missy," Suzette scolded once we were back in the car. "I thought I told you not to be doing anything stupid, like showing up at your dad's old bar."

"How was that stupid? I didn't go alone and look what happened. Besides, you're the one who took the cheap shots."

She whipped her head in my direction.

"That whole thing with Lance not being on any cold case team. You could've told me that yourself instead of embarrassing me with Warren." I was playing with her. Sort of. I knew she'd called me out like that in case I still had a morsel of interest in Lance. Exposing his lies in front of a stranger was also her not-so-subtle way of airing her disapproval. I couldn't be upset with her, since her instincts about him were right—and had been better than mine.

"Okay. Maybe you're right." Suzette sighed. "But I wanted you to hear from someone else that ol' Lance isn't working with CPD." Her eyes met mine. "That guy's not good for you. I can feel it."

"Point taken. I already know he's a jerk. He's proven it to me more than once." I'm sure he was planning to tell me he was Craig's nephew any day. But thinking he was going to use me as another notch on his manly conquest belt? The flowers, the compliments were all part of his ruse. That was the unforgivable in my book.

"So I didn't realize you liked your men…meaty." I stifled my laugh.

"Husky, babe, husky. And it's not like we can all date Rob Lowe like you." She shot me a side glance. "You are still dating Derek, right?"

I'm sure my smile beamed. "We're talking about getting married."

"No! Really? Lucky guy. So all this business with Lancey-pantsy is done?"

"Done." But I had an annoying feeling that Lance wasn't done with me. I'd lost track of how many messages he'd left—and I hated that he knew where I lived and worked, thanks in part to my stupidity.

"You know I was thinking," Suzette said, slowly as she started the car. "Since we're already out, how about we make a little pit stop."

"Where?"

"I figure it's our turn to drop in unexpectedly and visit our new gal pal."

It wasn't hard to guess what Suzette had in mind. She was feeling uppity, superior even, thanks to our chat with Buchanan and our education session with the case file. Her interrogation skills were itching to pounce.

"Let's do it" I clicked my seatbelt and made sure it was snug across my chest. "Let's visit Irene."

Like I said before, Mom claimed we lived in the ghetto, and maybe she had a point, since the south side of Columbus wasn't the wealthiest area. Growing up, I never knew we were poor, as she put it, but traveling into a neighborhood like Irene's—maybe considered the deep south side or inner south side—I felt up close and personal with the ghetto. Hard working, lower middle class, if that's what my parents were, lived like royalty compared to Irene and her neighbors.

Graffiti and barred windows covered every business, which were mainly drive-thrus for beer and pizza places, while litter and unkempt homes were the mainstay of residences. People didn't sit on the stained, spring-protruding couches on their porches. No. They opted for the more comfortable concrete step of their door stoops. Dogs and cats were plentiful, atop garbage cans and attached to heavy chains in front yards.

"Wasn't I against doing anything stupid?" Suzette said as we crept along in her car, searching houses for an address.

"Kinda had the same feeling."

"Think we should forget it?"

"No, because there it is."

We parked in front of a house with the address Irene had given us. A chain-link fence, in need of paint, outlined the perimeter of the front yard. Glares came at us from next door, where an older lady sat on her creaking porch swing with her hair in sponge rollers. Suzette said hello to her but the woman only responded with a scowl. At the doorstep lay a We_c__e mat that was no less than fifty years old. The light by the front door was busted and didn't have a cover. I think we both took a deep breath before Suzette knocked.

After what sounded like thunderous thumping from inside, a shirtless kid answered the door. More kids were zipping around in the background and the TV blared.

"Hi there." Suzette bent to the little boy's level and smiled. "Is your mommy home?"

I was terrible with both kids and guessing ages, so he was anywhere from five to ten. Without a word he left the door open and turned and ran. If that meant he was getting mommy or simply taking off, we didn't know. Yelling followed, along with more stomping sounds before Irene appeared.

"Well, never expected the likes of you two here," she greeted us. "Come on in." Irene wore a black tank top and jeans. I couldn't recall what she'd worn the day she showed up at the office, but her top revealed skeletal arms and a fragile frame. I also noticed slight bruising on the inside of one of her arms.

Okay, I was afraid. My parents did a poor job of monitoring my TV watching when I was a kid, so I'd seen my share of horror movies thanks to HBO. Seemed like every time innocent people entered a house unsuspectingly, they were goners. It also occurred to me at that moment that no one else knew where we were.

Suzette didn't hesitate, went right in. I followed helplessly.

"Sorry it's such a mess." Irene sounded hospitable, but the kitchen greeted us with the same aroma you experience when walking into Petland, combined with the stench of expired milk. "I watch my grandkids so there ain't no hope of keeping things clean."

Irene led us to her kitchen and had us sit at the table. Cheerios, spilled milk, and crumbs kept us from touching the table or sitting too close to it. Nestled in the corner of the kitchen, though I forced myself not to stare, was a rabbit in a cage. Shavings sprinkled in front of the cage, along with the pee-stained newspapers lining the bottom probably explained the offensive smell.

"You thirsty? I got Fantasia and Diet Pepsi."

"Actually," Suzette piped up, "we're good. We can't stay long. We just wanted a chance to ask you about something."

"Oh. All right." Irene joined us and, oblivious or resigned to the table's condition, plopped her folded arms onto the surface.

"We've been looking into your sister's case," Suzette shared, "and came across some new information that we could use your help with."

"Really?" Irene's eyes lit up, probably with hopefulness.

"We've recently learned that shortly before Marty's death she was seeing someone else." Suzette clasped her hands together. "Someone besides Craig and Gerald Reed. We were wondering if you knew about it, and if you could tell us anything about him."

Irene sat back in her chair, letting her arms fall from the table and taking a swipe of food debris with them. She rubbed the back of her neck with one hand. The underside of her arm was freckled with crumbs and Cheerios. But there was rabbit poop sitting four feet away, so what was a messy table?

"Yeah." Irene scratched the side of her head. "I remember but I don't think it was nothing serious."

"Can you tell us about him?"

"Not really." She lit a cigarette and closed her eyes as if she had to think about it. "He was a lot younger. I didn't like it and told her she was crossing the line, but I think she liked making Craig and Gerald mad, wanted all of them fighting over her while she took up with this other guy."

"Do you know his name?" I asked. "Or remember what he looked like?"

"Never met him. Can't think of his name off hand. Maybe Randy? No, that ain't right. Maybe she never told me. I don't know. Didn't do you no good to take stock in Marty's men. They came and went fast. Except for Craig."

"Where'd she meet this new guy?" Suzette said.

"I thought at the bar but don't know for sure." Irene paused and took a turn looking at each of us for a moment. "Are you serious about this? You really think that guy could've been involved?" An air of disbelief tainted her voice.

"It's possible," Suzette said. "The police also have fingerprints that didn't match any of their suspects. Did you know about that?"

"Well, of course I knew! My sister gettin' killed has just been my whole life since it happened." Her voice elevated.

"Okay, we understand." Suzette stayed clam. I appreciated that side of her and the way she knew how to handle people's reactions. "The police didn't know Marty had been seeing someone else, and we wondered why you didn't mention it."

"Because!" Irene sounded disgusted with us. "I already done told you who killed my sister. Craig did it! End of story! There ain't no sense in you or the police wasting time on some guy she had a fling with. She just used that guy, like a string of others. And those fingerprints don't mean nothing. You know how many people been in and out of that door?"

Suzette nodded slowly, rhythmically, as if that motion could soothe Irene's irritation. Irene muttered a few colorful phrases, more to herself than to us, and lit another cigarette.

A child toddled in wearing rumpled pajamas with teddy bears on them and a blonde fluff of bed hair. Kids scared me, but this little guy was undeniably adorable. He crawled onto Irene's lap and paid no attention to us. Irene nuzzled him as he rubbed sleep from his eyes. Suzette commented on how cute he was and asked his age; Irene said two and seemed calmer.

"So you never talked to this guy?" Suzette said, trying to get back on topic.

"No." Irene worked hard on her cigarette but was mindful of her ashes as she rocked the little boy. I expected her Marlboro to be a nub in two puffs.

"And after Marty died, he didn't come around, asking what had happened to her or expressing condolences? Didn't attend her funeral?"

Irene made a noise. Something between a giggle and a cackle, tinged with a smoker's cough. "They weren't like a regular couple. But no, no condolences or nothing like that. Never heard from him. Wouldn't expect any different. Marty wasn't the best picker when it came to men."

Maybe I was jumping to conclusions or trying to force pieces of this puzzle to fit, but if Irene never heard anything from Marty's new love interest after her death, wasn't it because he'd disappeared for a reason? That reason being that he killed Marty?

I couldn't get out of Irene's house fast enough. The smells, the sugar-buzzed kids, though how many of them there were, I couldn't say. Plus, I think we'd worn out our welcome.

"Would you call that a success?" I waited until we were safely encapsulated inside her car before I asked. I'd waved to sponge-curler lady and got the same response as Suzette.

"Depends on how you look at it. The good news is she confirmed there was someone new in Marty's life, but the bad news is we don't have anything else to go on."

At that, I had to question what my goal was now. So was there a next step? Or could I walk away now and leave it? Lay it to rest on the assumption that the new boyfriend was guilty and unfindable?

A couple things still bugged me. The timecard and the fact Mom lied about it. But there was something else there, attempting to burrow into my mind, and I couldn't quite figure out what.

The biggest question mark for me was my dad. Not as to whether or not he hurt Marty, but in his leaving. He'd left shortly after that infamous phone call where he claimed he was stuck, didn't have a choice. I guess he'd changed his mind, but what I didn't get was why didn't he move in with Marty when he left? Wasn't that what he'd wanted? Or had the new love interest changed that? My dad had no qualms about cheating on his wife, but drew a line when it came to a love triangle.

And then there was Lance. He'd started everything, unearthed those dormant memories, brought out a side of me that I wasn't proud of.

"Hey," Suzette said, "let's grab lunch before we head back to the office."

Great. Just what I needed to contend with. Food.

But I had a few things to come clean about with Suzette, and what better timing than an afternoon lunch.

Maybe it wasn't necessary at this point, but I told Suzette about my trip to the body shop, meeting Craig, and finding out he was Lance's uncle. Few things kept Suzette from enjoying her food. This was no exception, although she paused mid-chew in disbelief a couple times.

Luckily, she'd picked the Rice Bowl for lunch. Suzette knew my taste buds hardly wandered beyond bread, but that didn't stop her from encouraging me to try new places and flavors, especially when she was craving Chinese or other worldly cuisine. Worked for me because she wasn't surprised or upset if I was done or grossed out after three bites, which I was.

With everything I had to tell her, she didn't pay much attention to my lack of eating.

"I can't believe you broke your taillight just so you could check the guy out."

"I didn't know what else to do."

"Good thing, I guess. Otherwise, you wouldn't have seen that picture of Lance on Craig's desk." She slurped up some noodles.

"Yeah, but I don't understand why Lance went to all the trouble he did. Why come to my house and act like he's part of the investigation?"

"Sure beats me, babe. His uncle was in the clear, fell off Buchanan's radar early on, so what's Lance out to prove? Doesn't make any sense."

I agreed. Was Lance really on a mission to protect Craig, even though Warren confirmed Marty's case wasn't currently under review by their three-man unit of investigators? What was I missing? Why so many lies? Of course, if I wanted answers—if I wanted to confront him and demand the truth—all I had to do was call him back.

Back at the office, Crystal sprang from her chair when we walked in.

"You've got a ton of messages." She handed me several pink slips. "Is something wrong?"

"I don't know."

Flipping through the sheets, I noticed one call was from Lance, two from Shelia. Yes, three messages was a ton, considering I usually got none.

Her eyes wide with concern, Crystal said, "I could tell that Shelia was crying."

I darted upstairs to my office, grabbed the phone, and went to work. It took me a while to track Shelia down, but once I had her on the phone, her slight sniffles and muffled voice indicated her distress.

"What's wrong?"

"It's Trey. He's moved out and called off the wedding." She barely got the words out before sobs overtook her.

"What? When did this happen?"

"We've been having problems for a while but that was the whole point of getting married. We'd have to fix everything before the wedding. He wasn't supposed to just give up like this." More crying. "We're really trying and it's so complicated."

I didn't know what to say and I was sure we wouldn't get anywhere over the phone like this.

"Do you need me to come over?"

"I don't know. I just had to tell somebody. Trey wouldn't like this. He'd get mad if he knew I told you. He's like that."

She was right, and I didn't doubt that Trey wouldn't want me having insight to any of his problems, but I'd had no idea that things between him and Shelia were call-off-the-wedding-bad.

"If you see him," Shelia said, "tell him to call me, that we need to talk, but don't act like you know anything."

That was easy, because I pretty much didn't.

"Okay, I will." Although I'd already tried talking to him, when he was busy foraging for chips in Mom's cabinets with a bandage above his eye.

I told her I'd call later to check on her and for her not to worry. My crisis management skills were unrefined.

Like kids in teddy bear pajamas, love scared me. I was in a good place with Derek, despite a few bumps, but I felt hopeful about our relationship and about expressing how I really felt about him. Maybe committing to him. Was I wrong to embrace that euphoric feeling? Happiness was a fleeting emotion, right? Unreliable. It was a place you visited but never lived. And maybe that's when people got hurt, when they grew lax in guarding their heart or got swept into thinking that being vulnerable to someone was a good thing. Knowing that love was as fickle as it was fragile, and that it took very little to destroy, maybe I needed to re-caution myself about being too optimistic.

CHAPTER FIFTEEN

Suzette didn't say much else about our adventures or Marty's case for the rest of the day, and that worried me. I had a niggling feeling that she'd end up going to the Junkyard Lounge and trying to talk to Archie on her own. If CPD followed up on the info we'd passed along that came from Archie, I didn't know if Archie would appreciate having the police, and now possibly Suzette, showing up at his bar, asking questions. Not that he had anything to hide, as far as I knew.

Maybe I owed Archie a heads-up, especially since he'd been helpful. Thinking on it made me miss Linda. Had she still been alive, Linda would've been the one who could've revealed more about Marty's mystery man. Unfortunately, it seemed that whatever she knew about Marty and lover boy died with her. Sad circumstances all around.

My mind shifted from Linda to images of Carl. Maybe that's what I was missing. Carl! Since Marty often had a thing for her co-workers, what if she got involved with Carl, the creepy dishwasher at the Junkyard Lounge? Maybe that's why I'd caught him staring at Marty all the time. If Linda knew about it though, she might not have told Archie everything since Carl was his nephew. Of course, I couldn't ask Archie about it, but Carl was much younger than my dad. I also didn't know Carl or what he looked like now, or even his last name, so showing up at the factory where he worked wasn't an option.

There was only one person left that I could talk to. One person who'd been in on the whole affair. Literally. My dad. I hadn't seen my dad in well over a decade. I'd been a child, still able to fit in his lap when he'd left. How could I face him? I couldn't call him up or show up at his place and ask about Marty. But what if Suzette could? For now, I shoved those raging thoughts to the back burner of my mind. And burn they did.

I wanted to call Lance back but didn't. There was plenty I was ready to confront him about, but, pitiful as it sounded, I needed a chance to strategize, figure out how I wanted to expose him for the fraud he was. But I also considered turning the tables on him. What if I played along with his con and carefully plumbed for what he was really after?

Before leaving work, I talked to Derek somewhere in the course of the afternoon. My heart still pitter-pattered. Suzette made kissy lips at me when she heard who I was talking to. A sweet, feel-good flash of normalcy fluttered in my chest. Since it was Friday night, I was looking forward to a long evening with Derek. And to food. It was my night to eat.

Pressing on my mind, though, as I drove home was Trey. I didn't know what to expect when I got home. If he'd moved out of his apartment, Mom's house would have proof, right? Boxes, a Mt. Everest mound of laundry, his old stereo equipment, stuff.

But I walked in, got distracted briefly with loving on Maverick, then tiptoed around. Nothing was out of place and mounds of clothing didn't greet me. Plus, I was the only one home. Maverick and I enjoyed a walk and playing chase in the yard.

After leaving Irene's house earlier that day, I'd craved a shower. A long, steaming shower loaded with soap, disinfectant and sanitizer. I made good on that and readied for my date night with Derek.

I couldn't resist detouring into my mom's bedroom when I noticed the ring box sitting on her bedside table. Peeking inside, I saw the engagement ring from Roger, gleaming and lonely. Mom was a funny bird. I had a feeling I knew what was up. If she wore the ring, that told her co-workers and Roger that she'd accepted the proposal. While she'd enjoy the *oohs* and *ahhs* from everyone, she probably wouldn't enjoy the idea of getting married again. And once she made it official with Roger, that would give him a certain power over her, she believed, which was why she was holding him at bay. But here was the ring, as close as it could get to Mom without being on her finger, occupying a private, special place. She probably hated having the ring out of her sight, and I'd bet that she'd already had it appraised.

Leaving Mom's love life behind, I finished getting ready and went to Derek's. We went to Red Lobster for dinner. Seafood and those garlic cheese biscuits were two of my greatest weaknesses. I ate everything on my plate, including the crumbs from the biscuit. After the week I'd had, I savored the indulgence. My stomach gave up its complaining.

Over dinner I caught Derek up on developments with Marty's case, from the visit to the police station to meeting the detective who worked the case. I even mentioned stopping at Irene's, although I had to backtrack and explain who she was. When I reached the end of my long-winded narrative, one thing stuck out for Derek. My mom's falsified time card bugged him as much as it did me.

"Why would she lie about it if she didn't do anything wrong?" he said.

"That's what I wondered. Why fudge it in the first place?" That was one of those needling points I couldn't pin down until it came out of my mouth. Annette Reed wasn't guilty, so what did she have to lie about?

"I can't picture your mom lying to the police."

Neither could I. Mom walked the straight and narrow. Apart from her faithfulness to Salems and devotion to a few choice cuss words, the woman was a contender for sainthood. At least as far as women on the south side went, in my opinion.

I'd come a long way in trusting Derek. When this business with Marty resurfaced, I'd strung Derek along, not giving him much in the way of details and whys. Now, it felt right to trust him completely and to share my questions and frustrations. I'd let go of feeling ashamed of the Gerald-Annette-Marty triangle, almost like it didn't involve me, and I'd told him everything. Well, almost everything.

"I guess I never really told you how all this got started," I said.

"You mean with Marty?"

I nodded. "Yeah. My family never talks about it. Why would they, right? We can't hardly talk about what's happening now, so the past is way too difficult, I guess." I hadn't mentioned Trey and Shelia's break-up yet. Drama I could save for dessert.

Carefully, I explained about Lance and how he lied about being with the police and their cold case team. I left out details about Lance touching my hand, giving me flowers, and our late-night meet-up at the law office. I didn't feel good about holding back, but I wasn't sure how to be that honest without ruining my relationship.

"This guy sounds like bad news. Maybe you shouldn't meet up with him anymore."

"There's more. He's actually Craig's nephew." I shared how I found out and that I hadn't confronted Lance yet. "I don't know if he's going to keep calling me or if he'll get bored and disappear the same way he came." I didn't believe that but wanted to.

"I doubt it. Do you think he wants something more, something other than hashing through all this old case stuff?"

I kept my gaze steady as I looked at Derek and nodded. "He mentioned that he'd like to see me. Go on a date. He even brought me flowers."

"And what'd you say?"

It was one of the few times I'd heard Derek raise his voice.

"I didn't say anything, I just left."

"With the guy's flowers?"

I was too stunned by Derek's sudden anger to answer.

"Why wouldn't you tell him that you have a boyfriend, that you weren't available? Tell him to keep his flowers?"

"I threw the flowers away!" I had to check myself as heads in the restaurant turned our way. I waited a few minutes before leaning over the table and whispering, "Derek, there's nothing to get upset over. I never told the guy I'd go out with him."

"And you didn't mention that you had a boyfriend, either. What's that supposed to mean, that you're keeping your options open or something?"

Humiliation poured over me like that bucket of pigs' blood in *Carrie*. Being reprimanded in public was a first for me, while I'd never realized that Derek had a jealous streak in him. I'd like to think he was more interested in beating Lance to a pulp than embarrassing me, but I didn't think that was the case.

"Maybe we should go, talk about this someplace else," I said.

Derek slid from the booth and bumped into the table hard enough to make the silverware jingle. More patrons checked us out and watched as he bee-lined to the front of the restaurant, his anger apparent in his swift stride, leaving me stupefied and trailing behind him with my head tilted down and my heart sinking into the ground.

On the ride home, the tension paralyzed me. I couldn't think and had no idea what would make the situation better or ease Derek's irritation. Should I keep quiet and let him stew, or blanket the air between us with apologies and rambling explanations? I didn't know how to fix this. Feeling inadequate, nauseous, and worried that Derek would dump me on the side of the road, I went with quiet.

At his apartment, I went in and sat beside him on the couch, still not knowing what should come next. If I left, that might look like I was giving up on him and our relationship. I was the one who'd done the crime, so it was up to me to endure the punishment. Which, for now, was the silent treatment.

We sat there for hours. Him clicking through the TV channels with the remote, me saying nothing. He didn't bother with an arm around me, I didn't reach for him. I felt like Frosty the Snowman trapped on a hot seat, melting feverishly away yet never being gone. Just constant discomfort.

I finally felt I'd done my penance and spoke, "I'm sorry, Derek. I don't know what you're thinking, but I don't have any feelings for anyone but you. I love you."

"If you didn't want to go out with him why didn't you tell him you weren't available?" He slammed the remote onto the couch. "It's the same thing as saying you *are* available, or like you don't care about *us*."

He had a certain gem in his logic. And knowing that I entertained a slight attraction to Lance in the beginning, I couldn't argue or play Miss Completely Innocent. Maybe he sensed that.

"I was shocked," I said. "One minute he's talking about my mom being guilty of murder and the next he's talking about dinner. You're right, I should've said I'm taken, but I didn't and I'm sorry, Derek. I'm sorry a hundred times over. What else do you want from me?"

"I want to know I can trust you."

He wanted to know if I planned on being faithful to him. That was it, wasn't it? I suddenly realized that he was just as scared as I had been of getting hurt. He was hurting now but didn't want to say it. Acting out and being a jerk at the restaurant was all he knew to do. Maybe I deserved that, for what I'd put him through, and for what he still didn't know.

"I'm not perfect, Derek. I never will be, but I love you."

I pulled him close and kissed him, deeply and passionately. He returned my affection, and I could feel the hurt and tension drain from him. Just like me, Derek needed reassurances.

We stayed like that a while. Holding each other, not saying a word. Just the feel of this man that I truly loved worked like a healing balm. Tears escaped but I wiped them away so Derek wouldn't see.

The phone rang, forcing us to disentangle ourselves.

"It's your mom." Derek handed me the receiver.

"Kyle? Are you coming home soon?"

I glanced at a clock beside the couch. Only 11:17 p.m.

"Probably."

"Good. I'll wait up. I wanted to talk to you about Roger. I turned down his proposal."

Mom was just pulling my strings to get me home from Derek's but tonight it worked. As hard as it was to leave Derek, we promised each other that from now on we'd each do better in our relationship. I had more to prove than he did, but I got a boost, feeling that if two people loved each other they really could work through difficulties and missteps. Maybe the same could be said for Trey and Shelia.

At home, Trey had taken up residence in the rec room. No surprise that Maverick looked cozy beside him. Mom was in the recliner. The TV was on but they were talking quietly. I felt like an intruder.

"Party time?" I didn't know if jokes were appropriate. Guess it was my night for being the champion of awkwardness and not knowing the best move.

"It's a party everywhere we go." Trey's snappy humor suggested he was in a good mood. Odd, I thought, considering his girlfriend had been crying to me about their break up hours earlier. Maybe Trey had been giving Mom the details when I came in. It wasn't like I could ask.

"So what's this rumor I heard about you and Roger?" I eased onto the other couch. Maverick came over and helped himself to my lap. Nothing like a fifty pound marshmallow drop-landing on you.

"Not a rumor," Mom said. "I told him I didn't want to get married again."

"Probably for the best, since you don't really love him."

Trey laughed. "She oughta know, Mom. She's the expert on loooove."

I thought about delivering a stinger, such as, *And now you're the expert on break-ups*, but that saucy wit never worked for me the way it did for Trey. He got away with anything, especially where Mom was concerned. Had I said what came to mind, Mom would've scolded me, but it was fine for Trey to rib me.

So I did the only thing I could that didn't involve repercussions. I ignored him.

"Did you give the ring back?"

"I had to. Couldn't wear it. Can't get the milk for free."

I thought about correcting her, telling her that wasn't quite the expression, but I passed.

"Where do things stand between you two?" I asked.

"Oh, about the same. We'll still work together," she shrugged, "maybe go out to dinner from time to time."

"Guess this means the kitchen isn't getting remodeled."

"Roger wasn't too keen on that condition anyway," Mom said. "That's all right. There's more fish out there."

Disbelief left me speechless. Not so much in what she said but in how she managed to remain so emotionally detached from someone she was thinking about marrying. I still felt shaky from my argument with Derek earlier. A crushing sadness hit my chest when I thought we were breaking up, and I didn't know how I'd live without him. It wasn't like that for Mom. She probably cared more about losing the ring than Roger's love and devotion.

"What about you?" I tried with Trey. Since Mom was here, he could relent a little. "Where do things stand with you?"

"I'm good." He tossed a Cheez-Doodle up and tried catching it in his mouth but failed. "Looks like I might be single for a while."

"Oh?"

"Yeah, we postponed the wedding."

"How come?" Asking may have been the equivalent of dipping my toes into shark infested waters, but I thought I'd see how long we could play normal family.

"It's complicated, little sister. You best just focus on playing house with your John Stamos toy."

Again, a prime spot for a retort, but I let it go.

In some ways, Mom and Trey were alike. They were both practical, didn't talk much about feelings, had simple needs. And here they were, casting aside people they loved like it was a natural, ordinary thing to do when conditions weren't met or things didn't go their way. Essentially, two weddings had been cancelled and relationships redefined. And I was the only one confused about it.

Since Mom didn't need me there to hold her hand, I set Maverick up in the utility room and headed up for bed. I saw the door to Trey's bedroom was cracked open. Without pushing the door open further, I noticed boxes were stuffed against the wall. Maybe they'd been there earlier, I just didn't snoop enough. That also reminded me that I didn't call Shelia back to check on her. I hoped she was okay and taking the wedding *postponement* as well as Trey, though I doubted it. I wondered what he had told Mom.

In bed, I loved sliding my bare legs around the cool sheets. The sensation only lasted a few minutes but it was welcoming. What would it be like sharing that with Derek? Assuming that our relationship went that far and we got married. As of now, marriage didn't have the best reputation in my household. Could be that Derek was the most romantic guy ever, wanting to wait until we were married and legally bound together before going all the way physically.

There was a sudden tap on my bedroom door and Mom came in.

"Bitty, you sleeping?"

"Not yet."

She closed the door but didn't shut it. I rolled onto my side and scooted over so she could sit on the edge of the bed.

"How was work?" Here was a Mom specialty. When she used to work late at the Western Pancake House, I'd be in bed before she got home. She'd come in my room while I slept and would run her fingers through my hair. It was her way of seeing me and tucking me in, especially when I was younger. She told me that some nights I'd talk to her, tell her about school or what I had for dinner. I never remembered doing that, but on mornings when she'd congratulate me about a math test grade or remind me about a science project being due, I'd ask how she knew. "Oh, you told me while you were sleeping," she'd say, and I knew I had been talking. I think she missed those nights, and I know she missed tucking me in.

I kept it simple but shared tidbits about the office. Nothing exciting and nothing about my new investigative skills.

"How are things with Derek?"

"We're good." Could've gotten even better if you hadn't called.

"I take it you haven't told him about Lance."

Not that! "There's nothing to tell. I'm not seeing Lance."

Even though the only light came from the slit of the door jam, I could still see Mom's face. She gave me that cat that ate the canary look.

"Then why'd he show up here, looking for you?"

I pulled my knees closer to my chest and hoped Mom didn't notice.

"Lance came here tonight? What did he say?" I wasn't sure I wanted the answer.

"Just said he'd been calling, trying to find you. He was dressed nicely. Made me think you two were heading out to dinner or someplace."

"No, Mom, I didn't have any plans with him. He was helping with a case at work, but it's taken care of now. I don't need him anymore."

"I'm not sure he knows that. He didn't mention work, so I figured you two might be dating."

"I already have a boyfriend, Mom."

She shrugged. "Stranger things have happened."

"You think I'd do that to Derek?"

"Well, I've never been sure if he's right for you, or if you're all that attached to him."

In some ways, she sounded like a little devil on my shoulder, trying to make me doubt my feelings for Derek. I knew what she was up to. If I changed boyfriends, 'shopped around', I wouldn't become too serious about anyone. Marriage wouldn't come up. Mom didn't want any distractions on my career goal path—and she didn't want me ending up like her, pregnant with choices made her for.

But I wasn't totally innocent on the matter. I'd taken Lance to the office, led him on, because my subconscious had been trained to think that was okay. Funny though, I didn't think my mom liked being exchanged for Marty, yet she seemed okay with me fooling around on Derek.

"We're talking about getting married." As soon as I let that slip, I wished I hadn't.

"Aren't you too young for that? You have years of school ahead of you. Why, there's no telling who you might meet, especially once you start law school."

Because Derek just works construction with his family, that's not good enough was what she was thinking but didn't add. Mom was convinced a person had no hope of being successful without a college degree these days. She prided education more than a skill or talent. I got that but didn't necessarily agree when it came to having a degree.

"And what if you got pregnant before finishing law school?"

"Then I'd have a baby before I had a law degree. I'm sure it's happened before." I knew she wouldn't like that answer. Maybe it was insensitive on my part.

"I hope you take care of yourself and nothing like that happens."

"Sure, Mom." No way I was getting into a discussion on birth control or the sex I wasn't having.

"But I think you're gonna need to have a talk with Lance. I'm pretty sure he's not showing up here because of work." Mom was right about that, though I would've loved seeing her face as I explained how and why I knew Lance.

She kissed my cheek then stood. We exchanged good nights. She told me she'd be gone early tomorrow but didn't say where.

When she closed the door I could relax again. A little. I thought about Lance and wished he didn't know where I lived. For good measure, or because I was paranoid, I peeked out my bedroom window, making sure he wasn't parked outside and spying on the house. He wasn't. How long was it going to take for him to get the message that I didn't want anything to do with him? But maybe the bigger question was why was he being so persistent? I hadn't returned his calls and I'd made no effort to see him. Wasn't he suspicious that I'd done my own investigating by now, gotten wise to his phony tactics and meaningless accusations? So why did he bother? What did Lance want from me? More importantly, what did I have to do to get him out of my life?

CHAPTER SIXTEEN

When Trey took off the next morning, with no mention of where he was headed, I had a bad feeling. I couldn't imagine what had jolted him out the door early on a Saturday. Did that mean Shelia was on her way over and he was leaving me to deal with her? Wouldn't surprise me.

I took Maverick to the Obetz Animal Clinic for a nail trim. One of the perks of volunteering there during high school was that I could still stop in like that. Back home, I gave him a much needed bath, which he languished like the pampered baby he was.

After, I called Derek to see if we could spend the day together. He said he and his brothers were working but planned to cut out early. I could feel myself blush when he said he'd make up for last night's disastrous date. I told him that we didn't have to do anything big. Time alone with him was all I cared about.

With an empty day ahead of me, I showered and dressed so I wouldn't end up beached on the couch pilfering snacks all day. No eating was allowed until dinner.

As I considered various errands I could run, Carl came to mind. If only there was a way to find him and question him. With no idea of where he lived or even his last name, there wasn't anything I go on. For now, I had to let it go.

Then my thoughts circled around to my dad. Maybe, just maybe, I would drive by his place. For what exactly, I couldn't say. Maybe just to see him alive and breathing and moving. I always wondered if he spent any time thinking about me or if his days only revolved around emptying beer bottles. There had to be a bar close to where he lived, with a barstool that he parked his rump on regularly. Despite leaving my mom, abandoning his family, and Marty getting killed, I doubted that he'd given up his true love.

A knock sounded at the front door and broke me from my head ramblings. Maverick was lying on the slate by the sliding door, soaking up the sun. It'd take more than a knock to rouse him.

It had to be Lance. I balled my fists just thinking about him standing on the other side. This was my chance to call him out on his lies and get rid of him, once and for all.

But when I swung the door open, Lance wasn't there.

"Oh, hello there." Craig Cox stood before me.

My jaw fell open and words didn't come.

"I don't mean to disturb you," he said, "but when you came to the shop the other day you left this." He held out my jean jacket. Right then, I knew I'd left it in the chair by his desk. The pictures of him, Marty, and Lance had distracted me.

"Thank you." I took the jacket and felt strangely exposed. "I'm sorry you had to go to the trouble of bringing it here."

"Wasn't any trouble. I thought you might come back for it, but when you didn't, I just looked up your address from the sheet you filled out and saw that you lived pretty close. A nice coincidence, you might say."

I nodded. Thinking back to the file Suzette had obtained on Craig and his arrests, I remember noting that he still lived near his old place with Marty.

"I don't mean to be out of line," Craig said, "but do you mind if I ask you something?"

"No, of course not."

"I noticed your last name was Reed. It's been a long time, but a while back I knowed a guy name Gerald Reed. You wouldn't happen to know that name, would you?"

I thought about lying, but what for? In my opinion, Craig was harmless, and he'd done a nice thing for me. I was the one who'd shown up at his work under false pretenses.

"He's my father."

"Yeah, that name looked familiar, and when I found out where the address was, I kinda figured there was a good chance."

We stood there a second, neither one of us knowing what to say, or having so much to say we didn't know where to start.

"You were that little girl, all those years ago." He said it fondly, as though it were a pleasant memory. "I figured you came around because you were curious about me, had questions. I don't know what you may think or what people have told you, but I never did anything…" He looked as if he didn't know how to finish the thought. Or maybe he was worried he'd overwhelmed me.

"Can I buy you breakfast, Mr. Cox?"

His friendly smile emerged. "Only if you promise not to call me Mr. Cox."

I agreed and appreciated the irony of the situation. Moments ago I thought I'd be calling Lance out on his lies, when in fact, I was about to confess to my own.

If someone had told me that one day I'd be sitting down at Perkins Restaurant sharing breakfast with Marty Cox's husband, I wouldn't have believed it. But sometimes that's how life worked and the impossible happened. It was a good thing Mom and Trey had been gone. How would I have explained Craig showing up? I shuddered at the idea of Mom opening the door and facing him.

We each drove to Perkins and made our way inside. There was no getting around the awkward feeling of being near Craig and knowing we both had questions. As we settled into a booth, I wondered who else there was having their life changed.

"How did you find me at the body shop?" Craig started us off.

I held nothing back, telling him about my job at the law office and that we'd gotten a copy of his arrest record. It was difficult, because I didn't want him feeling embarrassed. I figured being raw and honest upfront was best.

"Yeah, I'm sure there's a lot in there I'm not too proud of." Craig filled his coffee cup from the pot our waitress had delivered to the table. "Those were bad years. I finally gave up drinking after my last stretch. It was never good to me."

"I know it's not my business, but what happened between you and Marty?"

"I think I fell in love with her when I first laid eyes on her. She was like a breath of fresh air and there was no denying when she walked into a room. I wanted to make her happy, but my drinking got in the way. I was never a good man when I was drunk. Always did and said the worst stuff. I'd lose my temper and sometimes…."

He didn't want to say it. I could understood and wished there was a way to make it easier for him.

"But Marty was a wild one," he continued. "That was one of the things I loved about her, until she started seeing other men. That didn't work for me and I let her know. She'd have a fling with a guy just to get back at me or to make me mad. We got stuck in an awful habit of hurting each other and couldn't stop. She'd leave me sometimes, go to her sister's, but I'd do and say the right things and get her back for a while. Never lasted though."

I thought about Irene and how she'd been a go-between for them. Her loyalties flip-flopped between them until Marty's death. Maybe it was best for me not to mention that I knew Irene, especially since her opinions of Craig hadn't been favorable.

He poured more coffee into his cup. "When she started seeing your dad, though, I thought she was going to leave me for good. I think he treated her different than most guys she ran around with, made her promises and all. That put me over the edge. You might not know this, but I came to blows with your dad. Hate to admit it, but he busted me up pretty good. Thought that was the end of me and Marty. She kicked me out of the house, said she and Gerald were going to live together, get married one day."

Craig echoed what I'd heard from Archie and Irene. A shudder glided through me. Marty's fairytale love for my dad, misguided as it was, didn't lead to a happy ending.

"What happened the night you found her?" I asked.

He regurgitated what he'd told Detective Buchanan years ago. Then added, "You know, I always thought it was strange, the way her body was laying. It was like someone was going to drag her out to the garage or like they were going to hide her body. I never understood it."

I thought back to the police photos of Marty's body. She'd been face down in a small hallway that led to the garage. Buchanan had mentioned something similar.

"What happened between you and Irene?" I asked.

"After Marty died, she was never the same. She helped me out a few times, but I think she always blamed me for Marty. Guess I could understand that."

I thought about the Marty-abused pictures Irene had spilled out in front of me and Suzette. Nervousness ticked in my stomach. Did Craig deserve to know about those pictures? And the fact Irene wanted him locked up for Marty's murder.

I slathered butter across a pancake I didn't intend to eat. "Did you know Marty was seeing someone new before she died?"

Craig stopped in mid-sip of his third cup of coffee and slowly set it down. “Where did you hear that?” A hard stare settled on his face.

“It was a rumor.” I didn’t want to mention Archie and Irene. “Marty was tired of waiting on my dad and she told him she had someone else.” I gripped the napkin in my lap, wishing I hadn’t brought it up.

Craig shook his head. The look of daggers dissipated. “Marty was the kind who always had somebody, even if it was for the wrong reasons.”

We both leaned back against the green padded booth. Mild stretches and sighs followed, relieving our tension. I focused on carving my pancakes into meticulous squares while Craig dipped his toast into his eggs. Small talk evolved.

Then Craig asked, “How’d your folks fare through everything?”

“My dad left us. Just walked out one day. I didn’t realize it until I noticed his clock-radio was gone from the bathroom. I thought that was weird so I opened the closet in my parent’s bedroom and found his side cleared out. It was a Friday night, right before *Dallas* came on.” Fitting, I thought. “My mom eventually divorced him, but I never saw him again.”

“Sorry to hear that. A life like that’s hard on a kid.”

“And you never had kids, just a nephew?”

“I don’t think Marty could conceive, but we spent a lot of time around nieces and nephews. Lance took a special liking to us out of the bunch. Losing Marty was hard on him, being young and all.” He shook his head and took a moment. “He grew up to be a good kid. Works over at the 7-Eleven on the south side.”

Somehow I kept myself from laughing. Lance had done a good job of posing as a detective. I guess he’d seen his share of *Hill Street Blues*. But to find out he was a clerk ringing up Big Gulps was too much.

“Did you talk to him much about the case?” I asked. “About Marty’s killer never being found?”

"He was about thirteen when it happened. Old enough to understand but not old enough to know how the law works. He didn't come around much after Marty died, and I had my own problems later on. Plus, Irene didn't want him spending time with me anymore."

"Irene?"

"Yeah, she's Lance's mother."

If there was an award for being the world's biggest idiot, I was about to own it. How had I not put it together that Lance and Irene were related? Why did I assume that Lance belonged to Craig's sister or brother instead of connecting him directly to Marty?

Craig and I finished breakfast and went our separate ways. Craig asked me to let him know if anything developed in Marty's case. He said I could call him or leave a message for him at the shop. I said I'd do my best, whatever that meant.

Since meeting Craig at the body shop, I had a good feeling about him, thinking that despite what he'd done and been through, he was remorseful and wasn't the same man from twelve years ago. But watching his expression darken at the mention of Marty's boyfriend had been unsettling. Had I seen a shadow of the old Craig?

Going home didn't feel right, so I went to the Main library downtown. I browsed for a while but all I could really think about was how I'd been duped by Lance. In more ways than one. I checked out a couple books but still didn't want to go home.

I cruised the empty streets of downtown Columbus. Aside from City Center mall, few businesses were open. With nothing around that could lift my mood, I gave in. Decided to head home. I went through German Village and cut over to High Street.

Driving the main stretch that held a lot of landmarks in my life, including Dan's Drive-in and the law office, I also passed the E-Z Sleep Motel. Nestled between highway 104 and High Street, the E-Z Sleep was where my dad spent his first nights after leaving me and my mom. That's what she told me. Only a portion of the building could be seen, since it butted against a bridge. The neon sign wasn't lit during the day, but you could always see the saw and log logo. A plain, white-wash, squatty structure, I couldn't imagine cockroaches wanting to stay there.

Fifteen minutes later, when I approached the road that led me to Jefferson Meadows, I kept going. Still heading south. My skin tingled with wrecked anticipation and I gripped the steering wheel a little tighter. It was probably a dumb idea, going to South Bloomfield. I didn't care. I only wanted to see where my dad lived.

Thirteen miles. For a man who abandoned his family, you'd think he'd make more of an effort, travel farther than thirteen miles to get away from us. But not Greaser. He was too lazy or too old to try an area that was too new. That was my guess.

South Bloomfield was a once-upon-a-time farming community that had grown into village status. Complete with three gas stations, an IGA grocer, hardware store, and a Dairy Queen, the village was a blip on the map between Columbus and Circleville. Railroad tracks crisscrossed Main Street with its one traffic light, and Fred's Used Tires occupied prime real estate across from the post office.

For early afternoon, traffic was non-existent. I took my time rolling down Maple Avenue, looking for number 75. It wasn't hard to find.

A simple two-story duplex, my dad rented the top apartment. According to Vinny's rundown, it was roughly 900 square feet of living space and cost $400 a month. The house showed every inch of its age with peeling paint, missing shutters and a cracked concrete porch. This was what my dad left his home and family for.

Trying to catch a glimpse of Greaser's blue Oldsmobile, I circled the block several times but didn't see it. I parked in the lot of the post office, which was closed, and had a fair view of the duplex. What I was looking for or expecting, I had no idea. It was the same as that afternoon I'd sat in the parking lot of the Junkyard Lounge, waiting for my past to come get me.

I thought about breakfast with Craig and a pang of jealousy hit me. Despite what he'd done and been through, Craig seemed changed. As long as I ignored the part where he seemed rattled at the mention of Marty's new love interest, Craig came across as level-headed. Why couldn't my dad have come to the same conclusions, that drinking didn't bring out the best in him, wasn't good to him? Being married with kids, my dad had more reasons to get his life together. How had it been so easy for him to let us go?

I kept my eyes on the duplex. The windows were open and curtains appeared to billow and breathe in the afternoon breeze. I noticed a wooden stairway on the side of the building that led up to the second floor. Greaser scaled those stairs everyday? It looked too dangerous for a guy who preferred being intoxicated.

After half an hour, no one came and no one went into the house. And the feeling that this had been a good idea was long gone.

Something told me that Greaser had found a contentment in his life. That he got up every morning, functioned, did whatever it was that he did, and gave no thought to that eight year old girl he'd left in Jefferson Meadows.

I drove home, telling myself I'd wasted enough time on him, thinking about him, even worrying about him at times, and now, I wasn't about to let one tear fall for that man, because he didn't deserve that kind of love from me.

Marty's House
1980

Dad told me to stay in the room. It wasn't a bedroom. More like a rec room but there was no TV. Marty said I could play with the stereo—but Dad pointed a finger and said I better not break it. Marty smiled at him and said it was okay. She gave me a glass of lemonade and oatmeal cookies. Dad gave me that serious look of his that meant, *Better do as I tell you* as he closed the door while Marty kept smiling and waved at me.

Grown-ups do weird things. I didn't know why I had to stay in the room by myself with nothing to do. Lemonade and oatmeal cookies weren't my favorite but I tried them. Still didn't like them.

A few minutes later, I thought I heard running water, like someone was taking a shower. Who takes a shower in the middle of the day? Maybe it was a dishwasher because I didn't know the sounds Marty's house made the way I knew how my house sounded.

I thought about testing the door and seeing if it was locked, but what if Dad was right there on the other side? He'd know I disobeyed, and I didn't want to get in trouble in front of Marty.

The stereo had two speakers at the sides, which probably meant it got loud. So I had to be careful. I opened the glass door and looked over the buttons and knobs. At home in my room, I had a Mickey Mouse record player and a Mickey Mouse Disco album I played all the time.

I picked up the record on Marty's turntable. It was *Rhinestone Cowboy*! I heard that all the time at the bar. Lots of guys would sing it there when it played on the record machine. I wasn't very good with the words but I liked that song and played it.

I turned the volume on low and played the song over and over. Ten times, maybe more. I jumped on the brown couch in the room since it only squeaked a little. I was pretending to be a cowboy! I didn't know what rhinestones were or how they made you a cowboy.

But I got bored. I checked the stereo cabinet for other records. Marty had good ones! Conway Twitty and Loretta Lynn, George Jones, and Barbara Mandrell. There were others I didn't know.

It felt funny being in Marty's house. I knew she was friends with my dad, but I didn't understand it. Were they supposed to be kissing and dancing the way they did? I thought you only kissed when you were married. Dad never kissed Mom like that. It made me look away. And why didn't Dad look that happy when he was with my mom?

Marty walked in while I was singing *Tight Fittin' Jeans* with Conway.

"Sorry," I said. My cheeks burned but I was glad I wasn't jumping on the couch anymore.

She smiled like she always did. She was wearing a shiny robe and my dad wasn't with her. Her legs were bare and she didn't have on any socks or shoes. Good thing it was hot outside. Wearing a robe seemed weird. Mom had silky robes like that but she only wore them before she took a bath. That made me think of the water. I checked but Marty's hair wasn't wet. She'd been gone a long time, though, so maybe she'd dried it and fixed it.

"You're fine, honey. Do you like singing?"

"Yes, but I don't sound good."

Marty always asked me stuff. I didn't know anyone else like her, but I couldn't tell if she really liked me or if she just did it because of my dad.

"That's silly," she said. "I think your voice sounds very sweet."

"Thank you." She sat on the brown couch and saw that I didn't drink much of the lemonade or eat the cookies. "You didn't like them?"

I was afraid of hurting her feelings or making her mad. "I wasn't hungry."

"That's okay." She talked about how she liked Conway Twitty and said I could sit beside her.

When I did she put her arm around me and held me tight. Then she put her head on top of mine.

"I wish I had a little girl like you."

I didn't know if I was supposed to say anything. Marty was being nice and she smelled like cherry shampoo. Maybe she had been in the shower. It felt like it was my turn to be nice.

"I like your necklace."

She wore that butterfly necklace all the time. I really did like it. The blue and gold were pretty together.

"Here, you can have it." Marty reached behind her long, skinny neck and unlatched the chain. Then she put it around me.

"Oh, I don't think I should take it from you."

She laughed. "You're not. It's my present to you for being such a sweet girl." She kissed my forehead and ran her hand over my hair.

I held up the butterfly so I could see it closer.

"It's beautiful."

"Then it belongs around your neck."

I didn't know what to say. Presents only came when it was my birthday or at Christmas.

"Thank you. I'll keep it forever." I really would, I loved it that much.

Later on, my dad didn't notice the necklace and I was glad Marty didn't say anything to him about it. I didn't want to give it back. But on the ride home, I pretended to scratch my neck as I took it off. I knew it wouldn't be a good idea for Mom to see it. She'd ask questions, and the last time I brought up Marty, she wasn't too happy. Mom didn't want me to like Marty. Maybe it was because of the kissing. I think I understood, but when I looked at the necklace before shoving it in my pocket, part of me couldn't stop from loving Marty.

CHAPTER SEVENTEEN

Throughout this whole Marty-thing, I'd been selfish. I'd rolled up my sleeves and gotten into papers and keepsakes that weren't mine, talked about Marty like she wasn't a person I'd once known and cared about in a weird, innocent way. I hadn't given much thought to Mom and what it might do to her if she knew what I'd been into over the last week. Her life with my dad had been a daily struggle, and for her, his leaving was probably the best thing that could've happened. I'm sure that once the murder investigation lost its steam and the divorce from Greaser was settled, all Mom wanted was a chance to build her own life, create her own contentment. And she'd done it. Had I been undermining her accomplishments, her resilience?

It weighed on me during the drive back home from South Bloomfield. I was glad to have the house to myself so I could clean up. Because whether it was from mourning my runaway dad or from guilt over the snooping and secrets from Mom, I'd cried and made a mess of myself. So much for being a big girl. I didn't need anyone seeing me like this.

Maverick seemed sympathetic and gave me that lopsided stare, along with kisses to my chin. He was also happy to enjoy the yard for a while on his leash.

Once I was reconstructed, I called Shelia at her apartment. No one answered. I left a message, saying I hoped she was okay and that everything would work out fine.

Then I was imprisoned with my thoughts. I hated that I didn't get to see my dad climbing those stairs to his shack of a living space. Hated that I didn't get a satisfying glance of seeing him miserable. What did that say about me though? That I was infected with bitterness? Maybe. But it was still hard to digest the idea that he'd moved on and rebuilt a satisfying-to-him life without his family. Where was the justice in that?

I busied myself with cleaning the house. At least that inner angst was good for something.

I thought about calling Suzette at home and getting her assessment of what had happened. She might not have approved of my breakfast with Craig, but I doubt she would've turned down a chance to talk with him. Also, I wanted to chastise her for not realizing that Lance was Marty's nephew and Irene's son, either. How could we both have been so dim-witted?

With Saturday afternoon winding down, I was surprised I hadn't heard from Derek. So much for him getting off early.

I perked up when I heard a car in the driveway. But when Trey walked in, I gasped.

"What happened to you?" I asked.

Trey made it into the kitchen and fell into a chair. He clutched his side with one hand and held a wad of blood-stained paper towels to his nose.

"Shelia."

I let that sink in and waited for him to explain.

"She's crazy. Always has been, I just pretended it was okay, that I could deal with it. But..." he looked at me and shook his head. "I told her it was over, that I wasn't going to live like this. That was Tuesday. I laid low, hung out at Brian's because I knew she'd come looking for me, crying, saying we could work it out. She's been in counseling but it's not helping her. I didn't know what else to do."

"The gash above your eye?"

He nodded. "Yeah. We got in a fight about the wedding. She didn't want Brian as my best man, said he'd ruin the image she was going for because he deals drugs. I told her that was years ago, and I wasn't getting married without him there. She went off, threw an empty beer bottle at me. I caught it with my head."

"I knew you two were having troubles, but I didn't know she was like this." It was odd, hearing about an abusive woman. Since we'd grown up with a father who was less than kind to our mom, I was surprised Trey had attracted a gal who was this venomous. Dangerous, even. "Did you ever hit her back?"

"No! Whenever things got heated and she started, I just took it, waited for her to simmer down. But over the last few months with all the stress from the wedding, she's gotten worse." A vacancy filled his eyes. "I couldn't do it anymore."

"Does Mom know about this?"

"Everything but today. I went over there to get the rest of my stuff, because she wasn't supposed to be there. But she was. She wanted to talk, make things right she said. I just wanted to get what was mine and be done. I ignored her, walked past her, but she was crying and holding on to me. I didn't even want to look at her. Then she snapped. She whacked me with the mop handle until it broke, then she threw a lamp at me."

Trey lifted his flannel shirt. Bruises stared back at me.

"We should get you to a hospital and have you checked out."

"No way."

I understood his reaction. He didn't want to admit to anyone that a girl had done this to him. The bruises and gashes were nothing compared to the blow his ego suffered.

"It's weird, isn't it?" Trey said with a weak grin. "All those years of putting up with Greaser, what he did to Mom. I swore I'd never be like him."

"You're not like him."

"Maybe. But you find out there's more to being a decent man. I think I understand him better now, and I get why he and Mom were wrong for each other." Trey's gaze became deeply serious. "I can't get away from him, no matter what I do, no matter how much time passes. There's a bad part to me, just like in him."

"That's not true."

He tried taking a deep breath but winced and grabbed his side. Shaking his head he said, "No, you don't understand—"

We were both startled when Mom came in through the sliding door. I guess neither of us noticed her pulling in.

She walked in with a smile, but that disappeared when she saw Trey. "What happened?" She went to him, hunched at the kitchen table, and gently removed the paper towels to examine his injury. Something about the way she moved and looked her son over told me she'd seen Trey like this before. I would've expected her to panic and fret, but she'd dropped her purse and knelt in front of him like a Florence Nightingale type.

Trey gave her a recap of what had happened.

"You need to get checked out."

"I'm not going to the hospital, Mom."

"I'm not asking. We've tolerated this long enough. It's time we do something."

I could tell Trey wanted to protest more but knew that Mom was pulling the strings now. He made it to his feet slowly. Mom wanted me to stay home and keep an eye on things. She said she didn't trust Shelia and there was no telling what she was capable of. I didn't quite get her logic. I mean, if she thought Shelia was going to show up at the house and go on a rampage, why leave me here? But whatever. Arguing would do no good. Maybe Mom thought I could handle Shelia better than Trey. I could hit back. Not that I'd hit anything besides houseflies.

I told Mom to call when she could.

Mom's priority was Trey and as long as she was getting him medical help, I'd go along. Trey's comment about having a bad part in him creeped me out. I'd had similar thoughts. Part of me was convinced I'd ruin my relationship with Derek because I wondered if I'd somehow turn out like my dad. Not that I wanted to, but who plans on being a cheater? Was it something inevitable and beyond a person's control?

Greaser had been gone from our lives for ages, but the effects of his lackluster parenting lingered. Were Trey and I infected with a degree of self-destruction? Did that explain Trey's abrasiveness and my insecurities? If so, how did we save ourselves? Despite my good girl grades and perfectionist attitude, there was something inside me that bucked against my values and what I knew was right. I just hoped I was strong enough not to let it destroy me.

There was no way I felt like going out with Derek, so I left a message on his machine that I was staying home for the evening. Maybe I was a little mad at him for slipping up on his promise of a half-day together, because I didn't mention Trey and the fallout. The message was short and probably terser than I wanted, but I'd deal with that later. After all, it wasn't often that I felt a degree of solidarity with Mom and Trey.

I thought about Shelia and wondered what had made her so violent. Her family seemed normal, but perhaps the Reeds did too at our Sunday dinners. Raking into a family's history though always caused secrets to surface. As far as I knew, her family didn't know about my dad's dead mistress, so whatever had led to Shelia's abusive behaviors probably put our families on a level playing field.

I felt bad, too, knowing that we were abandoning her, even though she clearly needed help. Better help than what she was getting.

When the phone rang an hour later, I jumped to answer it.

"Kyle?"

"Lance?" Just what I was in the mood for. "What do you want?"

"You never called me back."

"Yeah. Maybe you should take a hint."

"What's that supposed to mean?"

"I found out about Craig. You never bothered mentioning that he's your uncle or that your mom is Marty's sister!" I let the sting sink in for a beat. "And you lied about being with the police department. You must think I'm pretty stupid to go along with your scam for so long. So don't call me anymore, don't show up at my house anymore. Just stay out of my life!"

I hung up before he could respond. Of course, I thought of a million more things I wanted to say and it triggered my frustrations.

I hated feeling trapped at home. I should've gone to the hospital with Mom and Trey. That's where I belonged. Maverick kept to my side, as if he could sense my agitation. He'd kiss and nudge my hand in an attempt to make it better. I loved that.

Twenty minutes later when a car came into the driveway, I thought Mom and Trey were back.

But then came pounding on the front door.

I whipped the door open, finding Lance on the other side. Maverick jumped in front of me and started barking wildly at Lance.

"You own a pit bull?" Lance's face blanched white and he staggered backwards.

"He never acts like this." I had no choice but to put Maverick in the utility room.

"Why'd you hang up on me like that?" Lance asked when I returned. He'd invited himself inside.

"Because I know you're a fraud and a liar! How dare you show up here."

"How did you find out?"

"I talked to Craig. He told me everything." Not entirely true, but I didn't owe the guy an explanation.

Lance looked at me as if he was trying to decide if I was telling the truth.

"Why did you start all of this, Lance? What were you trying to prove?"

His demeanor changed. He stood in my living room brimming with cockiness and a defiance I'd seen in some of the guys Suzette had represented.

"Craig's lying to you," Lance said.

"He didn't kill Marty, if that's what you and your crazy mom are after."

"What makes you so sure?"

"Because unlike you, I read the case file, and I know there was someone else in Marty's life."

That stopped him in his tracks.

I stepped into his face. "You wanted me to think that my mom was involved in Marty's murder, then you wanted to blame my dad, but the whole time, you knew it wasn't true, that it couldn't be true. So why Lance?"

"You don't know what he did to our family—what he put my mom through! Everything with Marty was his fault. He deserves the blame and should be in prison for what he did."

"That's not how it works, Lance. Police build a case on evidence. There wasn't any evidence against Craig. He was a jerk for beating Marty but that didn't mean he killed her. Irene knew about Marty's new boyfriend. That's the information the police were missing."

"You think that's it? That some phantom boyfriend is the one?"

In truth, I didn't know. No one did. Even if lover boy was found and a fingerprint match was made with the prints from the garage side door, it didn't prove murder.

"If you really loved Marty you'd want the truth. You wouldn't settle for simply putting Craig in jail because your mom was mad at him."

Looking agitated, he paced liked a caged animal and ran his hand through his hair.

"And you never should've lied to me," I continued. "If you wanted help looking into Marty's case I would've done it, because I've always wanted to know, too."

With that he grabbed me and kissed me. His fingers clamped into me, making it hard for me to pull away. I used both my hands against his chest and shoved him away.

As my luck would have it, there stood Derek. He'd entered through the sliding door and was stock-still, staring at me and Lance.

"Derek, what are you doing here?" It was one of the dumbest things I'd ever said but it poured out naturally.

"I was worried when I got your message." He darted a glare from Lance then to me. "Looks like I shouldn't have bothered."

For a second I wondered if he'd lunge at Lance and punch him. After what Lance had put me through, I was hoping Derek would. But after a beat, I could tell that Derek's anger was aimed at me, not Lance.

"Don't!" I said to Derek. "Don't stand there and act like this is something it isn't."

"I'm not an idiot. We're done." He walked out and whipped the sliding door closed as hard as he could.

I went after him, blurting and rambling out an explanation as he walked to his truck. I tried grabbing his arm, making him look at me, but nothing worked.

"Now I know why you didn't want to see me," he said, ignoring my pleas.

"Stop it, Derek! This guy means nothing to me! I love you!" Tears stung my eyes.

He shrugged my hands from his arm and took off in his truck. I stood there, not sure what had happened.

Back inside, Lance was waiting for me, a proud smirk covering his face. Without hesitating, I slapped him.

"Get out of my house!"

He cupped his cheek for an instant then straightened. A darkness cast over his eyes. I thought for a second he was going to strike me back. Or worse. I didn't know the guy and what he was capable of. Did he have a gun? A knife?

His eyes narrowed and a blackness came over him I hadn't seen before as he said, "You're gonna regret that!"

CHAPTER EIGHTEEN

After Lance left, my body quaked, both from hitting Lance and from losing Derek.

I had no doubt he was done with us for good. That didn't stop me from calling his place and leaving eight or ten messages, since the dumb answering machine kept cutting me off. I explained everything, best I could with words choking me and tears gliding down my face. I told him Lance had shown up and made a pass at me. In the last two messages, I kinda turned salty, saying it was thoughtless of him to leave me with a guy like Lance, that I had no idea what the creep was capable of, and that Derek needed to have more faith in me. He, of all people, should know that I wasn't the kind of girl who haphazardly dropped her clothes for just any guy. And that after the past couple of days, I was more committed to him and more in love with him than ever. It wasn't okay that he acted like some kind of coward by running off and instantly thinking the worst of me.

I let Maverick out of the utility room. He bathed me with kisses. Then, his nose to the floor, he made a beeline for Lance's scent by the door and growled, something he never did. He spent the next several minutes sniffly loudly and retracing Lance's steps.

Mom and Trey came home not long after. Trey looked worse. More bruises were apparent and he looked like he felt the impact of each one. Mom said they didn't have access to a phone and that they didn't file charges against Shelia.

"Anything happen here?" Mom asked.

I wasn't prepared for that question but went with the easy way out.

"No." It wasn't a total lie, because she was really asking if Shelia had come by. Besides, there was nothing she could do, knowing about my showdown with Lance and getting dumped by Derek. I'd have to work on an explanation for why Derek and I broke up, but I had time. Right now, my concern was Trey, and how weird was that?

Loopy and dazed, Trey had enough medication in him to tranquilize a horse, which was probably a good thing since he had to be in agony. He conked out immediately after Mom and I got him situated in bed.

Mom and I relaxed in the kitchen afterward. She recapped their venture at the hospital but I wasn't really listening. We chatted about Shelia but didn't come to any finite conclusions on what we could do. I wanted to snicker *Told you so*, since her advice had been to leave Trey and Shelia alone, let them work out their own problems. But sometimes being right didn't feel as good as you imagined it would.

Mom made her toast-hot chocolate combo and offered to make me some. With my private world in shambles, I passed. Maverick lounged in the middle of the kitchen floor, looking both relieved and exhausted from the night's chaos.

"Did I tell you I saw Frank?" Mom said.

My body tensed, that old familiar feel of her setting me up for something. Of course she knew she hadn't mentioned Frank. Days had gone by when we'd barely seen each other or talked.

"How'd that go?"

"Pretty good. He's always been a good man."

"Better than Roger?"

She gave me that knowing half-grin of hers. "Two different souls. Can't complain about Roger, but Frank, well, he's…"

"Like being home?" I understood her feelings for Frank. He'd been there during her darkest days and knew a side of her that she'd never be able to fully explain to Roger or anyone else. Not that she'd try, either. On one hand, I would've thought that made Roger more attractive to her, since he'd never know the particulars about what she endured with my dad.

"Something like that. We went in next door, to his old house." Mom talked about how the place had changed, how the Whittiers had changed things Frank had done to the place. The butcher block countertops he'd crafted in the garage, and the wallpaper he'd hung in the dining room were gone.

"He's not thinking about moving back in there, is he?"

"No, but he might be around this area more often."

And there it was. That nugget of info she was building to. "So you two are dating?"

"I don't think people our age date. That sounds romantic. We've got a track record, been friends a long time. We're just…keeping each other company."

I nodded slowly in understanding. "Not ready to remodel the kitchen together yet?"

"There you go."

In many ways, Frank was a good fit for her, and I didn't mind the idea of them dating. Or enjoying each other's company.

"Not many men like Frank," Mom said. "You can count on him, the way you can't always count on a person."

Could you count on Frank to take out Marty? I wanted to ask but didn't. Had they discussed Marty and the painful events from back then, or did they treat it like it meant nothing?

My head hurt from the day's events. It was too late to play decrypt Mom's hidden messages, if that's what we were doing.

That picture flashed through my mind again. That memory of Frank and Mom sitting on the patio in the dark, that night when Frank had shoved my dad over the picnic table. He'd talked about looking out for her, having his rifle ready. Marty wasn't shot. That didn't exactly clear Frank, and I couldn't help wondering if his prints matched the ones from that side door to the garage.

Derek didn't call back that night. I was up past one and the phone never jingled. Did I really expect it to, though? I forced myself to be mad at him, because it was an easier emotion to manage than heartbreak.

Trey moved slowly the next morning with plenty of grunts mixed in. I had a feeling his last altercation with Shelia was worse than he'd admitted. He went straight for his meds.

Mom surprised us. We'd all slept in after such a late night, but Mom showed no affects from yesterday. She joined us in the kitchen, dressed to the nines, as she might put it, and said she was off for the day.

"Frank?" I asked. I kept my voice low, since I wasn't sure if the Annette-Frank friendship was public yet.

Mom smiled. It was neither an affirmation nor a denial. I couldn't picture where she'd be going, dressed like that, and Frank wasn't the type of guy who seemed to enjoy fancy places.

"Busy day ahead," she said. "Got an open house up north, then who knows."

I still wasn't in the mood to play decoder, so I let her have her secret.

"Probably be late." She finished her cup of coffee and put it in the sink.

Too bad I didn't have a number where I could call and bug her to come home.

But Mom wasn't out the door five minutes before she came back in.

"The police are here," she said.

We scrambled, best we could with Trey, and went outside. A Franklin County cruiser was parked at the curb. Two officers got out and joined us in the driveway at the side of the house. They introduced themselves, then came the bombshell.

"We're looking for Kyle Reed," one of them said.

I swear, my insides liquefied.

"That's me." A rising anxiety squeezed my throat.

"We're following up on a report of some vandalism down in South Bloomington," the other chimed in. "Someone busted two windows in Gerald Reed's apartment. I take it from the last name that you know him?"

Stares from Mom and Trey bored into me.

"Yeah, but I haven't seen him in years."

I stole a glance at my mom's pale face. I could only imagine the turmoil rolling inside her. Few things stoked her ire—maybe even her fears—like the mention of Gerald Reed.

"We have a witness who gave us a plate number. It came up registered to you."

"The lady gave us your description and said she saw you in the area yesterday."

Walking on hot coals had to be easier than facing this.

"Well, yeah, I drove around there yesterday." Heat, sweat covered me. "But I didn't break any windows."

"Would you mind telling us what you were doing down there?"

Did I have a choice?

I was mindful of every word out of my mouth but kept it honest. It was difficult, explaining to two strangers that I just wanted to see where my dad lived, maybe catch a glimpse of him after not seeing him for years. Mom chimed in with what a horrible father he'd been and how he'd been a coward, leaving the family. She surprised me, taking the situation and ambush of Greaser's name so well, but Mom knew how to put up a strong public front. Her years of practice paid off.

The officers were sympathetic, jotted notes, and didn't look too disturbed. I was sure they'd heard worse. They glanced over Trey and asked what happened. Mom said he'd been in an accident. The officers nodded and left it at that.

"I think we got everything for now," one officer said. "You might want to steer clear of Reed's place. I don't know if the owner of the house plans to press any charges, so you might want to be prepared for that."

"Sounds like a tough family situation," the other said. "I feel for you folks," then to me, "just make sure you don't go making it worse."

They prepared to go and said they'd be in touch if there were new developments. In a way, I hated seeing them leave, because I wondered if I'd be safer diving into the back of their cruiser and going with them than facing my mom.

"What possessed you to go see Greaser?" Mom asked when we were back inside.

We milled into the kitchen, each of us still standing. Maverick whined and sniffed each of us, then flopped into the middle of the floor.

Mom just heard my reason for going by my dad's place: that after all this time of being abandoned, I was curious. But I knew what she was really asking: *How could you care about that man after what he did to us?*

"It's because of Marty, okay?" There. I'd said it. "Lance, you know, the guy who keeps calling? He started everything. He showed up here and said you might've had something to do with Marty's death. He acted like there was a new investigation and you were a suspect. I couldn't sit back thinking that this guy was out to nail my mom for murder. So I got into it, started asking questions."

"And what did you find out?" Her lips were tight, jaw set, arms folded.

"A lot, but mainly that it wasn't you. Or Greaser."

"I could've told you that."

"Really? Because whenever I brought it up you wouldn't talk to me. You played it off and ignored me and acted like it didn't matter when it did matter to me."

My pulse kicked up. Accusing Mom of anything didn't happen. Neither did speaking to her with such raw boldness. Usually, I reigned in my words and those snippy impulses. But it was true, all along she'd discarded the fact that I wanted to be a part of my own past. I wanted to know what happened to Marty.

"I even sat down with Detective Buchanan, Mom. Remember him? I went through the case file and I saw the notes he had about you. He thought you were involved, too, especially because you lied and fudged your timecard at the Western Pancake House."

"What timecard?"

Her expression was unreadable. I didn't know if she was truly drawing a blank or lying straight to my face.

"According to Buchanan, your timecard showed you were working the night Marty died, but when Buchanan talked to your boss, he said you were off that night."

Mom looked to Trey then back to me. "I've got things to do." She flipped her curled hair over her shoulders and fluffed it. "If you want to see Greaser and talk about Marty, I'm sure he'd be more than happy to, but I've got more important things to do." She gathered her things and left, muttering under her breath the entire time.

Trey and I said nothing after she'd gone. Silence hung between us. Maverick had followed after Mom and stood at the sliding back door, whining. Trey began to move and scrunched his face in pain.

"Come on." I took Trey down to the rec room and helped him make camp on the couch. Armed with the remote, he popped his meds and nestled into the couch. Maverick joined him, making Trey wince as he settled down.

"I can't believe you went down there," he said while clicking through the channels.

"I didn't break those windows, if that's what you're thinking."

"Mmm. Doesn't sound good. If I'm one of those police officers, I'm not buying it."

He had a point. The coincidence was too rich. I guess that's what I deserved for sneaking around. The same day I'm creeping around Greaser's place, and some busy-body takes notice, his windows end up busted.

Then it hit me. Lance. Had he been following me yesterday? Maybe it was a stretch, but Lance had threatened me after I slapped him. *You're gonna regret that!* But he had no way of knowing which apartment belonged to my dad. Did he?

"Was that true about Mom's timecard?" Trey asked, a grogginess to his voice.

I nodded. Maybe I'd been cruel, bringing that up.

"Take it easy on Mom," Trey said. "She's been through more than you know."

With that he drifted off to sleep.

I didn't doubt what he said. Mom was the only person Trey defended. Ever. Perhaps he wasn't happy knowing I'd been poking around in Greaser's territory and in the whole Marty debacle. It wasn't to hurt Mom, but there was no explaining it now.

Since Trey was taken care of, I wanted out of the house. It seemed that I was subconsciously waiting around, hoping Derek would call. With each passing minute and hour, I knew that hope of us talking and working through the situation was wearing thin.

I decided to go to Suzette's. At this point, she was the only person I could talk to about everything from Lance and Derek to Mom and Trey. I was checking my address book for her home number when the phone rang.

"Is this Kyle?"

"Yes."

"Kyle this is Archie out at the bar. I's wondering if there's any chance you could stop out here today."

"Isn't the bar closed on Sundays?"

"Yeah, it is, but I got someone here that wants to talk to ya. It's your dad."

CHAPTER NINETEEN

A big part of me didn't want to go, but I had to face my father. It would be the most difficult thing I'd ever done, and I couldn't imagine what would compare to it later in life. But wasn't I the one who wanted to stop pretending, to face problems and deal with them? This is what I get.

Archie and my dad both knew the Junkyard Lounge wasn't far from my house, and I knew they were waiting. I got myself together, best I could, and went over.

The blue Oldsmobile was the lone car in the parking lot. He was really there.

Somehow, I made it up those steps and swung the door open.

My dad was at the bar, sitting in the same space I'd taken when Derek and I first went in. His back faced me and a trail of cigarette smoke wafted upward. Archie was behind the bar, drying glasses. He gave me a firm nod with his lips pressed together, then turned and headed into the kitchen.

I took the stool next to my dad. Neither of us looked over at the other, but with my peripheral vision I could see a mug of beer next to him.

"Still drinking," I said. Maybe I should've had more fear or respect in my tone, but both were overridden by indifference. This man was a stranger. I'd spent more of my life without him

"Sound like your mother." He smacked his cigarette with his lips and extinguished what was left. "Can't say I miss that. She know you're here?"

"No." I swiveled on my stool and drank in the sight of my dad. He looked scuffed and worn, like an old pair of tennis shoes you never throw out but have no use for. The rim of remaining hair that peeked out from underneath his cap was a dull gray, and white stubble speckled his sagging jowls. Had I passed him in the street his face might not have registered. He was that forgettable.

"I heard there was some trouble at your place," I said.

He shot me a side glance. "How'd you hear that?"

"Couple police officers stopped by and updated me."

Apparently, he liked that. He chuckled.

"I didn't break your windows, just so you know."

"What'd you come around for then?"

"To look. See if you were still alive." A chill hit me that went straight to my bones. He could've been dead, years ago or yesterday, and I probably wouldn't have known.

He shrugged. "Here I am."

Gerald Reed could've been the poster guy for the aimless and defeated. If I had to guess, that cap was the only one he had and he never left the house without it. His shoes probably had speckles of paint, mud splatters, and beer stain droplets. It wouldn't have surprised me if most of his clothes were the ones he'd had at Jefferson Meadows. In his left pocket he had a handful of change. In his right, keys and a handkerchief. I knew this because there were still a few things I clearly remembered about my dad that no one had told me. Those memories, those random sticklers, were all mine.

"Is that why you're here, you thought I broke your windows to get your attention and to get you to talk to me?"

Another shrug. "I ain't had any problems since I been there. Until last night. Then Mrs. Stevens from across the street said she noticed a red car parked there earlier with some young girl in it. Come to find out, it's you. So I got a hold of Archie, spent some time a-talkin', then had him give you a call."

I would've loved seeing Archie's face through all that.

"No windows were broken when I left." Defending myself probably sounded desperate. People rarely admitted to wrongdoing, even when they were caught. "But I didn't come here to argue. There's a lot of things I've wanted ask you for quite a while." Pressure built inside me. There were probably a hundred better ways to approach the subject, but this felt like the only moment I'd ever get the chance to blurt out that one question. "Did you kill Marty?"

It was the first thing that popped out. Maybe I said it so easily because I already knew the answer. He gave no reaction, only took a gulp from his mug.

"Heh. All this time and that's what you've waited to ask me?"

He was right. I wanted to know why he'd left me and how he'd managed to move on with his life. How could he sleep at night, not knowing if his little girl was safe, had food, or a roof over her head? That answer, though, wasn't one I was prepared for.

"No, I didn't kill her," he said. "You think I could smash someone in the head?"

Inwardly, I gasped. That reference again. *Capable of a blow to the head*, wasn't that what Buchanan's notes had said in the case file? I had to focus.

"And I don't know who did," he finished tersely.

"Did you know she was seeing someone else?"

He nodded and took a swig from his beer. "I was done with her when she told me that and I hadn't seen her in a while before she died."

I thought back to his statement to the police. Maybe that's why he'd sounded disconnected and as though Marty never meant much to him.

"Who was the guy?" I asked.

"No idea. Never laid eyes on him. Didn't care."

I swallowed hard before I asked, "Could it have been Carl?"

"Archie's nephew? Naw. He ain't right in the head. Got the mind of an eight-year old. That's why Archie had him wash dishes. Something he could handle."

Maybe that explained why Carl had freaked me out when I was little; I didn't understand his challenges.

I almost asked Greaser why he loved Marty better than Mom. But I already knew why. Marty was vivacious and had a sultry way about her. Considering her vast experience with men, she was probably fun in bed. My dad always had an eye for beautiful ladies and thought he had a way with women. With her flirty, playful nature, Marty had made my dad feel like a stud. Wanted and desired. A feeling of ick crawled all over me.

"I never thought I'd get over you leaving us." I refused to cry, but tears burned my eyes. It was one of those statements that had lived in my heart for ages, one I'd coddled and practiced saying, thinking I'd never really have the chance to let it out. There was a freedom that came with it, as well as a dread that I'd get a salty rejection in return.

Gerald Reed looked me straight in the eyes. "I never left you. I loved you more than anything in the world. I never raised a hand to you. I wasn't good at most things, but I was always grateful that I had you."

My body flushed—with what, pride, relief, justification—I didn't know, didn't recognize. But in that moment, I realized we were sharing the same experience, purging the things we'd wanted to say. That he'd waited just as long to say those words, feel his own release. It didn't undo what had happened. He didn't try to make up for any of it, or seem haunted by regret. It was probably the closest I'd ever get to an apology. I guess we both had accepted where we were at in life. Mistakes and experience had marred us both and left their disfiguring scars.

I was the first to leave the Junkyard Lounge, and that was probably best. Archie and Dad still had catching up to do, I figured. I left with no promises, no mention of how we could weave each other into our lives. We didn't hug or exchange a handshake. That felt right. No pretenses or phony sentiments. I realized, with a bit of pain, that he didn't ask about Mom or Trey. Maybe I could understand a lack of interest in Mom, but nothing, *nothing* about his son? The truth was, I couldn't imagine gaining anything from having Gerald Reed in my life again. Maybe that wasn't right or fair, but we both knew that was how it had to be.

I knew I'd relive that time with Dad at the bar for years to come, just as I knew it could be the last time I ever saw him. Even though it wasn't a Hallmark moment, I thought I could live with that. But his unexpected words had seared my heart, and I'd never forget that defeated, hardened look in his eyes.

I never left you.

There'd been an emphasis on you, and I understood what he meant. When I was little he'd told me he loved me more than anything in the world. He never lavished that sentiment on Mom or Trey. Sure, he'd dropped the customary Love you, babe on Mom, the same way he'd say Hey to Frank across the fence. But being the only one my dad loved hadn't amounted to much. Maybe it was another reason why Mom and Trey were bonded so tightly—and I was shut out.

Back home, Mom had returned. What had happened to her long day? I fervently hoped this wasn't a sign that her Mom-radar was spiking and telling her where I'd been.

When I went in, my first thought was to Derek. Had he called? I didn't see any messages but there was a chance Mom wouldn't have written it down. She'd just remember to tell me.

Trey was still snoozing on the couch. So was Maverick.

I found Mom in her room playing solitaire on her bed. She usually did that at night before turning in. She said it was her way of winding down and organizing her thoughts for the next day. But it was the middle of the afternoon.

"Have a good day?" My words tiptoed toward her. I figured we were breaking with our Sunday dinner tradition this week, not that I had the nerve to ask.

"Had a good showing." She'd changed her clothes and hardly glanced up at me.

I took that as a cue she was still mad about our morning visit from the Franklin County sheriffs.

"That's good." I turned to go, since she didn't seem interested in chatting.

"There was a reason," she said, "with the timecard."

I leaned against the doorway. "You don't have to tell me."

She swiped her hand across her bedspread, an indication for me to sit. So I did.

"I wasn't at work that night, but I'd told Greaser I was working then, that's why I had to lie." She lit a cigarette and took a few puffs before continuing. "I was with Frank. We'd gone down to his property in Marietta. He was giving me lessons on how to shoot his rifle. Frank had been looking out for me for a while, but he thought it'd be best if I could defend myself."

My imagination went wild, picturing Mom with a gun. Violence wasn't her style. Although she'd once 'spanked' Trey with his own rawhide whip, and she'd treated my bare legs to the flyswatter a few times when I was a kid, Mom wasn't one ruled by an unpredictable temper. I could envision her handling a rifle like a marksman, because few things intimidated Annette Reed. But *using* it against my dad? That went too far.

"Did you ever tell Greaser the truth, that you were with Frank?" Marietta was two hours away. That meant Mom and Frank had spent the day together. Just the two of them. How Frank managed to leave Nora and Mom avoided Greaser, I didn't know.

"No. He didn't care much about it, never asked why I lied."

"But you never told Detective Buchanan the truth either."

She shook her head. "Couldn't, 'cause there was more." She took more drags from the cigarette, as if to build her courage. Her attention drifted to the back of the playing cards. "I was planning on killing Greaser and making it look like an accident or suicide. Frank was helping me."

I felt my body sink deeper into the bed.

"I'd had enough with that coward. It was about time I did something before he ended up hurting me or crippling me. So Frank and me tried figuring out the best way to do it. But then Greaser left. Gone in the night. I was scared for a while that he'd come back, maybe try killing me so he could keep the house. Then Marty ended up dead. After that, we knew it was best to put things to rest. If Greaser wound up dead, well, that would've been too much for the police to accept as coincidence. I'd have gone to jail for sure, and you and Trey..." She pressed her lips together.

We said nothing for a while. I absorbed what she'd said, tried to figure out if she was telling me the truth while she worked on her cigarette.

"Does Trey know?"

"No, and there ain't no need. Not now. I couldn't say anything about Frank to the detective because it was too risky. Couldn't have Frank ending up in jail and Nora having no one."

"So if Marty hadn't been killed, then you might've killed Greaser?"

Mom shrugged a shoulder like it was no big deal. "I don't know. I hadn't made up my mind. I just wanted rid of him and to put an end to the misery. I should've stood up to him, shouldn't have let it go on for so long. I should've done more to protect Trey."

Life felt upside-down and inside-out. To hear that Mom was planning to kill my dad felt like a wrecking ball to the gut. Mom had always been my tough-as-nails hero, who occasionally took time off from that duty to pose as a thorn in my side.

To hear she'd plotted a murder tainted that image.

But even thinking that felt like a betrayal. I saw what being married to my dad had done to her, what it took from her. She'd watch Trey endure years of humiliation, and she had to entrust that her alcoholic husband would eventually leave his beloved bar and take care of his young daughter at home while she worked a double shift. Everyone had a breaking point. Maybe Greaser's affair with Marty was it for Mom.

Her frankness alarmed me. Sure, she'd burned through a cigarette, but she made no apologies along the way of her confession. And I'd never heard her mention being afraid of Greaser coming back. *...maybe try killing me so he could keep the house.* Had she truly believed that?

I didn't know what to say, perched on the edge of her bed. I nodded, accepted it, and ambled to my room. I curled on my bed and stayed there as the sun faded. When darkness colored my windows, I slipped between the sheets.

I wondered if Mom's night was as sleepless and restless as mine.

The three of us tackled Monday morning as if it were no different than any other Monday. Mom insisted Trey make it to work and lay off the pain pills for the day so he could function. It was one of the few times I heard her take a firm tone with him—and he agreed without a fuss. In the foggy dawn of this new world and its revelations, I only gave a fleeting thought to the fact Derek hadn't called. Maverick ruffed and jumped, wanting a walk. A good idea for both of us, but I felt like I was functioning on autopilot.

I went to work but couldn't fathom how I'd be worth anything. Once inside, Suzette called me into her office.

"Oh, I didn't know we had company," I said when I noticed a man standing beside her. "Good morning."

"Kyle this is Vincent Fox."

The name took a moment to register in my brain.

"Vinny?" I asked, looking at Suzette.

"The one and only." She said it with a va-va-voom in her voice that embarrassed me.

I shook hands with him and traded greetings. Vinny Fox was probably the opposite of the images that came to mind with a name like Vinny Fox. Short, bald on top, and thick around the middle, Vinny's appearance was anti-climactic in person.

"So you're Annette's daughter?" His eyes darted over me, as the corner of his mouth curled. Something about the way he said it put me on edge. Maybe it was having him know personal things about me and being at a disadvantage. All I really knew about Vinny was that Mom had once hired him. Oh, and he and Suzette had enjoyed a fling at some point in time. "Suzette tells me that your parents were involved in an old murder case."

"My mom never mentioned it to you?"

"No, she'd hired me for the divorce proceedings. By that time I think she and your dad had been separated a good number of years. I had to hunt down your dad so he could be served with papers and all. You know, I'll never forget your mom. That Annette Reed is something. Knew exactly what she wanted."

Sounded like Mom.

"I told Vinny what we've been up to," Suzette said, "and how we're piecing a few items together. I also told him we might need his help in talking to your dad."

"What?"

"Yeah, I thought if Vinny tracked him down again, we could figure out a way to orchestrate a meeting, maybe sit down and hash through the case. I know it would be hard on you, babe, but Vinny and I could do it, if you didn't want to get involved."

I paused a moment before laughing. Suzette and Vinny traded confused glances.

"What am I missing?" Suzette held out her hands.

I was reluctant to tell her about meeting my dad with Vinny there, but what could I do? So I filled her, and Vinny, in on my bar stool conversation with Greaser. For good measure, I added in the bonus content that someone had broken his apartment windows—and warned her that I might need a lawyer.

"All this went down and you didn't call me?" Suzette seemed offended, maybe a bit embarrassed in front of Vinny.

"I thought about it," I said, "but it was Sunday. I didn't know what you were doing."

She darted a side glance at Vinny, who suddenly had an ornery look on his face.

It was a good thing I didn't eat much. That exchange almost made me ill.

"Okay," Suzette said, "so what did he say about Marty? Did you get to that?"

"He was a dead-end. He confirmed that there was another guy in Marty's life, but had nothing new about the night she died. No confession." The mention of confession made me think of Mom and what she'd told me. I wanted to tell Suzette but not with Vinny around.

"Mr. Fox, I have a question. My mom kept a file on all the info you gave her. There's a sheet of paper that reads like a list of demands. I always wondered, how'd that come about?" I described the paper and the words written on it while he seemed to search his memory banks.

"Yeah, I remember that. She had me write it down. She thought that would make the divorce come through faster. Those terms about custody and child support, all that came from her. I wasn't kidding when I said she knew what she wanted."

After work I drove by Derek's. More than anything, I was desperate for a break and wished I could empty my head of all-things-Marty. At the same time, I felt like an emotional weakling showing up on Derek's doorstep. He'd heard my messages and knew where to find me. But he didn't want to talk to me. What was next, me begging outside his window?

He wasn't home. I missed him. Everything about him. During downtime at work, I'd written him a lengthy letter, going over the Lance situation and reiterating—again—that I didn't want anything to do with Lance, that I wanted what (I thought) we had. I slipped it underneath the door to his apartment, feeling that I wasn't welcome to use my key anymore. I told myself this had to be it, that the next move, good or bad, had to come from Derek.

Throughout our relationship, I thought I'd maintained certain barriers, that I'd guarded my heart well enough so that if we broke up, I wouldn't feel distraught. I'd even told myself it wasn't a question of *if* we broke up but *when*. That was meant to serve as a reminder not to get too close to him. Or too attached. I'd been worried that having sex with him would be the one thing that would cement such an attachment, but I was wrong. Intentional or not, he'd coiled himself around my heartstrings. I hadn't counted on that.

I also wished I could just talk to him, especially about Mom's new revelations. He knew her and the circumstances well enough that I could spout off my fears and vexations. I wouldn't have to explain everything to him. I could just be me. He'd understand and probably tell me that it was okay now, that back then my mom was only desperate to save herself and her family. And I wanted to tell him about seeing my dad, wanted to melt into his arms so he could hold me while I cried out what was left of my feelings.

But I couldn't hope for that anymore.

When I got home, I switched from semi-depressed to mildly panicked, seeing Shelia's car in the driveway. Trey was home too. I hurried inside, terror pinching at my heels. Had she come to finish him off? What if she was in there on a rampage, what would I do? Did I have it in me to fight back? Considering what she'd done to Trey, I knew it could get ugly.

But when I entered, Mom and Shelia were sitting at the kitchen table, cups of coffee between them. Trey stood, slightly leaning against the counters. Had it been two weeks ago, I never would've guess that anything could be wrong.

"Hey," I said. What does a person say to the woman who thrashed her brother?

Her eyes were puffy and pink, indications she'd been crying.

"Hey." Shelia lifted her fingers in a mild wave. "I just came by to bring Trey his stuff and see how he was doing. And I wanted you all to know how sorry I am for what's happened. I never meant for it to get so out of hand." She cupped her mug as she spoke, her voice close to cracking.

"You've been under a lot of strain," Mom said.

Astonishment gripped me, because I never would've imagined Mom extending a kindness towards Shelia after what she'd done to her precious Trey.

Shelia replied with trembling lips and a weak nod.

"I should probably go now." Shelia stood and slid her purse strap over her shoulder. She seemed confused about what to do next, or maybe it was that overwhelming feeling of knowing it would be the last time she would be in our crappy little kitchen. The last time she'd see Trey.

She moved to the sliding door then turned back to us.

"I'm so sorry, Trey. I really do love you." Tears and sobs collided as she scurried out the door.

None of us moved. A muffled grunt and thud came from Maverick, protesting his position in the utility room. Then Mom sighed before sipping her coffee.

"Good riddance to that one."

CHAPTER TWENTY

Mom and Trey were quick to say nothing after Shelia left. No explanation. No recap of things I'd missed. My pining for details went unfulfilled. Mom rinsed out the mugs and stated that she had two listing appointments to go to. The good thing about that was no dinner. Trey and I were on our own.

But to make sure I couldn't corner him and leech him for info about Shelia, Trey took Maverick for a walk. If taking him to the end of the driveway counted as a walk, since Trey was still hurting from his injuries. Maverick would be thrilled, having Trey around permanently now. I forced myself not to feel jealous.

Trey retreated to his bedroom when he came back in. He probably needed time alone. What I doubted he would ever need was me.

I ignored the gloomy thought. Now that Derek was out of my life, the urge to sulk and feel sorry for myself wrapped around me like a wet blanket. Refusing to give in, I took Maverick out to the yard and we played with his toys. As I rolled in the grass and got assaulted with slobber, gratefulness swelled in me. I did my best to roughhouse with Maverick and to mimic Trey's playfulness. Maverick and I worked ourselves into a panting, sweaty mess.

Evening crept in. My first Monday evening without Derek. I'd have to get used to it, along with suffering through a lengthy list of *no more 'insert everything' with Derek*.

Leaving Maverick in the kitchen, I headed upstairs for a shower. With Trey around now, there'd be no more parading through the house in towels. I made quick work of drying my hair and changing into fresh clothes. Before going down to watch TV, or whatever it is single people do, I paused in front of Trey's door, wondering if I should check on him. With my knuckle ready, I was about to softly knock but held back.

Trey must've heard me, though, because as I turned to go, he opened the door.

"You heading over to Derek's?" He didn't seem as groggy as he had been.

"Not tonight." I tried playing it casual. "Sorry about Shelia."

"Yeah, me too."

"You need any help?" I nodded toward the stack of boxes.

He shook his head. "It's probably better if I work on getting my own place."

We stood there a beat, then I nodded and turned to go.

"I was going through some of my stuff and found this." Trey slipped a necklace out of his pocket and gave it to me. "I thought you might want it."

The delicate chain pooled in my palm and I picked up the charm. A sapphire-blue butterfly trimmed in gold. Marty's butterfly necklace, the one she'd given to me.

My gaze snapped to Trey. "Where did you get this?"

"I took it. It was a really long time ago. I saw it in your room, lying on the dresser. I thought Mom might see it. Maybe she wouldn't know it was Marty's but she'd be curious where you got it. So I took it. I didn't know if you'd be smart enough back then to lie about it."

Holding the necklace was like holding a sacred relic, like having a tangible piece of all those scattered memories. I remembered looking for it in my room and feeling sad that it was gone. But with the churning chaos between my parents, I couldn't afford being too upset.

"I was mad at you for the longest time," Trey said, "keeping that thing. I didn't get how you could touch something from Marty, knowing what she'd done to Mom. That's why I never gave it back. But I guess you were just a kid, and what does a stupid kid know about a drunk father who's screwing around with a barmaid." He seemed to swallow a lump in his throat. "Then I just forgot about it, until now and all this garbage with Shelia."

Nostalgia suffocated me. Images of Marty and of Marty and my dad together zipped through my head. Grief joined in—a genuine sadness for Marty and the way her life ended.

"You're right." I choked back the battling emotions. "I was eight and didn't understand what was going on. And I never kept it to hurt Mom." I couldn't explain the feelings I'd had for Marty, how she'd been a bright spot through that mess and treated me sweetly. He wouldn't understand what it was like, being little and lost in a sea of adult turmoil, just like I couldn't understand the humiliation my dad put him through.

But then, it hit me.

"How did you know this was Marty's necklace?"

A strange expression dawned on him. The kind of look that weighed how much he wanted to say and how far he wanted to take the subject.

"I saw her wear it," he said.

"Where? When?" The words dribbled out.

"When I was at her place."

I started feeling lightheaded and wasn't sure I was hearing this right. "You spent time at Marty's house? You...*you* were the guy she was seeing?"

He didn't admit it. He didn't deny it.

Suddenly, it all came crashing in. Trey, that day he'd eaten the hotdog outside his office building, had asked me if I could picture Mom, *busting someone's skull*. But he couldn't have known that, even the papers had reported Marty had been strangled.

"But how?" I couldn't find the right words.

"I wanted to get back at Dad. For everything. But the way he treated Mom was the worst. So I thought I'd get him where it hurt. I sat outside the bar and saw him with Marty a few times, so I knew who she was. Then I started following her near where she lived. I ran into her at the grocery store. It didn't take much with her. She was flirty and liked attention. She invited me back to her place and we drank beer and listened to records. All I had to do was talk about how beautiful she was. Next thing I know she's wanting rid of her husband and married boyfriend."

"I can't believe this! Dear God, how old were you then?"

"Close to seventeen."

Back when he had that mop of fluffy, feathered hair Greaser was always telling him to get cut. He'd looked like a cross between Andy Gibb and Shaun Cassidy. No wonder Marty fell for him.

"How far did you take it, Trey?"

"I wasn't doing it to have sex with her. I just wanted her to dump Greaser."

"She wasn't exactly a choir girl, Trey. I've talked to her sister and know how she was with men."

"Yeah, but she was nervous about how old I was. Said she had a nephew close to my age. So it freaked her out."

Lance!

Maybe Marty had her own set of flawed morals, too. Greaser didn't want a two-timer; it was only fine if he was the one doing the two-timing. And Marty probably loved the idea of a love-sick teen infatuated with her, but she couldn't go all the way with him.

Trey moved his mouth as if he were tasting a strange food for the first time, trying to decide if he liked it or not.

"It's a long story, Kyle, but I was there the night Marty died, and I saw everything."

Marty's house
1980

She didn't ask if he had his driver's license yet—which he didn't—and she didn't ask how he'd ended up waiting for her in the parking lot of the Junkyard Lounge. She was just happy to see him and proved it with a squeal and a dramatic embrace. She tossed him her car keys and told him to wave up at Linda, who was standing at the entrance waving at them. He returned the gesture but didn't look up. It wasn't that Linda knew who he was, he just didn't want to risk her getting a good look at him.

It'd been three weeks since he'd started seeing Marty, if that's what it was. He hadn't expected her to be so easily enamored. Was she this way with every guy who gave her a wink and a smile? He understood why his dad liked her. Plump and perky in all the right places, with a personality that was a cross between a Hee Haw Honey and Charo.

He'd rushed up to her at the Super-Duper when she was reaching high for a can of green beans that almost toppled on her.

"Here, let me get that," he'd said and handed her the can.

She thanked him and gave him the kind of smile most guys wished for, one that was flirty and curious, that threatened to set his groin on fire.

"What's wrong with the cans down here?" he'd asked.

"I read somewhere that the fresher ones are always higher."

"Oh." The logic didn't make any sense to him, but he wasn't there to get schooled on canned vegetables. "You better be careful. I'd hate to see a beautiful lady like you get hurt."

She laughed.

"Maybe I should keep an eye on you, in case you need corn."

As simple as that and he was carrying home a bag of groceries for her. He lied about everything, his age, his family, where he was from. Compliments distracted her from being suspicious. So did her attraction to him.

The biggest struggle had been avoiding both his dad and her husband. He knew when his dad would be at work or looking after his little sister. Gerald couldn't spend endless hours at the bar on weeknights; he had to check on Kyle or Annette would start with her griping. Trey counted on that, and the fact he could come and go from home as he pleased, since his dad never asked about school or kept track of his work schedule at Gold Circle. His dad preferred it when he was out, Trey knew.

Marty's husband was a different story. She said she'd kicked him out, that their marriage was over. But once, he'd shown up, came in through the back door in the kitchen like he still lived there. Trey had just enough time to escape through the garage.

But now, he had all night with Marty. He knew his dad was upset with her. She'd told him there was another guy. Gerald even went to another bar to get his fix and prove to Marty how mad he was.

"You look so good tonight, Brian," she told him, running her fingers through the side of his hair.

He couldn't pretend she didn't turn him on. She knew how to touch a guy, tease his sensitivities.

"I might just have to take advantage of you." She giggled and her head lolled to the side. Sure signs she was drunk. It happened often because Archie didn't mind Marty and Linda doing shots with some of the regular customers.

He'd chugged a beer earlier. Needed it to calm him. Tonight was going to be that tipping point. His plan, loose as it was, included sleeping with Marty, then telling her who he was. That way, he figured, she'd be done with his dad for good, and with Marty out of the picture, maybe his mom could have a sliver of peace.

He didn't doubt that his parents hated each other, that their togetherness was only a formality. Divorce was expensive, and his mom was terrified of supporting herself and two kids. Although he knew his mom gave up on the marriage long ago, that didn't lessen the sting of embarrassment she'd endured since Gerald began the affair with Marty. Gerald had been blatant, taking Kyle to the bar and letting her watch the two of them dance and kiss.

Trey would put an end to it.

Marty scooted closer and slipped her hand inside Trey's shirt. His breath caught and he wished that he had more chest hair.

"You're gonna feel so good next to me." Marty cuddled as close to him as she could get.

Trey felt his body responding. At least he wasn't a virgin. He could handle the physical part, or thought he could. He had to shut off the reminders that his dad had been with this woman. That his dad's primary attraction to Marty had been the sex.

He pushed it from his mind.

Marty ramped up her groping, started whispering into his ear. Perspiration coated Trey as he smelled the alcohol on her breath and the sweet lure of her perfume.

He drove Marty's car inside her garage and hit the button for the opener to close it. Slow and noisy, the garage door shimmied its way down.

"Maybe we should do it right here," Marty said.

Trey didn't know what to say. He couldn't think.

She laughed, apparently pleased with herself, then let out a sigh. She tumbled over into Trey's lap and didn't move. Trey froze until he realized she'd passed out.

He cursed.

What now, he wondered. He rubbed his hands across his face. This wasn't supposed to happen. He looked down at her face. Her mouth hung open slightly and her lips were dangerously close to his belt buckle.

She ruins everything.

The rage that surged inside him had never felt so tangible. He'd punish her, do whatever it took to get her out of his dad's life. Revenge on Marty would be revenge on his dad. For all those times Gerald Reed had embarrassed him, come at him, slapped him in the face, and for never being a real father. Trey wanted to destroy the one thing Gerald cared about.

But a fog tried settling in his mind. His thoughts derailed and a hazy sleepiness threatened. He realized the car was still running and the garage door was closed. Were the fumes starting to get to him?

His mind shifted gears. He had to get out of the car and drag Marty out. He decided he could take Marty in and wake her up. Even if it took all night, he was going to seduce her—then tell her who he was. The look on her face would be worth the trouble.

Trey went into motion. He cut the engine and got out. Then, he had to pull Marty over into the driver's seat because he hadn't left enough room to open the passenger door. It didn't take much effort with Marty's thin frame.

As Marty slumped in the seat, Trey knew his mom was right. Marty was nothing but trash. A worthless hussy who deserved everything she got, because if it wasn't Gerald Reed's life she was messing up it'd be someone else's. He didn't have a thing to feel guilty about.

But a sound came from inside the house. Trey feared it was Marty's husband. He darted out the side door of the garage, just like he'd done before to avoid getting caught.

Trey didn't run. He hunkered down outside the garage and listened. The door that led into the house opened.

"Mom, she's out here," someone called.

More noise. Footsteps.

"What's she doing out here?" came a female voice.

Trey risked a peek. He couldn't say for sure, but he thought the woman was Marty's sister. Irene, wasn't it? There was a guy with her—not much younger than Trey. Was that the nephew Marty had mentioned? She shook Marty by the shoulder and yelled her name. Marty groaned.

"Lance, help me get her in the house." Disgust tainted Irene's voice.

Lance did a sloppy drag-carry combo of Marty's limp body.

Trey couldn't help himself. He was irritated these two had ruined his set-up, and he wasn't about to leave. He'd wait them out. Keeping crouched low, he went around the back of the house. Marty wasn't one for curtains on the rear windows. With no light coming from the moon or shining on the patio, Trey had a concealed vantage point. Hunkered down, he peeked inside through the back windows. The sliding back door was open slightly, an indication of where Lance and Irene had entered the house?

Lance dumped Marty onto the couch in the family room. Her body contorted, Marty was rousing with a slight cough.

"What are you doing sleeping in your car?" Irene asked, a bit too loudly. "In the garage? How'd you get yourself home if you're that drunk?"

With her hands covering her head and face, Marty worked her way to full consciousness. Suddenly, she made for the kitchen, on wobbly legs, and hurled into the sink. Irene shook her head in disgust while Lance looked like he wanted to remove his skin. Marty ran the water and splashed her face several times.

"You're pathetic," Irene said. "Were you stone cold drunk out there? Passed out again?"

Watching Marty, Trey noticed a wrinkled look of confusion cross her face. Clearly, he thought, she didn't remember passing out, and maybe she was wondering what had happened to him, why he wasn't around.

"What are you doing here, Irene?" Marty grabbed a paper towel and dabbed her face and mouth.

"Checking up on you, as usual. You said you'd watch the kids tonight but never showed."

"Watch the kids? I just got off work and it's after midnight."

"Yeah, you were supposed to be at my place over an hour ago. You said you'd get off early and come over so I could go out."

"I must've forgotten." She said it with a cold nonchalance. She turned and reached inside her fridge for a bottle of Jack Daniels. After several swigs, she replaced the cap and set the bottle on the counter.

"That's so typical of you, Marty. You never think about anyone but yourself. The world's gotta revolve around you, and when you screw up, there's never any consequence."

"So I forgot, big deal. It's not like you need to be out all night anyway. Unless it's time for you to pad your welfare check with another kid."

Irene trembled and balled her fists. "I've always been there for you and stood up for you. All the trash talk about you growing up, I defended you, even when you kept whoring around with every guy you could find. And every time you call me when Craig knocks you around, I'm there."

"Shut up, Irene! Don't act like you've been a saint!" She glanced at Lance.

Irene struck her across the face. Marty took it, didn't react. She touched her fingers to her lips.

"Go home, Irene. No one cares about you. Your only talent is getting knocked up, and even that doesn't keep the men around. They all know you're worthless. *All* of them."

Irene stood there as Marty's words seemed to claw at her. Shaking her head, she snapped her gaze in Marty's direction. Irene looked ready to hurl a verbal insult, but instead she screamed and thrust her hands around Marty's neck. She pushed Marty against a wall, smacking Marty's head into the paneling. Marty arched her back and kicked, trying to get Irene off her. They staggered into the living room, Irene with an unsteady grip. Marty bumped into an end table, spilling items to the floor. Lance yelled for them to stop but the women ignored him.

Marty chopped at Irene's arms and broke from the choke hold. She gasped and coughed. When she caught her breath, Marty jabbed Irene in the throat. Irene made a wheeze-gasp sound and fell to her hands and knees. Marty grabbed a lamp and raised it in the air.

"No!" cried Lance. He snatched an iron skillet from the stovetop and whacked Marty in the back of her head.

Marty crumbled to the floor. The lamp tumbled down beside her.

Lance stood above her body, heaving in breaths as his lips curled strangely. Marty didn't move. Irene, sitting on the floor, stared up at her son.

"What did you do?"

He shook his head. "She was hurting you….I just wanted it to stop. I didn't mean to hurt her."

Irene reached over to Marty and checked for a pulse.

She looked up at her son. Her lips trembled as she spoke.

"She's dead."

CHAPTER TWENTY-ONE

"My God, Trey, you were there? You saw Marty get killed? How could you live with a secret like that?"

"There wasn't anything I could do! It all just happened." He ran his hand over his face. Was he reliving it, watching Marty die all over again in his head? How many times had those scenes haunted him over the years?

"They huddled together for a few minutes," Trey continued, "then Irene said something about getting rid of the body. They argued, because the boy didn't want to. Irene convinced him it was best. They started dragging Marty's body toward the garage door but got interrupted."

"Craig showed up?"

Trey nodded. "Good thing it was dark out that night, otherwise, he would've seen me. He walked right by me and in through the back door. But he was drunk. He called out for Marty, said he wanted to talk. The way he came stumbling in and as loud as he was, I thought he'd wake the neighborhood. People were probably used to those two arguing. But he must've gone back to the bedroom, probably thinking Marty was in there with someone. That gave Irene and her son just enough time to get out through the garage. They had to step over Marty and they took the skillet with them. I almost lost it, thinking they were going to come around the back and find me, but they didn't. When Marty's husband came out of the bedroom, it took him a few minutes but he found her by the door.z He stumbled back and fell in the living room, then crawled around till he got to the phone and called for help. By then, I knew I had to get out of there."

"How'd you get home?" I asked.

"I ran down to that grocery store. It was closed, but there was a payphone outside. I called Brian. He came and got me. I stayed the rest of the night at his place, that way I could say I'd been there all night. I knew it was best not to tell him much, so I told him my night didn't go well and I needed a place to crash."

"And when the investigation started, why didn't you tell the police what you saw?"

"Because Mom wanted me to stay out of it."

"You told her?"

He nodded. "I wasn't going to, but you know how she is. She can detect when you're keeping something from her, and maybe I wasn't doing a good job of playing it cool around her. I laid it all out, and she never acted too surprised. I think she was disappointed Greaser wasn't involved, but she didn't want me saying a word."

I knew what he meant about Mom's ability to leech out the truth when her suspicions were on alert. She wouldn't let it go until she knew every detail. I can't imagine how let down she must've been, hearing that Greaser wasn't responsible for Marty's death. More importantly, I realized that Lance *was* responsible for dealing the fatal blow to Marty's head. He'd barely been a teenager. From what Trey described, it sounded like Lance was defending his mom and probably didn't intend to kill Marty.

I needed time to think, to process. Instinct told me to call Suzette. Trey would have to talk to the police and give a thorough statement, but I wasn't sure if he'd be charged with a crime, especially since he'd been a minor at the time. And what would it mean for Mom?

My streaming thoughts were broken by the barbaric pounding on our front door. Trey and I dashed down the stairs. Maverick started barking from the backyard, which distracted me from snagging a peek out the bay window.

"Where is she?" shouted someone from the other side.

I don't know what possessed Trey to open the door. A sick curiosity? A brain lapse from those pain pills? Whatever the cause, he did.

And in barreled Craig Cox.

"I know it's you! Why are you doing this to me?" He came at me with a pointed finger.

"Craig, calm down! What are you talking about?" I'd held up my forearm as if to defend myself, but the truth was, if Craig went for me, full-on, there wouldn't be much I could do.

"The phone calls at night, telling me to turn myself in. Sending me notes at work, saying I hurt Marty! How dare you!" He shook as he spat out the words. Then, he staggered, as if his coordination suddenly failed.

His wavering steps and sloppy speech told me he was drunk.

"I just wanna be left alone, get my life back. I told everybody I never hurt Marty." His voice whimpered. Sobs came. "Not like that. I loved her."

I looked at Trey, who stood frozen. Did he recognize Craig? Whether Trey was paralyzed from memories or a dose of fear from Craig's entrance, I didn't know.

"Craig, I don't know what's going on, but I'm not the one taunting you."

He shook his head harder.

"It's gotta be you! All this started after you came around, after you were in my shop. The day after. And I didn't know who could do such a thing! But there were calls. Someone whispering about what I've done, about how my secret would get out, about Marty seeing someone else. I've worked hard being good."

He whimpered a moment, then sank into an armchair and dropped his head into his hands. Trey and I traded glances, both of us at a loss for what to do. Was there any hope of getting through to Craig in his current condition?

Craig snapped his head up.

"That day with the pancakes," he said, referring to our breakfast at Perkins, "you asked if I knew Marty was seeing someone else, someone new. So it had to be you. I didn't want it to be you. I thought...you were like me. Innocent." He gasped for breaths and seemed as though he might start crying again.

But no.

He rocketed out of the chair and straight for me, tackling me to the floor. I couldn't manage a scream, having the wind knocked out of me. He grabbed handfuls of my hair and banged my head on the carpet.

"You're not gonna do this to me! Not letting you ruin my life!"

Had he thumped me a little harder, I would've been out cold. Or worse. I brought my knee up and tried prying him off me. He didn't budge. Craig's weight made it hard to breathe. I wanted to explain everything and help him if I could. But Craig was beyond listening.

"Hey! Get off her!"

Suddenly, a whack sounded. I guessed Craig had been kicked in the side, but I had my eyes squinted shut. Several more hits landed on Craig. Grunts followed. Craig must have passed out, as his body went limp and heavy on top of me. I slid out from under him and rolled onto my side. Eyes still closed, my hands reached for my now-sore head and I worked to catch my breath.

"Kyle? Can you hear me?"

I expected to hear Trey, but it wasn't him.

"Derek?" I peeked between my fingers. He was looking down at me as if he was too afraid to touch me. I reached for him. On bended knees he held me, held me, and despite the ache it caused, I thought it was the greatest feeling of my life.

"What are you doing here?" I asked Derek after a few tears of relief and gratefulness.

"I came to talk to you and see if we could patch things up. It isn't really safe leaving you alone, is it?"

I laughed a little, paid for it with some pain.

Trey stood over Craig. "You walloped him."

"Do we need to call for an ambulance?" I asked.

"Oh, and how do we explain this?" Trey held out his arms. The chair Craig sprang from had toppled, along with a side table and knickknacks, but I knew what Trey really meant. How did we explain why a virtual stranger was unconscious in our living room? And after having a recent visit from the police, Trey and I were apprehensive about where things could go.

"I knocked him out, but I think he's okay," Derek said.

"Based on what?" Trey asked.

"I'm the youngest of four brothers, so speaking from experience."

"Right. Well, what are we going to do? Wait till he comes around then ring the bell for round two?"

"He seemed pretty drunk," I said. "He might be out for a while."

"Let's check his wallet," Derek said. "Maybe we can take him home."

"Are you crazy? You want to go to the guy's house?" Trey asked.

"Unless you've got a better idea," Derek replied.

The three of us waited, but no one came up with an alternative. I doubted Craig wanted the police involved, considering his past record and convictions. And no way I wanted to explain why the husband of my dad's murdered mistress had shown up to attack me.

Derek fished Craig's wallet out of his pants and found his address on his driver's license. He knew the city fairly well from having construction projects all over and had a good idea of where Craig lived. Plus, he kept a city map in his truck, which helped us find Craig's street. I figured the best plan of action was for Derek to drive Craig's car while I followed. Trey was fine with staying home and straightening up.

We agreed for now it was best not to tell Mom what had happened tonight in her living room.

Crazy as it seemed, our plan worked. We got Craig into his house, thanks to his house key being on his keychain. It was a good thing Derek was used to heavy lifting. He managed to flop Craig onto his bed without much problem. I left a note on Craig's kitchen table. There was no telling what he'd remember about tonight, but I apologized for what he'd been through and said I'd like to talk to him when his head was clear. Maybe I could've included a sentence about how we made sure he got home safe and that I still had nothing to do with the harassment he'd endured, but it didn't seem fitting for a simple note.

After that, Derek and I scurried out of there.

Riding back to my house in his truck, with his hand in mine, I felt like my heart was getting nourishment. It scared me though. Break-ups, even temporary ones, were brutal.

"I'm glad you were there tonight." It sounded pitiful, like Baby carrying a watermelon in *Dirty Dancing*, but it was true.

"Me too." He kissed the back of my hand. "And I'm sorry about everything. I don't know what got into me. Except that seeing you with that guy, I don't know, it just made me crazy-mad."

"It's okay." That sounded even worse. Truthfully, it wasn't okay, and I'd be a fool to make this easy on him. "I mean, it's not okay-okay, just that I understand why you got mad. But I never thought you could shut me out like that, not even care or listen to what I had to say."

He was quiet a moment. "Yeah. I played your messages over and over and kept reading your letter. I knew you weren't lying to me, and I didn't think for a second that you wanted to be with that guy or that you had a thing for him. But it was like I couldn't stop myself from being mad. Just seeing him there, I don't know, it set me off, and I didn't know what to do."

"You let a misunderstanding and your jealousy come between us." The words came gently but delivered a punch. If I hadn't made the effort—hadn't called and cried to his answering machine, explaining the whole mess—would Derek have come to me for the truth otherwise? Or would he have accepted the faulty perception of events and thrown our relationship away? "Was it worth it?"

More quiet. I don't know what I wanted him to say. Maybe I hoped he'd realize that he'd almost lost me to a foolish slice of his pride. He might not have agreed or seen it that way. I promised myself I wouldn't go through that again, that I wouldn't shackle myself with unnecessary blame and worry. If a relationship was the wrong fit, I'd have to let go. At least I'd learned something from Trey and Shelia.

"Proves I'm not perfect," he said.

"It proves neither of us are."

At that moment, I'd never loved his smile more.

Mom wasn't home when we got back, which seemed odd but at the same time gave me a sense of relief. Trey, Derek, and I piled in the rec room and rehashed the evening. Trey made no mention or excuse for why he didn't jump in and save me from Craig. Maybe the outbreak of violence paralyzed him. Those years of verbal abuse and taunts from our dad had left their mark—and rendered Trey helpless in Shelia's wrath. That's was my unprofessional guess anyway. Who knew what would've happened if Derek hadn't been there.

Maverick plopped in my lap and took turns sniffing me and kissing my chin. He knew I'd had a bad night and how to make it better. I glanced at Derek, knowing how he didn't care for dog licks, but he simply reached over and patted Maverick on the head.

Trey and I didn't bring up his confession about witnessing Marty's murder. I figured it'd be best to tell Derek later, when we were alone, but I wanted a chance to go through and sort the particulars. For that, I knew I needed Suzette.

"So what happened to you?" Derek asked Trey.

Trey shot me a glance, probably having forgotten how battered he looked. He responded with a half-grin. I gave him a slight nod, indicating that he should be the one to tell Derek what had happened with Sheila. Trey responded with his own nod and began the tale. That—that little step of progress—made me wonder if the walls between me and Trey could come down, bit by bit.

While the guys did their thing, I called Suzette at home. I told her I didn't have time to comb through every detail but I'd found out who killed Marty. She surprised me with a mixed reaction of sound effects and silence, even when I told her it was Lance.

"Get to the office as early as you can tomorrow," she said, "because I've got some news for you, babe."

"Really? What?"

"Mm-hm. You've been holding out on me a little, so now it's my turn, missy, but trust me, it'll be worth the wait."

When Mom got home, we didn't ask too many questions about where she'd been. It really wasn't like her to be secretive or out late, but since we still didn't want to tell her about Craig stopping by we thought not pressing her would serve as some sort of tacit courtesy.

The only wrinkle was Derek. He wanted to spend the night. Mom's sense of propriety ruffled, since she didn't allow a boyfriend to stay over, but Trey acted like his pain was flaring up, and maybe it'd be best if he and Derek slept in the rec room, that way Derek could look after him. Mom was no dummy. She knew something was up but must have sensed no one was willing to talk. Not tonight. But I couldn't help being even more suspicious about what she'd been up to when she didn't protest the arrangement.

I liked that Derek didn't want to leave me, and that he was willing to spend the night on the couch in my mother's basement just to be near me. It also gave me a soothing feeling, knowing he was there, in case Craig made another appearance. Right now, I didn't want to think too hard on our relationship. Were we over a hump with a lesson learned or did we need to realize we weren't going to make it as a couple? No firm answer came to me. Not tonight.

CHAPTER TWENTY-TWO

In the morning, it was a race for each of us to see who could get out the door the fastest. Except for Derek. I think he was hoping for time alone with me, but with Mom's radar alert after her first cup of coffee, I had a feeling she wasn't leaving until Derek left. Luckily, Derek picked up on this and left when I did, which was good. It meant I didn't get trapped with Mom and a stream of questions I didn't want to answer.

I wished I could've talked to Trey but there wasn't time.

At the office, Suzette was already there with piping hot coffee and donuts. And a satisfied-looking Vinny.

"Okay," I said, not sure if I should start with questions about them or questions about the big news. "I take it you two have been working together on something?"

"Vinny has been checking out Irene," Suzette said. "Come to find out, our girl is sick."

"Uterine cancer," Vinny added, as though he had to toss in a bit of info.

I let that sink in. "She's dying?"

"Don't know," Vinny said.

"She's finishing chemo," Suzette said. "Probably has to undergo a round of tests to see where she stands. But remember that whacky hair of hers?"

I nodded.

"I'm thinking it's a wig. Bet she's lost her hair."

"Wow. She doesn't really look sick." But as I thought about it, maybe that explained her skinny arms and the bruising I'd noticed.

"Maybe that's good," Vinny said, "means she's gonna beat it."

"Yeah, hopefully."

"But this could explain why she's set on having Craig arrested," Suzette said. "She wants Craig taking the blame instead of her son. If she's dying, she wants to tie up loose ends, and she doesn't want Lance in prison. Craig gets arrested, case is finally closed. That's my theory anyway."

Silence beat. I wondered if Suzette was right. After twelve years, had Irene and Lance poked this hornet's nest in a crazy attempt to get Craig charged and sent up the river? No doubt, they hadn't counted on Marty's boyfriend poking a gaping hole in their plan. Just like I hadn't counted on said-boyfriend being my brother.

"All right, missy, now it's your turn, you bozo." Suzette folded her arms, gave me the stink eye.

"Uh, excuse me?"

"You heard me, skinny britches. Sit yourself down and spill it. I want to hear every bit and grit about how you found out Lance Turner killed Marty Cox."

"First, I need to ask a favor." With a bit of hesitation, I looked to Vinny.

"From me? Ah, well, Vinny A. Fox at your service."

Indebting myself to Vinny teetered between gross and desperate, and while Suzette enjoyed a mild chuckle at my expense, I hoped I wouldn't regret it.

Before I dove into Trey's confession, I preambled with Craig Cox's intrusion at my house last night. Suzette wanted to make a fuss and file a report and skin the guy alive. Her reaction was touching, but I talked her down. Then I shared how Derek and I ended up taking Craig home and essentially tucking him in bed, which led to the most flabbergasted expression I'd ever seen on Suzette's face.

Relaying Trey's story wasn't as easy as I'd thought it would be. Suzette and Vinny hung on every word and asked minimal questions. It was still disturbing that my brother was making moves on my dad's lover. Finally knowing what had happened to Marty brought a degree of relief and cemented the fact that my family was even more messed up than I'd known. We still had to look at each other and do holidays and Sunday dinners together somehow.

"So let me see if I got this," Suzette said. "Trey, who was outside, saw Irene attack Marty. The quarrel escalated, then Lance hit Marty in the back of the head, killing her?"

"Yes, in a nutshell."

"All this time, and your brother said nothing about it?"

"My mom told him to keep quiet."

"And even let herself look guilty, probably for the sake of protecting him."

I hadn't considered it, but Suzette could've been on to something. Was the falsified timecard a means of distracting Detective Buchanan? I wondered if she'd planned on lying and telling Buchanan that *she'd* witnessed the whole thing. Not Trey. Almost like a Get Out of Jail Free Card, if Buchanan put too much heat on her.

"It's a wild story." Vinny shook his head, finished his third donut.

"You know Trey's going to have to talk to CPD," Suzette said to me.

"He knows that."

"And what about your mom, she's okay with that now?"

I waited a beat. "I don't know. We didn't get into it last night. My mom doesn't know that Trey told me everything. Not yet."

Suzette threw her hands in the air in disbelief. I could tell she had a dozen things to say, but they jumbled together and nothing but groans came out.

What would it do to Mom, bringing Marty's case to a close? Could it hurt Mom's career? Had I been stupid to push this so far? She'd never forgive me if her life came crashing down—again—because of Marty.

"Well, we have to take action, Kyle." Suzette slapped her hands against her hips. "We can't just sit on this. I think you know what you're going to have to do."

Suzette was right that our next step depended on me. Maybe not so much on me as it did Trey. I had to convince Trey to tell his story to the CPD and to Franklin County prosecutors. They'd decide how they'd want to handle it, and I wasn't sure if an arrest could be made on age-old eyewitness testimony alone. However, Trey's story confirmed the weapon used to strike Marty, explained the marks on Marty's neck, and why her body was lying in the nook area that led to the garage. His fingerprints on the side door to the garage would also prove he was there.

Suzette told me to find him and talk to him.

I left work and went to his office, without calling. Again. This wasn't the ideal set up for a heart-to-heart with my brother on why he needed to meet with the police and discuss the murder he'd witnessed a dozen years ago, but I was willing to chance it.

At Trey's office, though, they told me he'd called in and taken the day off.

That was odd. He'd been the first one to leave the house that morning.

But I had a good idea where I could find him.

That old adage that some things never change proved true when I walked into Brian's loft and found my brother. Slumped in a faded blue bean bag, with an empty pizza box, cans of Pepsi, and a stack of videos from Blockbuster at his side told me he'd made a day of it. *Blue Velvet*, one of his favorite movies, played from the TV.

"This is how you deal with your problems?" I said.

He didn't respond.

"Where's Brian?" I turned off the TV.

"Work."

I squatted down beside him. "You have to go to the police and tell them everything."

Trey folded his arms across his chest. "I need time."

"You've had twelve years."

"You think you're so much smarter than everyone else."

"No, I just know what's going to happen. If you don't go to them, they'll come to you. It's time to quit hiding the truth."

"You don't care about hurting Mom."

That remark landed in my chest like a fistful of poisoned arrows. Of course I cared! He was the one who could've settled Marty's case years ago. By not telling the police, he'd only made it harder on himself.

I thought we'd made progress last night, surviving Craig's wrath and not telling Mom. One of those moments that would live in our sibling history, become an only-between-us secret, like driving by our dad's place. But now it felt as though whatever cracks and breeches we'd made in the walls between us were suddenly repaired and made thicker than before.

I stared at him, waited for common sense to dawn on him, but he didn't budge.

"Do what you want." I stood. "You always do."

There was a hopelessly-sick part of me that believed, or wanted to believe, that one day, Trey and I would get our act together and turn out like the siblings on the *Brady Bunch*. Like we deserved a partial happily ever after, of sorts, for what we'd survived. But maybe I had to accept that the universe didn't work that way, that at best, we'd be like the kids on *Roseanne*.

After leaving Brian's loft, I was glad for the walk home. It was only a distance of nine houses and saved me the minor hassle of parking on the street and announcing my presence. The warmth of the afternoon sun was revitalizing.

I figured I'd have the house to myself and a chance to mull over my next step, but to my surprise, Mom and Frank were having lunch on the patio. Astonishment gripped me for a moment, because I couldn't remember the last time Mom had done something as carefree as enjoying lunch outside in the middle of the afternoon on a work day. She'd become a pro at maintaining that laser focus on work and survival, and when the work was done, she switched her attention to more work, like plans for remodeling the kitchen.

When I glimpsed the exchange of smiles between her and Frank, a dozen sensations hit me like a geyser. Never had I seen my mom look at someone with such adoration. Sure, she'd perfected her pleased smile around Roger, but this was different. True, uninhibited. Watching them now, I knew for certain that this relationship had been on-going, cultivated for a while. Mom wasn't flirty or the type to fall for someone easily. She'd loved Frank for a long time.

Maybe that explained those hours of her missing. I had to give Mom credit. When it came to being secretive and crafty, she had an impressive skill set. Interesting how I kept rediscovering that fact.

Mom and Frank weren't surprised to see me walk up the driveway, didn't even ask where I'd been. Maybe because my car was parked in the opened garage. Maverick, with his tongue lolling and eyes wide, had apparently found a new pal in Frank. His tail thrashed with every word or rub Frank gave him. Mom invited me to join them but I said I needed to get back to the office. No way I could sit there eating fruit salad while I knew Mom and Trey were on the verge of being called in to the prosecutor's office or to meet with detectives at CPD.

And what would Frank think, hearing that we were eyeball-deep in bringing closure to Marty's case? I also felt a pinch of guilt for having suspected him.

Playing the third wheel with Mom and Frank felt like an intrusion. I headed back to the office and shared my lackluster results with Suzette. At least Vinny wasn't still there, making the misery worse.

"Maybe it's okay for now," Suzette said. "The day's winding down. I left a message for Warren, and I haven't talked to Buchanan yet. But instead of waiting around, we can cover our bases. Tie up loose ends."

"Okay...meaning what exactly?"

"We drop in on your friend, see how he's doing."

My stomach knotted, because a big part of me was apprehensive about showing up at Craig's place with a lawyer who'd been ready to thump him a few hours earlier.

CHAPTER TWENTY-THREE

Although Suzette promised—promised—that she wouldn't go off on Craig for last night's outburst at my house, I didn't know if she'd hold to it. I reminded her that what we had to tell him would change his life. In response she gave a curt nod.

We called the body shop and were told Craig called in sick. That made sense, considering Derek and I had driven him home and delivered him, unconscious, to his bed the night before. My guess was that he'd had a difficult morning. A hangover coupled with a fog of how the night's final moments had played out. I also wondered what he thought about the note we'd left him.

Suzette figured it was best for us to just show up on his doorstep since I knew where he lived. That move made me nervous and hadn't proven to be the best approach. I worried Craig might be fuming still, or that he might be working on getting drunk again. Last night proved—harshly—that I didn't know the guy.

A couple knocks on his front door and Craig appeared. Not surprisingly, he seemed unsure about how to greet us.

"Craig," I said, after introducing Suzette, "we wanted to check on you, after last night, and we have some news for you about Marty's case."

He invited us in, though it was awkward for all three of us.

I did a subtle, precursory glance of Craig's place, checking for weapons. Nothing alarming was around. Strange how my perception of the man had changed. I guess being lunged to the floor did that to a person.

"I'm glad you're here," Craig said. "I wasn't sure how to get in touch with you, and I didn't want to show up at your house again." He hesitated, probably considering how much he should say. "And I wanted to deeply apologize for my behavior. You might have a hard time believing this, but I never meant to hurt you. That wasn't my intention when I got to your place, but I got upset and then it all just got away from me."

Actually, I believed him. Craig could've crushed my neck in seconds, so deep down, maybe he only meant to scare me. His present tone, his mannerisms, ripe with an awkward tenderness, that was the Craig I'd quickly and briefly come to know. I took in a deep, smooth breath, and it felt good. Even so, I kept my nervous hands wadded behind my back.

"I haven't had a drink in years," Craig continued, "Turns me into everything I don't like about myself, and I can't seem to control what happens. I promise you it won't happen again."

If I were one for gambling, I'd bet he'd said that a thousand times to Marty. Probably to his former girlfriend, too—the one he'd beaten and gone to jail for. I guess there was always hope that a person could overcome their demons. Just as there was always a chance of a slip up.

"Thank you," I said. "I appreciate that."

"And thank you for what you did for me, getting me home." His cheeks flared red.

I felt my own cheeks heat up in return.

"I don't mean to sound insensitive, Mr. Cox," Suzette put in after a beat of silence, "but were you drinking on the night you found your wife?"

I appreciated her moving the conversation forward.

"Yeah," he said. "We were having a lot of problems back then. I drank a lot in those days. Took me longer to get my life straightened up than I like to admit. But yeah, I'd had quite a few beers that night. I was miserable, because she was talking about getting divorced. She'd been having an affair..."

Again, he seemed to hesitate because he wasn't sure how much to share with Suzette.

"It's okay," I said. "Suzette knows everything, including my dad's affair with Marty."

Craig nodded but that didn't appear to make his admission easier. He shifted and stuffed his hands into his pants pockets.

"Right. Well, Marty and I weren't living together at the time. I was staying with her sister. She couldn't keep me from tying one on though and losing my temper. I remember earlier that week she'd been talking about Marty seeing someone new and how she didn't like it, because he was a young fella. Knowing that didn't help my temper. I got drunk, went over to Marty's, determined to shout some sense into her, I guess. Only, I found her lying on the floor. I had that sick feeling in my gut when I saw her. I knew she was dead."

"And you didn't have a clue what had happened to her?" Suzette asked.

"No. She was by the door to the garage, not breathing."

"Craig, before we go any further, I need to ask you, what kind of support system do you have in place? Is there someone you'd like to call or talk to about your drinking?"

He snickered. "I've got my parole officer and a couple friends from the body shop."

"I'm only asking because it might not be a good idea for you to be alone. I know going back in the past can be hard for a person, and I know you don't want to start drinking again."

Few people surprised me the way Suzette did. A while ago I was concerned she might create a scene, but now, I knew her humanity had taken over. She recognized that even though Craig would be cleared of any suspicion or involvement in Marty's death, finally, that he was still susceptible to self-destructive behaviors. Despite the fact that Craig was a worse drunk than my own father, and putting aside his actions from last night, I still believed he was a good guy.

"You're right about that," Craig said, "and maybe I do need to talk to someone. Be more accountable."

We went on to share that we'd found Marty's mystery man but didn't reveal that it was my brother. No need to give Craig another reason to come breaking my door down if he ended up in another drunken stupor. Trey's identity would eventually become public knowledge, but for today we kept it to ourselves.

Suzette also explained that mystery man had witnessed everything, and that Lance was responsible for Marty's death.

The grimness of the reality crawled over Craig's face. His features furrowed and no doubt his thoughts plunged down that rabbit hole of grief and despair.

"No! It couldn't be Lance. He was always a good kid, never in trouble." Craig struggled with the news. He shook his head in disbelief and recounted stories about Lance and Marty, how Marty loved him like her own and he loved her.

Remembering how Marty had treated me, I could see that. Maybe she'd ached for children of her own and projected that need onto Lance. It only made the facts of the case more painful.

"What's going to happen to him?" Craig managed after a few minutes.

"We don't know yet," Suzette said. "There's a lot of factors to be considered, but the DA will decide what charges will be brought."

"And Irene?"

"She might also be charged. Again, we'll see what the DA has to say."

"You do know that Irene's been trying to convince the police that you were the one who hurt Marty, right?" I asked.

Craig nodded. "Irene's always been hot and cold toward me."

"Did you know she's been sick, fighting cancer?"

More nodding. "She told me, but I haven't seen her or talked to her in a while."

"Last night, when you came to my house, you mentioned that someone had been harassing you with calls. You said it had started right after I first saw you at the body shop. Do you think it could've been Irene, trying to push your buttons and get you to do something stupid?"

He dropped his face into his hands and seemed to smear the idea into his head.

"I don't know. I probably didn't think it through. Anything's possible with Irene, and I should know that better than anyone."

"There's no sense beating yourself up over it." Suzette paused a moment, no doubt regretting her word choice. "The only way to find out for sure is to check the phone records. But I think Kyle is right, someone wanted you upset and acting out. Even getting arrested again. Makes Irene's claim that you're guilty look valid, at least to her."

"Irene's not a bad person," Craig said, "She's had it rough, being a mom all by herself to those kids. Luck and favors haven't visited her much."

Craig reminded me of my dad, in not taking any blame on himself. He probably could've pitched in, helped with the bills and kids, since they were family. I bit the inside of my cheek as the thought penetrated.

On the other hand, Craig didn't dwell on Irene's shortcomings or rage with bitterness that those two had killed his wife.

We stayed a while longer, talking about the case and what might happen next. That look of despondency never left Craig. Suzette advised him not to call or see Lance and Irene for now, saying it was best to let the authorities handle the situation. Craig nodded in agreement.

Suzette promised to make some calls when we got back to the office and help set Craig up with counseling and guidance. Craig was appreciative and said he didn't want to lose his job. Before we left, we shook hands. He clasped my hand in both of his.

"I really can't thank you enough for what you've done. Not just last night and not calling the police but also for finding out about Marty. It means everything knowing the truth after all these years."

"You're welcome, Craig. I hope you can find some peace."

He was right. An exhausted relief had come, finding out the truth. But it wasn't over and done. A new anxiousness festered inside me as I wondered if Mom and Trey were positioned to lose pieces of their lives, all because of that truth.

Back at the office, Suzette and I spent the rest of the afternoon on the phone. Not only did she find resources for Craig, but we heard from Detective Buchanan, a rep from CPD, and the DA's office. It was really going to happen. Marty's case would come to a close and my family would have to spill their secrets to make it right.

The DA wanted to review the case and all evidence. He set up a meeting for next week and was clear that Suzette and I were to be there. He planned to notify my mom and Trey as well. Of course, I was free to pass that info on, but I wasn't anxious to bear the news.

After a numbing day, I headed home, only then realizing I hadn't eaten since having pancakes with Craig, four days ago. I felt it, too. My insides cramped as though they'd been scraped out. Usually, that gave me a twisted sense of self-depriving victory and made me feel strong. Not today. Today it felt empty and hollow. Barren. I wondered if I'd been lying to myself, that controlling my waist size and those three numbers on a scale didn't mean anything. It gave me no super power, nothing to show for it. Wasn't that my dirty little secret? That being successful at starvation impressed no one, because it wasn't an accomplishment I could boast about.

Tears surfaced. The avalanche of what was to come overtook me, and I knew I had to get this out of my system before I talked to my mom. Crying wasn't welcome. I wasn't sure 'sorry' would be either.

At home, the first thing I noticed, besides Mom rinsing off dishes, was the Possum Holler Pizza box sitting on the stove. Although it was a local favorite, it also had a reputation for poor service and hit-or-miss quality. Hungry as I was, I'd pass on finding out which element was suffering tonight. Noise from the rec room told me Trey was down there, probably sitting in the floor with his share of the pizza, watching TV, and tossing Maverick pizza crusts.

"You look beat." Mom finished wiping down the sink before handing me a plate. "Trey brought home dinner."

"We need to talk." I set the plate aside and slipped into a chair at the table.

"Trey told me."

My mouth fell open.

"How much did he tell you?"

She shrugged a shoulder. "He said he'd filled you in about that night."

It didn't surprise me she didn't say Marty's name.

"You know the police are going to want to talk to you both, right? Next week, actually. It's all been set, and the summons are probably on their way. You up for all that?"

"Don't have much choice." She placed her hands on the edge of the sink and took in the view outside the window.

"I didn't know it would turn out like this." In a strange way, this was my attempt at a veiled apology, not only for letting myself get taken on a ride by my curiosities but also for opening that can of worms known as my dad. I knew that hurt Mom.

"Life in the city, I guess."

That phrase again, and I wasn't any closer to understanding what she meant by it.

She joined me at the table, looked me straight in the eye. "You've seen him and talked to him, haven't you?"

My breath caught and I couldn't respond.

By now, with everything that had happened, I suppose it wasn't a big stretch of the imagination that I'd seen my dad. Still, there are things in life you never want to admit to your mom. I bit my lower lip and nodded.

"Guess I can understand," Mom said. "He's your father, no matter what's happened. Maybe it's natural to be curious about him, where he's been. But as far as I'm concerned, he doesn't exist. You might want to think long and hard before you start spending any time with him, treating him like he's done you any favors, because you might not want to listen, but I'll warn you anyway: you can't count on him. Never. Not for anything. I don't care what he's told you, either. If it's anything about me, you can set it on the pile and light it on fire."

I understood her need to be defensive. She'd admitted to crafting a plan to take the guy out, but she didn't have to justify her reasons to me. I'd been there, living the turmoil with her. Plus, I still wasn't convinced she could've seen that plot all the way through. Maybe the time with Frank, the reassurances that he was looking out for her were all she'd genuinely needed.

"It's okay, Mom, I know." Would that defuse her? "I never had any fantasy that he'd changed. I know bringing back all those memories must be hard on you. I'm sorry."

Tension left her as her shoulders relaxed. I was glad I could put her at ease, but I had to dip into forbidden territory.

"But what about those envelopes?" I was referring to the three I'd found in her keepsake box. "The empty ones addressed to me, they were from him, weren't they?"

Mom set her jaw, cast her glare away from me.

"You might want to remember who put a roof over your head, made sure you never went without, whether it was braces or trips or college, I've been there putting in the labor, laying down my life and ever' dollar I made."

Braces, the school trip to Washington, D.C. Both had been mentioned in Vinny's file.

"What did he send me?" I deserved to know, didn't I? Why was she making this a contest or acting like I had to choose between them?

She swallowed, pressed her lips together.

"He sent a hundred dollar bill for three months. That was it. No letters. Nothing on your birthday or graduation. That's all you were worth to him. Never called and checked on you. Just mailed three hundred dollars."

Hearing the truth was as awful as it was liberating. I'd had my suspicions about the envelopes, and a certain vindication bloomed knowing I'd been right. Three hundred dollars went nowhere in the course of raising a child, but it was more than I'd given him credit for.

Her harshness came as no surprise. She didn't want me feeling sorry for him or romanticizing his meager token. He'd walked away, left us both to fend on our own. It only took three hundred dollars to soothe his conscience.

But what would she think if she'd seen him sitting on that bar stool, looking worn and hopeless? Would her compassion have moved?

I stood and embraced my mom. It wasn't a norm for us, but neither was this river of emotion. As I held her, I felt Mom tremble. Whether it was because she was on the brink of crying or because her anger had reached its limit—or because she feared losing me to Greaser—I didn't know.

Mom went to bed early, which she never does. She didn't even watch the news.

I followed her lead, thinking it was best to get this day behind me as fast as I could. Not that I expected much sleep. Still, there was an odd comfort, laying alone in the dark.

Trey came into my room without knocking. Something he'd done maybe twice before. He sat on the floor with his back against the side of my bed. Instead of asking if I was awake, he went on assumption.

"I heard you and Mom earlier," he said. "Can't believe she didn't go off on you. She was kinda upset when I told her I'd come clean about everything."

"Everything?" As in, Did you tell her about Craig stopping by?

"Not *everything*, just that night at Marty's."

"If she had it her way the truth never would've come out."

"Did you have to tell Suzette and get the DA involved?" he asked.

"It's the right thing to do."

"But it won't change what happened."

"No." Finding out Lance had been responsible made me feel cheated in a peculiar way. I hadn't pulled a Sherlock Holmes and figured out that it was Greaser or my mom who'd gotten away with murder. It was a teenage boy who'd reacted to an altercation between his mom and aunt—and he'd accidentally killed a person he loved.

"Why'd you do it, Trey? Why tell me all this now?"

He was quiet a moment. Then, "I wanted out from under it. Back when it happened, Mom didn't want me telling the police what I saw because she thought I could get in trouble somehow. I went along, thinking she might be right. But then it felt like she had this power over me because we had this big secret. You know how Mom likes being in control. Not sure what's going to happen with the DA, but I'm not too worried for Mom. She seems to come out of these things okay. She gave up playing the victim long ago."

I knew what he meant. Mom knew how to work her charms and how to manipulate when it suited her.

"So how was it, seeing him?" Trey asked.

Inwardly, I smiled to myself. Despite the painful events of growing up, Trey, like me, couldn't let go of wondering about Greaser. Curiosity had its grip on us like an ever-tightening tourniquet, because nothing good, nothing healthy could come from our need to see him.

"Weird. Strange. Tense. Uncomfortable."

"Yeah," Trey said, "it was the same way for me."

"You saw him?" I rolled onto my side.

"Years ago. Met him at a bar in Circleville and bought him a beer."

"Oh. How'd it go?" A stupid question, but how could Trey drop that on me like it was a normal thing?

"Wasn't anything special. We didn't exactly leave friends. I just wanted to face him, say some things to him."

I pictured it in my mind. Trey showing my dad he'd turned out all right. Buying them beers as if they were pals; Trey's way of taking the high road, proving he was a better man than my dad. The closest Trey would come to forgiving Gerald Reed.

Maybe it explained why we hadn't shared a drive-by to our dad's place. Trey had found a way to make peace with the situation, and he didn't need to cruise by that aging duplex anymore.

"He didn't leave, Kyle."

"What are you talking about?" I perked up, lifted my head.

"Mom threw him out. She couldn't take it, the way he carried on with Marty. It was humiliating. After he got laid off from Buckeye Steel, all he cared about was Marty while Mom worked double shifts at the Western Pancake House. She told him to get his stuff and leave. And if he ever came back, she'd kill him."

"Is that what he told you?"

"No. They were in the garage. He'd just pulled in from being out all night. I don't know if he was with Marty or just didn't bother coming home. By that time he was about done with Marty. She was putting too much pressure on him, and he knew she was seeing someone else. Mom didn't know or care about any of that. She confronted him, right when he got out of the car. I was sitting out back behind the garage, skipping school. I heard them through the window. He packed up what she'd let him take and he was gone."

Trey's knack for being invisible had paid off again.

"But all this time, why would Mom say he left? Why wouldn't she brag about throwing him out?"

"Because you were the one who loved Greaser. And this whole time, with everything revolving around Marty, she's been afraid you'd find out the truth and hate her for it."

I couldn't confront Mom about her decision to make Greaser leave. From what Trey said, I knew he was telling the truth. Mom had admitted that she and Frank were on the verge of taking Greaser out, so maybe giving him an ultimatum had been the alternative. And it made more sense why she feared he'd come back to exact revenge—and take the house for himself. Those were her decisions and I couldn't hold those against her. Once upon a time I'd loved my dad just the way he was, because that's all I knew. Unconditional love is probably natural for most kids. It takes bad experiences and injustices to wreck it and teach otherwise.

I didn't ask but I wondered if Trey had been upset with Mom. Why did it take Greaser having an affair for Mom to reach her limit? Why wasn't she outraged by the way Greaser treated and embarrassed Trey? Maybe I was wrong and the affair and Greaser's unemployment were the final insults she needed to get her life on track.

I woke before my alarm on Wednesday and darted for the office early. Tension fueled me rather than food. I felt like every time I looked at Trey and Mom they were becoming more distant strangers to me. Relying on automatic responses and treating them with kid-gloves was tiresome and surreal. And I got the feeling Mom was upset with Trey, so there was no point lingering, waiting to see if she gave him the silent treatment or her grumbling tirade about how no one appreciated her. The office felt like a safe refuge.

Once I was there, I found a handwritten note on my desk from Suzette:

Vinny came through on that favor, Babe. 1544 Lockbourne Road
Don't go alone!!!

Knowing the area's reputation, I took Suzette's advice.

When she got in an hour later, I practically turned her around and ushered her out the door. She went along, not quite as anxious as me to get there.

"Babe, you don't even know if the guy's gonna be there," she said.

"Actually, I already called. Some guy told me his shift ended at eleven this morning. Guess he worked all night."

"You talked to him?"

"No. Just said I had a delivery for him and needed to know how long he'd be there."

Suzette looked at me sideways. "And some co-worker said he was in?"

"Basically."

Her crinkled expression told me she was dubious. "I'm not convinced we should be doing this. Remember our advice yesterday?"

She meant Craig. "I know, and maybe that's why I want to do this."

Suzette gave a flimsy okay and we rode in silence until we pulled into the lot.

"I think I should go in alone," I told Suzette.

"You're not serious. Have you looked around?"

The 7-Eleven looked as if it was situated in the middle of a prison yard rather than an economically challenged neighborhood south of downtown. It made Irene's place look tranquil and desirable. Two distinct groups of men clustered in the area. Some smoked and others tossed their fruit pie wrappers onto the parking lot while lounging on top of a beige Monte Carlo. Others sat atop a splintered picnic table with chipped sky-blue paint. They smiled and eyed us like hungry predators who knew how to be patient.

"I won't be long. Just sit tight." I got out before she could say more and I changed my mind. Maybe it didn't make sense, but I had to face Lance. I'd been furious, discovering his lies, but now I pitied him knowing the DA would bring charges against him for killing Marty. If he got too upset, couldn't temper his reaction, then I'd duck out.

His eyes went wide and his face blanched when he saw me walk in. I stood in line, two people deep, and waited to make my way up to him at the counter.

"What are you doing here?" he asked, once it was my turn.

"I wanted to talk to you." Immediately I regretted being there. Not only were the stares from other customers intimidating, I got concerned that leaving Suzette outside had been a bad idea.

Lance and Rufus, according to his nametag, were the only ones working the front of the store. Several other people, who weren't in line for gas or lottery tickets, drifted around inside. Some were chatting with Rufus. All took turns staring and checking me out.

"So you just show up like it's nothing?" Lance said, a bitter tang in his tone.

"Look, I know what happened at Marty's that night—and I know it was an accident."

Lance met my stare and seemed to be judging me for truthfulness. The irony!

"I came here because maybe I can help—"

"Hey, Ru," Lance said to Rufus, "mind if I take a few?" He pointed to the back of the store.

Taller than Lance and with muscles piled onto muscles, Rufus had an imposing presence. Probably came in handy if the customers got out of line. Rufus looked to me, then back to Lance. A devious smile appeared. "Do what you gotta do, man."

I didn't like the implication in Rufus' words. I wasn't Lance's girl, here for a spat or money for smokes. Not that I could explain that to Rufus.

Lance bent down behind the counter a moment, then popped back up. I noticed that Rufus' smile dropped. Lance came around the counter and led me toward the EMPLOYEES ONLY-marked doors with his hand at my back.

"Hey, now—" Rufus said.

"It's cool, Ru," Lance replied with a slight wave. On the other side of the doors he took us to the break room. "Who do you think you are, showing up here and starting something?"

"That, coming from you? A guy who lied to me the minute he walked up my driveway. If anyone started this fiasco it's you. I only came here because I felt sorry for you."

"You're lying. There's no way you could know anything."

"You killed Marty with an iron skillet."

He shifted his weight nervously from side to side and blinked repeatedly, as if he were fighting off the memory.

"No, no. Where did you hear that?"

"It's a long story, but once the DA reviews the new evidence, he might bring charges against you—you and your mom."

"You're lying." A sheen of sweat coated his face. "Who told you this, Craig? Cause he's gotten away with it? All he's ever done is lie about the whole thing. That's all he does and all he knows. If anyone goes down for Marty it should be him."

"This crazy scam you and your mom cooked up isn't going to work, Lance. I know she's sick and—"

"No! You know nothing about it!" He shouted in my face then backed off. "That's your problem. You're one of those who thinks she knows everything, but you don't! Want me to enlighten you, college girl? How 'bout this—"

He reached under his shirt and pulled out a gun.

My pulse quickened. "Lance, whatever you're thinking, don't do it. This isn't the way to go."

"You think Craig's something special? He's playing some poor guy who lost his wife? No. He's not even a real man. My mom took good care of him." His voice started to falter. "She did everything for him but he skipped out. Never stepped it up."

My focus darted from Lance to the gun in his hand. A slight tremor had set in his hand. I'd never been around guns. Lance's agitation seemed to be ratcheting. Along with my nerves. What if he accidentally pulled the trigger?

"I don't care about Craig." Somehow I kept my voice steady, my hands open and defenseless. "I'm here for you, Lance. To help."

"You got cops out there?" He glanced over my shoulder. A useless, nervous move.

"No. I just want to talk. Marty's death was an accident. You were a minor at the time. I can help you out."

"It's too late for that." He cocked the gun and pointed it at me. "You want me cuffed and in jail. Craig's been putting lies in your ear, but I bet he left out a couple highlights. Bet he didn't tell you about how he used my mom—or that I'm his son!"

The tension, the gun barrel looking my way, I swear I couldn't breathe.

"What, he didn't mention that? Not even over pancakes that day?"

He had been following me. I felt like a deer trapped in the headlights. Stunned. Frozen. Scrambling in my brain for a way to stop the oncoming disaster.

"Craig never owned up to it," Lance said, "never took me in, or treated me as his own. Told my mom he couldn't know for sure that I was his. Said she got around too much like her sister. Never helped her out. He cared more about Marty finding out and losing her than he did about taking responsibility."

"I'm sorry, Lance." Tears burned my eyes, knowing my words were feeble, not good enough to pull him from the ledge.

"Don't you pity me and act like you're so much better than me. Here's what we're going to do." He grabbed my wrist. "You're coming with me for a little ride down to Kentucky. The DA and all your cop friends will have to back off, unless they want me to mess up that pretty face of yours." He pressed the side of the gun against my face. "You understand? 'Cause I'm not doing time."

My body tensed, pulled away from him best I could. "That's only going to make this worse, Lance. We'll talk with the DA, he'll take all the circumstances into consideration. It'll work out, Lance, but you have to face this."

"No!"

The door to the break room squeaked opened and Rufus walked in. Lance swiveled the gun toward him. Rufus held up his hands and froze.

"Whoa! What are you doing, Lance?" His posture stiffened.

"Don't make me do this, man!" Lance tightened his grip on me and shook his head. "You know I will!"

"Easy now." Rufus had his fingers spread wide.

"I'm about to get out of here. Give me the keys to your car, Ru. I promise you'll get it back."

Rufus shifted his glance from me to Lance. "This ain't no good, and I'll be a dead man 'fore I let you touch my car."

Lance let go of my wrist and snatched me around the waist. He started pulling me to a nearby exit. He put the gun to my temple. My legs started to give way but he hoisted me up.

"I'm not playing, Ru." Lance spoke through gritted teeth. "Get the keys, now!"

"Kyle!" Suzette yelled from the doorway, behind Rufus. A handful of faces filled in behind her.

Rufus turned slowly, as if he were about to leave the room, but I caught that glint in his eye. He pivoted and charged toward me and Lance like a linebacker. I tried screaming as Rufus tackled us, but only one sound came—the metallic click of the trigger.

CHAPTER TWENTY-FOUR

Whatever Suzette told the dispatcher in her 9-1-1 call, it sent the Columbus PD and the SWAT team to that south side 7-Eleven in droves. Within minutes most of the casual crowd fled the parking lot and the store.

The impact from Rufus sent the gun skidding across the floor. Being a good thirty pounds heavier than Lance—or more—Rufus laid on top of Lance like a bagged grizzly bear. I'd squirmed my way from under the pile. Lance kicked and thrashed until two officers plucked him up, cuffed him, and placed him in the back of a cruiser. Rufus and Suzette stuck to my side as paramedics checked me over, despite my claims that I was winded but fine.

Suzette, Rufus, and I sat atop the splintered picnic table outside. Two officers stood nearby. The fresh air helped clear my head.

Come to find out, Rufus Peoples, the store's manager, kept the gun behind the counter because the place was a favorite for armed robbers.

"But I ain't never kept no bullets in it," Rufus explained. "Most of the fools who show up are cowards anyhow. They run once I turn it around on them. It puts the word out not to mess with my place." He looked at me. "I always had a feeling about Lance. All he was good for was trouble. I saw him swipe the gun from behind the counter and knew there was gonna be problems."

"Thank you for saving me." Bullets or no, I knew when Lance grabbed me that he'd do anything for his freedom. Hearing that gun click against the side of my head, I thought I was dead. In the long seconds that followed, I realized the impact and flood of pain came from smashing into the floor. Nothing was broken. No ache or throb that a couple Tylenol couldn't soothe. When it dawned on me that I'd see my family again, that I'd learned a hard lesson about confronting someone guilty of a crime, my pain dissipated.

"You probably could'a handled yourself fine." Rufus patted my shoulder and winked at me as an officer called him over to give his statement.

"Well, that wasn't exactly what I had in mind," Suzette said when we were alone. "Way to inject a little Jerry Springer action into the day."

"Yeah, more than you know." I told her about Lance's admission—that he was Craig's son. "Maybe that explains why he and Irene were set on having Craig arrested for Marty's murder. They wanted to get back at him for rejecting his daddy duties."

"Something tells me Craig isn't fatherly material," Suzette said. "With two stints in jail, he wasn't able to provide financially for Lance, and he wasn't much of a role model when he was around, if beating up Marty and his girlfriend were any indications."

"Maybe Irene thought she could take Craig away from Marty." I shrugged and felt like I had Rice Krispies for brains. I pushed through the popping and crackling, trying to fit pieces together. "Craig and Marty never had kids. Maybe Irene got pregnant on purpose, thinking she'd have some kind of leverage on Craig. Maybe she was jealous or tired of Craig always going back to Marty. Having Craig's baby, she could steal him from Marty, but it backfired when he didn't want anything to do with fatherhood." I thought about the pictures Craig kept on his desk at the shop. Maybe that was his way of acknowledging Lance as his. It didn't make him a father, but maybe that was the best Craig could do.

Suzette stared at me a beat, then said, "You gotta lay off *Falcon Crest*, babe. But yeah, who knows." She sighed. "People are bizarre, and you know what, that's a good thing because it keeps gals like you and me employed."

"Kyle!"

Derek came running toward us.

"Your mom called me. She was watching the news and swore she saw you," he said. "I got here as fast I could. What's happening?"

Suzette and I took turns telling the story.

"Lance? That the same guy—"

"Yeah, him." Shame shot through me.

"He had a gun to her head and pulled the trigger!" Suzette added. "But thank God the gun wasn't loaded."

For a few seconds, Derek was paralyzed by the same fears and thoughts that I'd experienced—and he knew this moment could've ended a lot worse. A mash of emotions spiked within us. He slid his fingers along my cheek and drew my lips to his. It was the only thing I wanted.

"Now that's my kind of rescue," Suzette said.

After Suzette and I gave our statements and were cleared to leave, Derek offered to take me home. Suzette gave one of her Cheshire cat grins of approval.

At home, Trey, Mom, and Maverick were waiting. I can't remember the last time I held my family so tightly. When I went over the day's events one more time, Mom was a tornado of questions about Lance, about Craig, about everything. Finally.

Trey ordered pizza again and we took it down to the rec room. Maverick on one side of me, Derek on the other. I didn't stick to my two-square limit. I paced myself though, since my stomach was in agony and ecstasy. Feeling this miserable, I decided, wasn't worth it. My dad leaving me wasn't my fault. Though it would take time, I'd have to forgive myself, let go of the reserves of hatred I'd stored up against my physical imperfections, and love myself for who I was working to be.

For the first time ever, we talked openly about Marty and Greaser and their affair.

"How did you find out?" I asked Mom.

"You told me, that night in the kitchen when you came in and said, *Let's dance like Dad and Mawty*. I knew Greaser was foolin' around, but that's when it became real. All those nights he didn't come home." She shook her head. "After that, I couldn't ignore what was going on."

"Remember that time you went looking for him at Marty's place?" Trey said.

I wondered if that was the night I was with her, or if there'd been other times.

"Pitiful." Mom swatted her hand at Trey. "Can't believe I wasted time on those two. They deserved each other. Him leaving was one of the best things that ever happened."

Trey and I traded glances. We'd never call her out on that or let on that we knew otherwise. She could keep her secret.

My mind drifted to the Polaroid of Marty tucked in Mom's bedroom closet with the word "HIT!" written on it. Now would've been the time to ask what it meant. But I held back. For once, I didn't need to know. Whether it was part of a plan to attack Marty or simply my mom expressing her frustration with the situation, I'd let her keep that secret, too.

Suzette called later to check on me. She also said that the DA had been in touch and wanted to meet in the morning instead of next week, since she'd filled him in on our morning at 7-Eleven. Exhausted as I was, this was good news, because I was ready to put Marty to rest and get on with my life.

My family and I, along with Suzette, filed into the Franklin County Courthouse early the next morning for a long day of depositions. Mike Matheson, the DA, wasn't a fan of media attention and, in light of yesterday's events, wanted to move on the developments in Marty's case as quickly and quietly as possible.

Mike and three other prosecutors and two secretaries took turns questioning the three of us. Harlan Buchanan was also there and added his own questions. When Trey detailed his night at Marty's, Buchanan hung onto every word. Trey's fingerprints were taken when we'd arrived, and although it would be a few days before a match could be confirmed against the prints found at Marty's, Buchanan seemed satisfied that the case was finally closed.

Buchanan even asked Mom, under oath, why she falsified her timecard. Mom, now the sentinel of family secrets, replied, "Well, it's been so long ago I can't remember why." Buchanan left it at that.

The three of us waited in a separate conference room while Suzette spoke privately with the DA. She wanted to get an idea of how he would proceed and what charges he'd consider against my mom. She was technically guilty of obstruction of justice by telling Trey not to discuss what he'd seen. It was hard to say who was more nervous. Though she kept her composure throughout and was her usual talkative self with the DA, Mom had to be a wreck on the inside.

After a good thirty minutes, Mom decided she wanted to go outside for a cigarette. Trey went with her. While they were gone, I took in the view of the Columbus skyline, flipped through a couple *People* magazines that were on a side table, and even caught myself praying.

Suzette finally came in.

"Where is everyone?"

I hooked my thumb toward the window. "Smoke break. What did he say, is he charging her?"

"Relax, babe. Mike's a good guy. He's not after your mom. What she did was wrong, yes, but all things considered, prosecuting her is a huge waste of time and taxpayer money. He might—might—at the very worst charge her with negligence, which will mean a fine. That's it."

"And Trey?"

"He's in the clear."

I sighed heavily. "Thank God!"

"I asked about Lance and what was in store for him. Mike said he'd probably get charged with involuntary manslaughter, which might get plea bargained down. According to Mike the bigger hurdle for Lance is yesterday's show. I doubt either case goes to trial, but Lance will probably do time."

"Yeah." The pity I'd had for Lance was gone. I didn't hate the guy. After all, it was because of him I understood more about my past than ever before. Knowing how the pieces fit together gave me a better sense of who I was and helped me understand Mom and Trey on a deeper level. But when I thought about how he almost put a bullet in my head, I forced myself to feel numb, indifferent about him. That was the best I could do.

"Come on." Suzette put her arm around my shoulders. "Let's go find your family and tell them the news."

We left the conference room arm-in-arm, but when we saw Irene being led in with two officers at her side, our cheer fled. She didn't look well.

"Nice to see you got something to be all happy about while my boy's sitting in a jail cell." She spat the words with an undeniable venom.

I could've snapped back with a number of tart, true remarks, but I didn't. Irene was angry, and I wasn't sure her outcome would be as pleasant as mine.

"There's a good chance he won't get a lengthy sentence," Suzette said to her calmly.

"That supposed to comfort me? I went to you two for help and now I'm gonna lose my boy because of you!"

Thankfully, the officers escorting Irene nudged her and resumed their stroll to the DA's office. But Irene fired several obscenities over her shoulder at us.

"Ignore her," Suzette said. "If Lance goes up the river, it's partly her fault."

"I'm just ready to get out of here."

Leave it to Trey to want to celebrate after a full day of depositions. Suzette came with us and we dined at One Nation, a restaurant located atop the Nationwide building. The glass elevator, positioned on the outside of the building, was a one-of-a-kind in Columbus. Mom faced the door, despite our encouragement for her to enjoy the view of downtown as we climbed thirty-eight stories.

Vinny joined us. I was less than delighted about that fact until I saw Mom's face light up. She and Vinny acted like long-lost friends throughout lunch. Trey and I were taken aback at their camaraderie while Suzette enjoyed their banter. Seeing Mom have a good time was worth it. And I owed Vinny. Not only had he found out where

Lance worked, like I'd asked, he'd also clarified that Lance's last name wasn't Turner. It was Slater, same as Irene. So as far as Vinny's talents went as a PI, I could vouch for him.

After the party broke up and we got home, Trey said he'd take care of Maverick. I changed and told them I was off to Derek's. That wasn't entirely true, but it was best Mom and Trey didn't know that.

I didn't know if it was worth doing, but I stopped by Craig's house. He welcomed me in, just like the first time I met him at the body shop.

"I saw the news yesterday," he said.

"It's part of the reason I'm here." I briefly explained why I'd gone to see Lance at work and how the situation deteriorated. "Lance kept saying you'd lied to me and left out the fact that he's your son."

Craig looked at me and didn't deny it. "I don't know for absolute certain, but yeah, Irene told me he was mine."

"I know it's none of my business, but Irene doesn't look good, and both of them are dealing with a lot of anger over the issue. Lance has a tough road ahead, especially if Irene's health isn't good. He needs you."

I told Craig about the depositions and the charges Lance could face. I also shared the theory that Lance and Irene were probably the ones who'd taunted him with phone calls in an attempt to push him over the edge. He hadn't received any more calls in the last few days.

"You can't go back and change anything," I said, "but you've got a chance to make things better from here on out."

"I don't think either one of 'em wants anything to do with me."

"Maybe, maybe not, but I think you should try. It's not the best circumstances, but they need you. If you make the effort and they turn you away, at least you'll know you tried to do the right thing."

He considered that a moment. "Ironic, isn't it? Who knew that little girl sitting on a bar stool would be helping me out one day?" Apparently, Craig had seen me at the Junkyard Lounge. Maybe when Marty first started working there he'd been around, before she got involved with my dad. Maybe we'd played pinball and twirled around on the dance floor together.

"I hope it works out for you," I said. "All of you."

I meant it. Despite the long, rocky history, Craig had a slim chance of a reconciliation with his son. Unlike my dad.

Craig had also missed the chance to work things out with Marty. There was no way to tell if their marriage would've survived the bedlam of Craig's alcoholism and abuse and Marty's unfaithfulness. Their flaws had gotten the best of them. It was unfortunate, because from what I knew of both of them, they were capable of great love and affection.

August, 1992

It was one of those calls I didn't think I'd ever get, and the finality of the situation I was about to walk into didn't escape me. I glanced down at my new engagement ring before I left my car, hoping the flash of sparkle from the diamonds would help stiffen my spine and beef up my courage.

Derek had proposed a week ago. Totally surprised me. He'd even asked Mom for permission—and received it. Both of which floored me.

Derek suggested eloping, having suddenly grown anxious to abandon his virginity, but we'd come this far and I'd grown attached to the feeling of pride of doing this the old fashioned way. But as dreamy and romantic as a Christmas wedding sounded, I couldn't focus on those details just yet.

Mom and Frank were officially an item. Whatever that meant. Although I knew Mom wouldn't burden Frank with the same conditions she had Roger, I didn't bother asking what their plans were. But over dinner one evening Frank shared that Nora had passed peacefully. Watching Nora deteriorate over the years, he said, had been trying, and he was grateful for Mom's help with arrangements. As tears welled in his eyes, he reached for Mom's hand. She responded with a look of adoration and strength. I had a feeling they would be good for each other.

Mom, Trey, and I were still finding our way with one another. It was new territory, now that secrets were out and perceptions were marred. I didn't feel like the baby anymore, always clueless and uncertain of where I fit, but that had come at a price. Time was the best remedy for us.

Archie had called yesterday, saying my dad had agreed to meet me today at the Junkyard Lounge. There were things I needed to say, and until Archie's call, I didn't know if I'd get the chance.

We couldn't keep this up, my dad and me. We'd both used up favors with Archie, and it wasn't as though our meetings would repair or grow our relationship. Nothing could. And that was probably for the best.

When I walked into the bar, my dad was already there, sitting on the same stool he'd occupied before, and a half-empty mug of beer at his side. His forever-faithful companion. I eased in beside him and realized how awkward it was not feeling as awkward as the last time. Archie wasn't around to buffer and kickstart our conversation.

Dad slowly tapped his fingers on the bar top, his only move that acknowledged my arrival. Maybe he felt a notch less of discomfort, too. A hundred more times and maybe we'd make eye contact when we met.

"Heard you wanted to see me." A pinch of annoyance in his voice, perhaps from waiting on me to say something.

"Yeah, I, uh, just wanted to clear the air on a couple things."

"Like what?"

"For one, the windows in your apartment. I'm sorry it happened, but like I said before, I didn't do it." I paused, uncertain if a full-blown explanation about Lance and Irene would mean anything. And maybe I was afraid—afraid to admit I'd been duped by Marty's nephew and what my father would think of me. Such concerns probably wavered on irrational, but that's where I was, like a tightrope walker who'd made a wobbly step. "But I want to help pay for the repair."

"What for? You didn't do it, you don't owe me nothing."

He was right. This whole scene between us was backwards. Here I was feeling guilty for something I didn't do and acting overly anxious to please him. Wasn't he the one who should've suffered from a guilty conscience?

He darted a glance my way. "Keep your money."

Goosebumps pimpled along my arms and I nodded. "I also wanted you to know that Mom"—*Do I call her that in front of him?*—"She told me about the envelopes, about the money you sent. I asked her." I'm sure he would've enjoyed hearing that it wasn't easy on her, and that the admission had flared a jealousy I didn't know existed in her.

"And I know that you didn't leave on your own, that she made you go." A lump jumped in my throat on that last bit, as I felt like I was betraying my mom. I wasn't, not really. I was letting him know that I realized Mom wasn't perfect, that she had her flaws—not that I'd ever mention her strategy with Frank or the threat she'd used to kick him out. That didn't undo everything she'd done for me and the fact she'd managed with me and Trey on her own. In my heart, nothing could deprive her of my love and respect. I could forgive her the same way I forgave my dad for almost ruining all of us.

Gerald Reed nodded steadily for a moment. "That was the way she wanted it. I knew I couldn't stay with her no more. We never should've looked twice at one another." When he reached for his cigarette, I glimpsed the tremor in his hand. If it was from nerves or a lingering condition, I couldn't say. "She told me I couldn't ever see you again or she'd...." He shook his head as the words seemed lodged in his throat. "I didn't have much choice."

Those same words he'd said to Marty over the phone. In reality, Gerald and Annette began their relationship on *I don't have a choice* when my mom ended up pregnant. Marriage was their only solution, they thought, but it didn't fix them or make them compatible. The fact that I unexpectedly came along eight years later only prolonged and intensified their misery.

"Wasn't nothing I could do, so I took my things and left. I figured you didn't miss me none." He turned to me, gave me that hard, long look of his. Meeting his weathered gaze, I could sum him up in two words: sad and tragic. "But that never stopped me from loving you and being proud of you." His lips stumbled over the last few words.

My head buzzed. Tears threatened, and I looked away, because I couldn't let him think that everything was okay, that the past and its damage was undone. Hugging him would be crossing a line. He'd said he loved me, but I was rock-solid sure that he had no idea what love really was. I'd learned that loving someone costs you everything you have emotionally and physically. Words, on their own, didn't mean much.

But I believed in being fair. He loved me in his capabilities, in whatever it was that defined love for him. Our definitions of that one word would never match, and there'd be no middle ground between us.

“Despite all that’s happened,” I said, “I never hated you.” That was as close as I could get to saying I loved him and mean it. “Growing up wasn’t all bad.” Christmastime had always been a bright spot for me back then. I could remember peace in the house and moments where my parents were kind to each other. My dad always made a point of getting me that one special item I was desperate for each year, and whether it was a Barbie camper or a bike, he struggled through directions without a beer or a curse word until it was finished. Those were among the few, untainted memories I had of my dad. Funny how they were so ripe and clear.

I couldn’t say Trey fared the same. Mom usually bought Trey’s gifts and Dad discovered what they were the same way Trey did. Maybe that was another reason Trey was embittered against me.

I stood, knowing this meeting was on borrowed time.

“I don’t speak badly of you, and I’ll always hope the best for you.” I took out one of Derek’s business cards that I’d prepared for this. On the back, I’d written the phone number to Derek’s apartment. By winter, that would be my place, too. “Just in case,” was all I could muster as I slid the card toward him.

He looked at it but made no move to put it in his pocket.

Our eyes met again. We could’ve filled a gorge with all the unsaid words that passed between us. Some good, some not. In the beats of silence between us, I think we both felt the heaviness and impact of those unspoken words. A mild agony pounded my head as I refused to give my resentment a voice.

We didn’t hug or even shake hands. I walked out of that bar with my chin up and my heart lighter, though. Just like Trey, I’d shown Gerald Reed that I’d turned out okay and I was making a pretty good life for myself. Every single thing I’d dreamed of saying to him, yelling at him, fell away. Because in that moment—that one chance—to unload every insult and curse I’d imagined, I knew it wouldn’t make me feel better. The angry words, the tears, none of it would undo the hurt that had been done, and nothing would erase the scars on my heart.

I didn't expect Gerald Reed to call. Ever. As I abandoned that emotional baggage at the Junkyard Lounge, a grim reality cloaked me and sank in. I wouldn't see my dad again until he was sick or dead. Maybe not even then.

I could live with that, because I had today. A discrete memory I could tuck away and revisit when I needed reminded of the closure. Because we all had that place inside ourselves, where we kept every little secret. Those things that defined us, meant something in the time capsule of our lives. Like Marty and her butterfly necklace.

ACKNOWLEDGEMENTS & AUTHOR'S NOTES

This story is a work of fiction. However, certain elements are based on facts. From a young age, I can remember my dad taking me to his favorite local bar. My mom worked second shift as a waitress, and I was too young to stay home by myself. Pinball, Juicy Fruit, and playing The Kendalls ("Heaven's Just a Sin Away") are vivid highlights from those long nights. Most memorable was my dad's behavior with a beautiful woman. I'm not sure how long they carried on their affair, but my mom (eventually) threw my dad out of the house. Also fuzzy are the details on how and why my parents reconciled. My guess is that a divorce would've been too expensive, and if nothing else, my parents were practical and frugal. Their union disintegrated, once and for all, six years later.

Both of my parents have passed, each taking secrets with them. Writing this book has served as cheap, effective therapy. For part fun and part research, I revisited several of the places that could be considered 'landmark' status for Columbus' South Side. If you're interested in journeying with me on a Then & Now photo-tour, please check out my website.

As always, I owe my family, friends, and writer-friends a great deal of thanks for all the support they pour into me while working on a project. Most of all, I'm forever grateful for my Husband and the beautiful life we've created together.

If you are a victim of domestic violence, please reach out for help. The National Domestic Hotline is a place to start. https://www.thehotline.org/

If you are struggling with eating disorders, please reach out for help. The National Eating Disorders Association is a place to start. https://www.nationaleatingdisorders.org/help-support

ABOUT THE AUTHOR

MERCEDES KING is a Columbus, Ohio, native and founding member of Buckeye Crime Writers. With a degree in Criminology from Capital University and a passion for writing, she enjoys exploring the depth of criminal behaviors through her stories. Mixing fact with fiction is her specialty, as is setting her tales in not-so-distant decades, which she's dubbed Modern Historicals. In 2016 and 2017, Mercedes was a finalist for the Claymore Award. When she's not elbow-deep in research, reading, or enjoying the local bike path, she might be at Wrigley Field or sinking her toes into the sand somewhere along Florida's coastline. Join her mailing list at MercedesKing.com

Every Little Secret follows Kyle Reed, a young college student determined to unravel family secrets entangled around the unsolved murder of her father's mistress.

Columbus Noir features Mercedes' short story, "An Agreeable Wife for a Suitable Husband", set in Columbus' gritty South Side during the 1970s.

A Dream Called Marilyn (novella) focuses on a psychiatrist who is hired to treat and subdue actress Marilyn Monroe, no matter what it takes.

Plantation Nation, follows the journey of Emma Cartwright, a 16 year old Southern girl who disguises herself as a young man and joins the

Union Army.

You can connect with her on Facebook, Twitter, and Instagram.

Made in the USA
Monee, IL
29 October 2020

46252059R00173